LEASE ON THE BEACH

A DAMAGED GOODS MYSTERY

JENNIFER L HART

ELEMENTS UNLEASHED

PRAISE FOR JENNIFER L HART

"....*difficult to put down.*"

— Kirkus

"...*a very likable, sympathetic, savvy and smart heroine.*"

— Gemma Halliday, New York Times Bestselling Author

"*Jennifer L. Hart brings a whole new meaning to family togetherness....*"

— Night Owl Reviews

Copyright 2015 Jennifer Lynn Hart
Cover design by Click Twice Design
All rights reserved.

This ebook is licensed for your personal enjoyment only. This ebook may not be re-sold or given away to other people. If you would like to share this book with another person, please purchase an additional copy for each person. If you're reading this book and did not purchase it, or it was not purchased for your use only, then please return it and purchase your own copy. Thank you for respecting the hard work of this author. To obtain permission to excerpt portions of the text, please contact the author at laundryhag1@gmail.com.

All characters in this book are fiction and figments of the author's imagination. All rights reserved.

❦ Created with Vellum

LEASE ON THE BEACH

Lease on the Beach
Hart/ Jennifer L.
978-1-951215-44-6

Lease on the Beach/ Jennifer L. Hart

Contemporary Romance—Fiction 2. Mystery Romance—Fiction 3. Strong Female Leads—Fiction 4. Miami—Fiction 5. Mystery—Fiction 6. Beach—Fiction 7. Mystery—Fiction 8. Property Management—Fiction 9. Humorous Romance — Fiction 10. Contemporary—Fiction 11. Murder—Fiction 12. Amateur Sleuths—Fiction 13. Women Sleuths—Fiction 14. Alpha Male—Fiction
I. Title

A new lease on life....

After a brush with death, Jackie Parker has big plans to lie low for a while. The best laid plans didn't check in with her stressful job as part of Damaged Goods property management—or her drama queen mother.

When one of their clients is found brutally murdered, and a recently evicted tenant is a suspect, Jackie vows to Luke and Logan that this time she'll stay out of the fray. After all, she's not a detective and they have more than enough on their plate. A rogue RV, drug dealers, furries, snakes and monkeys, oh my!

Plus there's a rival property management company determined to ruin Damaged Goods, a kidnapping and a sexy animal lover looking to cause trouble in Jackie's already rocky marriage. The Magic City's sassiest process server is sitting on a powder keg of crazy and the two men in her life are playing with matches. One thing's for sure, for Jackie, this isn't a day at the beach.

LEASE ON THE BEACH

CHAPTER 1

It's not every day you see a 300 pound man wearing a sweater and an elephant bathing suit. Unless you're an eviction specialist in Miami, then you just gotta hope the trunk doesn't move.

I wasn't so lucky.

"How you doin'?" Joseph Santino—the man with the unibrow and questionable taste in attire—made a kissy face at me. He ignored the towering masses of my husband and his brother who flanked me on either side of the small stoop.

Luke, my husband, stepped forward. "Mr. Santino? We're here on behalf of the property owner. You are trespassing on her property."

"Huh?" Santino scratched his chest and my jaw dropped as I realized that the tenant *wasn't* wearing a sweater, that dark matte that looked like wool was actually his chest hair.

Ick. Ick. Ick.

"You don't have a lease to live in this apartment," I said.

Santino moved closer until I caught a whiff of garlic, rum, and BO. "Says who?" His Jersey accent was as thick as the humidity.

"The woman who owns this apartment complex." I folded

my arms over my chest and glared at him, intentionally ignoring what was going on south of the border.

"Jackie," Logan's voice held a warning tone. "He's been drinking."

No shit, Sherlock. "Mr. Santino—"

"You can call me Big Joey, sweet cheeks." He waggled the unibrow.

Not even if he paid me would I call him Big Joey. I was already too familiar with him for my mental comfort. "Mr. Santino," I began again. "Without a lease—"

"I do too got a lease." Santino turned, gifting us with the view of his patchy back hair.

I exchanged a surprised glance with Luke, just as Logan muttered, "I thought you said this guy was a squatter?"

"That's what Mrs. Pomeroy told me over the phone," I hissed.

Santino shuffled back over, trunk swinging with every step. I didn't bother to stifle a shudder of revulsion, but reached out and took the crumpled paper. It was stained with what smelled like marinara sauce.

"See, whatch yous got here is a case of mistaken identity," Big Joey said. "I pay the guy every month on time. No way am I giving this gem up."

"Is it legit?" Luke asked, reading over my shoulder.

At $500.00 a month for a two bedroom apartment on the beach, not in this lifetime. These places usually went for four times that amount. But saying so in front of the man who thought he had every right to let his freak trunk fly wasn't smart. The battered paper was a standard rental agreement, though the owner's signature was illegible. "Where did you get this?"

"From the woman who showed me the place."

"What woman? Do you have her name?"

"I'll do you one better, sweet cheeks. I's got her card." The trunk shifted as he plucked a small, white business card off a white wicker end table and offered it to me, making sure to brush his fingers over mine. I didn't look down, but I was fairly certain the trunk lifted.

Behind me, Logan uttered a quiet, "Man, that is just not right."

Yup, there had definitely been movement. "Kay, sorry to disturb you." I backed up swiftly, almost falling off the stoop.

Another kissy face. "You come back and see Big Joey any time, sweet cheeks."

Not if I could help it. I didn't run to get back in our big black truck, but I didn't dawdle either.

"Another name to add to your fan club roster, huh Jackie?" Logan said. "I bet if you went back he'd let you sit on his lap like Santa Claus."

"You only think you're funny, Logan Parker. It won't be so funny when I shove my foot up your ass."

Logan looked at me over the rim of his sunglasses. "Who told you I was into that?"

At times I found it hard to believe I'd left my last job due to sexual harassment in the workplace only to wind up dealing with Logan, Big Joey, and the elephant trunk of doom. What was that expression about a frying pan and fire?

Luke, who'd been focused on his smartphone screen, murmured "Jackie, what was the supposed realtor's name?"

I looked at the card. "Marlena Cruz. No address or company logo, just an email addy and a phone number. Should I call her?"

Luke shook his head. "No, call our client back first. Find out if she knows Ms. Cruz and why she had access to the apartment."

I retrieved my own phone from my pants pocket, swiped at the screen and frowned when nothing happened. "That's weird."

"Did you try turning it on?" Logan sneered

"I could swear it was on."

"Maybe the battery's dead," Luke suggested.

"I just charged it last night." That was the third time this week my phone had spazzed out on me. "Damn it, I'm going to have to go home and get the number off my desk."

"Is it in your email account? You can access your email from my phone," Luke offered me his device.

"The IT guy is doing a system upgrade today. We can't get online until he's done."

Logan groaned. "You mean we have to drive all the way back through midtown traffic just because you didn't remember to plug in your phone?"

I bit my lip to keep from snapping. It would only start an argument. Logan had saved my life a few weeks ago and I had made a mental promise to be nicer to him. But he'd come by the nickname, the Dark Prince, honestly—he was evil incarnate and he'd made no such vow. Every time we went out on a job he was there, needling me and I was closing in on my breaking point. Unfortunately, old habits die hard.

If at all.

"It's cool, we'll call it a day." Luke, my savior, shifted the truck into drive and made a broken K turn to head back into downtown Miami. "No rush."

"Maybe not for you," Logan muttered. "You already have a house."

Our property management company, Damaged Goods, wouldn't get paid until we got the job done. In this case, managed to get the squatter out so Mrs. Pomeroy could re-rent the beachfront property for its market value. Somehow I doubted Joey the elephant man wanted to pay two large when he'd been living there for a fraction of the cost.

"I'll fix it," I told Logan and squeezed Luke's shoulder in thanks for smoothing my screw-up over. Though I couldn't see my husband's chocolate brown eyes behind his dark shades, I knew he must have glanced at me in the rearview mirror. He didn't smile though the way he would have a few weeks ago. Things had been rocky since we started our own property management company. And not just professionally either. Working with family was trying at the best of times and drawing the line between work and personal lives was tricky. I'd pushed to be a part of this team because I wanted to be closer to my husband, but I knew less about him now than I had before we'd started Damaged Goods.

"First thing's first," Logan groused, breaking me out of my melancholy. "Get a new cell phone."

"I HATE SHOPPING FOR PHONES," I grumped as Logan dragged me into the nearest tech superstore. "Phones and cars."

"As is evidenced by that piece of crap you drive."

Them was fighting words. "You talk bad about Bessie Mae and I will post naked pictures of you on the Internet."

He frowned down at me. "You never took naked pictures of me."

"I'll have Marcy do it."

Logan smirked as he held the door for me. "You don't have that kind of influence."

"Hos before bros," I said, and made a face. "Wait, that didn't come out right."

Logan's expression soured and he stalked off toward the big screen aisle without another word.

"Too soon?" I called sweetly after him, unable to keep from pressing my advantage. So much for being nice to him.

Okay, on the surface it wasn't weird that my lifelong friend was dating my brother-in-law. What *was* weird was that I'd slept with said brother-in-law once a long, *long* time before I knew what part he'd play in my future life. Like that I'd end up marrying his brother and working with both of them.

In a word, *awk*-ward.

I was determined to make Damaged Goods work though. And in order to do that, I needed a phone that didn't flake out and have the technological equivalent of PMS.

The phone I currently had had come free with the service contract I'd signed up for no more than five years ago. Technologically speaking, it was a relic and though I was loathed to admit it, Logan was probably right. I needed a new phone. I just didn't want a new phone plan to go with it.

"Can I help you?" A bored looking sales associate with wire rimmed glasses and a prominent Adam's apple— whose name tag, oddly enough read Adam—asked in a flat tone.

"I need a new phone." I proffered my ancient device.

He didn't even glance at it. "Are you looking to sign up for a new plan?"

"Not if I can help it." I hated those damn phone plans that were only x amount a month in the store but once they tagged on data, texts, fees and taxes, the monthly bill totaled the GNP of a third world nation.

Adam meandered through the rows, prattling about features I'd never use, apps I'd never download. I sighed and wished Luke had come with me instead of Logan. My husband was much more tech savvy than I was and he could speak geek with the best of 'em. But he'd volunteered down at the local animal shelter for the third time this week.

I'd wrestled with the idea of asking if I could go with him. Two things stopped me—the worry that he didn't want me with him and the worry that he did. I wasn't really an animal person. Growing up in a trailer park full of the stereotypical junkyard dogs, one of whom had taken a chunk out of my calf when I was nine, had soured me on the whole man's best friend shtick.

"Are you even listening?" Adam's irritated tone broke into my reverie.

"Sorry, no. Look, I'll be straight with you. I really just need a phone that works. Like all the time."

He rolled his eyes. "Good luck with that."

Ten minutes later I left with my new phone, charger, and damn it all, a two year contract.

"I feel dirty, like I just signed away a piece of my soul." I told Logan as we waited at the light. "They practically want my first born in order to terminate the contract early. Loan sharks are more forgiving than those services."

Logan didn't comment, just stared out the open window. His expression looked very far away.

"Hey, Dark Prince, you okay?" I asked, not really sure if I wanted to hear his answer, but feeling the need to ask.

"Do you and Marcy talk?" He asked out of nowhere.

"Um, yeah, all the time. Why?"

"No, I mean *talk*. About me."

I frowned as I made the left out of the parking lot and merged with traffic. "Your name has come up a few times. Again, Why?"

He blew out a stressed sounding sigh. "I mean, do you guys like, compare notes on…things."

"Things…?" I trailed off and had what felt like a mini seizure as I realized what he meant. "Cripes, Logan, no!"

"Calm down," he said, which of course only wound me up further.

"Marcy doesn't even know about….about that."

One sardonic eyebrow lifted. "You mean that we slept together. You joke about it all the time yet you can't just say it outright? Why is that, Jackie?"

"Because..." I trailed off, unsure how to finish that statement.

"Because...?" he prompted.

Damn it all. I didn't know why. Instead, I retrenched for attack. "Just because I don't go around blurting out my personal information. It's a tricky situation and frankly, it's no one else's business. Do you and Luke discuss *me* like that?"

The second the question was out I wished I could have recalled it. I didn't want to know if they engaged in locker room talk behind my back now that everyone was in the know about it. Damn, why did every encounter with Logan have to be the verbal equivalent of traversing a minefield?

"Don't answer that." I reached forward to click on Bessie Mae's radio. Something had to fill the engulfing silence. I cringed when Air Supply filled the car's interior and quickly changed the station. Anything but that.

He grabbed my hand, not hard, just to still it mid-motion. "Don't be stupid. You're his wife and Luke's not like that."

"But you are?"

"You know I can keep a secret," he released my hand and I tried to ignore the tingling sensation left from the shared contact.

He was right. Logan had sat on our shared history for over seven years. Though he'd prodded me to tell Luke and get it all out in the open. In the end it hadn't mattered because Luke knew about our hook-up all along, which was part of our current marital damage.

But this conversation wasn't about me and I couldn't afford to let my mind wander. I had no idea how Logan would react if he discovered all was not peachy-keen with me and Luke. "So, why would you think Marcy and I would discuss you like that?"

He shrugged. "Women are different."

"The entire point of Men are from Mars, Women are from Venus summed up oh, so eloquently."

Logan rubbed the bridge of his nose. "Having a conversation with you makes me tired."

He wanted succinct? I could spell it out for him. "No, Logan, Marcy has said nothing to me about your sexual prowess. Is that what you wanted to hear?"

The hand dropped away. "Thank you."

I should've left well enough alone, but that wasn't my style. "Should I keep you updated? Text alert you if she brings up the subject? You never know when she might feel chatty."

"Shut up and drive the car, Jackie." Logan said with a smile.

CHAPTER 2

"Stop here." Logan said as we approached the turn off to the animal shelter where Luke was volunteering. "I want to ask him something."

"Can't it wait? I've got things to do." I really didn't but the thought of all those animals made me nervous.

Logan sent me a disbelieving look over the top of his sunglasses. "Oh yeah? Like what?"

"Work. I thought you wanted to get paid?"

"It'll just take a second."

I made a face and the turn at the same time. It was easier to stop than to argue with the Dark Prince, no matter how much fun I had baiting him. And I really did want to get back home and do a little online sleuthing to discover the identity of the realtor who had rented Big Joey the beach house.

I shuddered when I realized I *was* thinking of him as Big Joey. Stupid power of suggestion.

Logan had been scrunched up pretty tight in my Barbie blue civic and he looked like a well-equipped Ken doll as he climbed out of my girly accessory. "You coming?"

I cast a wary glance at the shelter. The animals were in

cages, I'd be safe enough from lunging jaws. Besides, if one got out I didn't have to be fast, just faster than Logan. "Kay."

I powered the windows up and followed him across the gravel lot to the squat red brick building. The Florida sunshine beat down on our heads, and perspiration dotted my upper lip. God, it was hot and summer wasn't even in full swing yet.

Logan held the door open for me and we entered the relative cool of the dark office space. The place reeked of musty cedar chips and furry animals. Several dogs started barking frantically as the door slammed behind us.

"Huh, would you look at that. I guess animals really can sense evil," I teased.

Logan ignored me, probably because he didn't have a good comeback prepared. No one sat behind the wood paneled desk, though what looked like hundreds of files in every color of the rainbow stuck out from the built-in raw wood bookshelves along the back wall. At the corner of the chest high desk, an ancient desktop computer hummed indicating whoever worked here had just stepped out and would be back shortly.

"Luke," Logan called, though I doubted his voice carried over the cacophony of yips, barks, and howls. I shivered involuntarily.

"Can I help you?" a feminine voice asked from behind us.

I jumped, startled that she'd been able to sneak up on us. She was young and pretty, one of those women who looked gorgeous without an ounce of effort. Despite the heat she wore jeans that clung to her perfect figure and her hair was pulled back in a messy blond ponytail through the back of her Dolphins ball cap. I disliked her on sight, though I tried to hide it with a phony smile. "We're looking for Luke Parker."

"Oh, he's around back with the new litter." Her big blue

eyes barely flicked toward me, all her attention on Logan. "You are just the spitting image of Luke. You must be his brother. He talks about you all the time. I'm Justine."

Her voice was thick with southern honey. She tilted her head in that beguiling sort of way that was oh so obvious to me but turned normally intelligent men into mouth-breathing idiots. Logan was no exception.

"Actually, I've got sixteen months on him so he's the spitting image of *me*." Logan winked at her in a flirty sort of way and leaned against the desk to better display his "image."

I ground my molars together and put a hand to my left eye. Was it twitching?

Justine grinned up at Logan then sent her noxious smile my way. "And you are?"

Irritated. Apparently my husband had spent enough time with Justine so that she recognized Logan on sight but I didn't ring a bell. My tone was sharper than I intended when I said, "Jackie. Do you think you could get him for us?"

"Sure. Come on 'round back."

"What's your problem?" Logan asked, his eyes glued to Justine's swaying butt as she led us past several rows of cages.

"Nothing," I muttered. Only that I was sweating profusely and looked tired and frazzled while the woman who my dear husband had neglected to mention he was spending all his free time with appeared daisy freaking fresh. I could tell Justine wasn't the type to actually sweat. No, she glistened, radiating a dewy freshness through and through. Damn it, I should have stayed in the car.

A snarling German Shepard lunged into the chicken wire mesh as though to tear my throat out and I slammed back into Logan, hard.

"It's okay," he soothed, though I wasn't sure if the tone was for me or the dog. His hands gripped my shoulders.

"Jeeze, Jackie you're shaking. He's confined, he can't hurt you."

I exhaled an unsteady breath. "I know. I was just startled."

"That's weird," Justine frowned, her delicately arched eyebrows meeting over the bridge of her nose. "Adonis is usually so friendly."

"I'm an acquired taste," I said, my gaze glued to the sharp looking canines Adonis bared for my benefit.

Logan still held me by the shoulders and I was reluctant to step away from him and move any closer to the snarling dog.

"Try to calm down," Justine said. "Dogs can scent fear and it works them up even more."

I was tempted to snarl at her for telling me to calm down when Luke came around the corner up ahead. "Hey, what's all the commotion over here?" His tone was light, teasing even, and a pang of hurt went through me when I heard the flirty tone he intended for Justine.

"You've got visitors," she said with a wave in our direction.

I shrugged off Logan's touch a second before Luke's gaze shifted from his brother to me and some of the light went out of his smile. Freaking ouch. I winced and both the Parker brothers noticed.

"What are you guys doing here?" The smile was back, though not nearly as genuine as it had been for Justine.

Logan waited a beat to see if I'd detonate but when I remained silent he cleared his throat. "I just wanted to ask you if I could borrow the truck later. I have a date with Marcy and she's not a fan of the bike."

Really? *That* was the question that couldn't wait? The reason why I was enduring this awful moment? Ignorance really was bliss.

Luke tossed him the keys. "Sure. Take it now if you want. I can walk home."

Or slither, the snake.

"I can give you a ride." Justine volunteered, suggestion loaded into her voice. "I'm dying to see your place."

I'd had enough. With a vicious glare at Luke, I stalked back out to the parking area, climbed in Bessie Mae and roared off, hands closed tight on the steering wheel. Part of me wanted to go back and make a huge scene that involved cussing and throwing things, but I didn't make a habit of sticking around when the odds weren't in my favor. The dogs had me unsettled to begin with and it was Justine's home turf. Losing my shit would only make me look like a nut and I hadn't done anything wrong.

Haven't you? A demonic inner voice prodded. *You've been treating him differently.*

"Shut it, self," I said aloud in the empty car. "I'm not in the mood for your pearls of wisdom."

Think about it. Ever since the incident...

I slammed the mental garage door square on top of that thought, hoping to cut it in half and silence it for good. There would be no ruminating about 'the incident', as I'd dubbed my near death experience. The nightmares were bad enough, I didn't want to dwell on morose thoughts while the sun was up, too.

But that just left more room to be hurt over Luke's betrayal. Not that I thought he was sleeping with Little Miss Perfect. But it was blatantly obvious he hadn't mentioned the fact that he was married, or even bothered to introduce me as his wife. And the way he'd looked at her... so happy. It made me want to cry. When was the last time he'd looked at me that way? Damn it, I should have checked to see if he'd been wearing his wedding ring.

Honking brought me out of my downward spiral and I

caught a glance of the big black truck in my rearview mirror. With the tinted windows I couldn't make out the exact features of the driver but the passenger's side was empty. My heart sped, flipped then sank somewhere down in to my stomach. Which Parker brother had come after me?

I pulled up in front of our work-in-progress bungalow and shut the engine off but made no move to extract my sorry carcass from the vehicle. The truck pulled up behind me and I shut my eyes when I heard the door slam. My windows were still up but with no AC it was too hot. I rolled them down and heard the steady footsteps approach. Felt the energy of the man who crouched beside my door.

He didn't say anything. I leaned my head back and sighed.

"Did you know?" I asked Logan. "Is that why you just had to stop there?"

"I'm sorry," he murmured.

I laughed and rolled my head to the side to look at him. "No, you're not."

"I am. And believe me Jackie, if I'd known, I wouldn't have rubbed it in your face that way."

My eyes stung with unshed tears. I thought about crying but it seemed like too much effort. "What, you're not even going to try and convince me that there's nothing going on? Isn't that what you guys do, have each other's backs?"

"I wouldn't do that to you," he said simply. "Not ever."

Despite my earlier conviction, a tear slipped out.

Logan rose and opened the door. "Come on, you need a drink."

"What about your date?" I sniffled.

"I'll call Marcy, she can come over too. Hell, maybe she'll bring Gertie and we'll have ourselves a party."

"You're a wild man, Logan Parker." I said and let him lead me into the house.

Marcy did come over, though sans Gertie, her shut-in older sister. Excellent friend that she was, she went out of her way to get *Frankie's Pizza*. Whoever said you couldn't get decent pizza in Florida had never had Frankie's. Some of my best childhood memories revolved around my mother bringing home a steaming pizza in that familiar box. Granted, I was a Frankie's Fanatic thru and thru but when you're born into a line of women who are kitchen cursed, it's second nature to become a take-out aficionada.

I made us frozen mudslides, heavy on the marshmallow vodka and chocolate ice cream. The blender, one of the few kitchen items I could operate without risking life and limb, whirred in a steady reassuring thrum.

Luke still hadn't come home and I refused to think about where he was and what— never mind who— he was doing. Instead, I watched Logan and Marcy's courtship. They'd been dating ever since my in-laws vow renewal, about six weeks now, though they didn't really act like a couple. There were no subtle touches, no smoldering glances or even sparks. At least not that I could detect. They were comfortable with each other, talking and laughing, but there was something missing. Weird, Marcy had pushed hard for me to set her up with Logan, yet they acted more like brother and sister than lovers, or even potential lovers.

I poured the batch of mudslides into parfait glasses I'd already coated with chocolate syrup and topped them off with whipped cream.

"Those are fru-fru girly drinks," Logan grumbled. I later noted that he was the first to go back for seconds.

"So babe, how's tricks?" I asked Marcy. "Anything new and exciting?"

She shrugged. "Not really. You?"

I did what I always did when my personal life was less than stellar, I talked about work. "We have a squatter with awful taste in swimwear that swears he has a lease. Had paperwork and everything."

Marcy's perfectly sculpted blond eyebrows drew together. "How'd that happen?"

"Not sure." I'd been in no frame of mind to set to work when we got home and the mudslides weren't helping. "It's probably a scam of some sort. Someone finds out which apartments are empty and which owners aren't vigilant and move people in under a phony lease. If it goes on long enough the squatters have to be evicted, just as if they were regular tenants. Could cost the owner thousands in court."

"Sounds like a headache." Marcy said.

"And you didn't even see the guy. Evicting him is not going to be pretty. " Logan described the scene that we'd stumbled across and Marcy laughed until tears rolled down her face.

"How you doin', sweet cheeks." Logan did a startling good imitation of Santino's Jersey accent. "You should have seen the look on Jackie's face—"

"*My* face?" I interrupted. "What about you?"

Logan was looking at me with a raised eyebrow. "I was stoic, as always."

"Stoic, my Aunt Fanny." I dropped my voice to a much deeper pitch which sounded both stupid and hilarious. "Man, that's just not right."

We were all laughing when the screen door slammed. Logan and I sobered first and exchanged a look.

Logan pushed back his chair. "Marcy, maybe we should head out, catch a movie or…" He was halfway out of his chair when the newcomer appeared in the doorway.

"Celeste?" I asked, frowning at my mother's haggard appearance. I hadn't seen her so bad off in years, mascara streaked down her face, eyes bloodshot. Wouldn't it figure she'd go on a bender and show up on my doorstep? The last thing this day needed was her puffed up drama. "What's the matter?"

"Oh Jackie, sweetheart. It's awful." She foisted a crumpled piece of paper at me and broke down into sobs.

Logan guided her to a chair and rubbed her back soothingly. Marcy hopped up and fetched a glass of water that she placed before Celeste. I sat there stupidly afraid to read the message in my hand, an awful sense of foreboding snaking through the pit of my stomach.

Seeing that I'd gone inert, Logan took the paper from me and opened it. His gaze darted back and forth as he read.

"What is it?" Marcy asked. "Is she sick?"

Logan shook his head and set the paper on the counter. I bit my lip so I wouldn't scream, somehow sensing what was about to happen, what he was about to say.

"No, she's been evicted."

CHAPTER 3

"There's such a thing as Karma, and she's a vindictive bitch," I muttered, mostly to myself.

"What do you mean?" Marcy asked. We were in the office, A.K.A the second bedroom that contained Marcy's old desk, my laptop, and heaping boxes full of God alone knew what. After putting my mother to bed in the guest bedroom, Marcy and I had retreated to the office to dig into Celeste's eviction. Logan had disappeared, and there was still no sign of Luke.

I ran a hand through my hair, wincing when my wedding ring snagged on a tangle. This was so not my day. "How many people have I helped to evict from their homes over the years? What goes around comes around, right?"

"You were just doing your job. There are plenty of people out there who abide by their rental agreements, pay the rent on time, and have no problem whatsoever."

I clicked through my mother's online bank statements. "I just don't get it. There's money in her account and the land rental has been paid every month. She owns the trailer outright. Why would she let it go this far before telling me something was up? You know how it works, notices and all. She had plenty of warning."

"Well, maybe it was something else, other than her not paying her rent. Do you have a copy of her lease agreement? Maybe she violated some obscure HOA rule."

There was a sharp stabbing pain behind my right eye that only came at the mention of a home owner's association. Theoretically, an HOA was supposed to help the residents of any given community by keeping property values up but that was rarely how it worked. It was more like high school, where the popular kids banded together and the outcasts were given swirlies by a group of douchenozzles on a power trip.

Referring to Celeste's lease, I waved my hand at the stack of files in the corner. "Yeah, I have it around here somewhere. I just can't deal with this right now."

Marcy nodded. "Yeah, you look like hell."

I rolled my eyes at her. "I can tell you've been spending time with Logan. His charm's rubbing off on you."

Marcy smiled but wouldn't meet my gaze.

Uh oh. "What, trouble in paradise?"

"I don't want to dump my problems on you, too."

I held both palms up. "Hey, what are friends for? But I do reserve the right to say I told you so about the Dark Prince."

Marcy shot a glance to the open door and then leaned down and lowered her voice. Whatever it was she had to share, it was going to be juicy.

"Nobody here but us chickens." I reassured her.

"Do you think—?" She cleared her throat and tried again. "Is there any chance that Logan's...gay?"

I blinked, stunned. Of all the complaints she could have had about dating him, that was one I'd never in a gazillion years expect. I was suddenly glad he hadn't taken me up on the text messaging suggestion. "Why would you think that?"

"It's just that he never wants to...um...go there."

"There?" It was either the mudslides or the stress but something was making me stupid, as was evident by the exasperated look Marcy gave me.

"Sex, Jackie. He doesn't want to have sex."

For maybe the first time in my life, I didn't know what to say. Logan Parker oozed testosterone and I had first-hand knowledge that he wasn't batting for the home team, so to speak. But should I *tell* Marcy that? Would that make things better or worse?

Before I decided, she pressed on. "I've made the suggestion, *multiple* times. But he always shuts me down, you know? Politely, but the message is clear, he's not interested. We have a good time when we hang out but he's got this whole just friends vibe kicking. It's weird. I mean, do you think he's like really deep in the closet because he's worried about what Luke or his parents would think?"

I shook my head. "No. They wouldn't care even if Logan was gay. Which I'm one hundred percent certain that he isn't."

Her face fell. "So, then it must be me specifically he's not interested in." She wrapped her arms around herself.

"No. It's all him," I said with conviction. "Maybe he just wants to take things slow because he really likes you. Did you ever think of that?"

She snorted. "He hasn't showed me his purity ring, if that's what you mean."

I rolled my eyes. "Look, I'm not saying Logan's perfect but I know for a fact that he's been burned before. If he likes you, it's only natural he'd want to proceed with caution."

The way he hadn't done with me. And look at how well *that* had turned out.

Marcy nodded. "Maybe you're right. I should get going."

I rose and shut the office door quietly so I wouldn't wake

my mother. "Thanks for coming over. And helping with Celeste."

I watched her taillights disappear around the corner. Still no sign of Luke. Had he really gone home with the puppy-lovin' tramp? The thought filled me with despair. How had my life turned into such a bubbling cesspool in so short a time?

I headed into the master suite and turned on the shower and combed through my hair while waiting for the water to heat up. My reflection was an unhappy woman in her mid-thirties with red rimmed eyes and sallow skin. Despair was *not* a good look for me.

Six years. I'd spent six years waiting for Luke to get out of the military, six years of waiting for my life to start. Was this what I'd been waiting for? Doubt, uncertainty and betrayal?

"You don't know that he's done anything," I told the sad eyed woman in the mirror. "So just stop being a melodramatic loser."

Stepping under the spray, I let the hot water course over me, concentrating on relaxing my tense muscles. The problem stemmed from the secret of me and Logan, the secret Luke had known almost the entire time. Was it two-faced of me to resent that he'd never told me he'd known I'd slept with his brother before we'd met when I'd almost taken that information to my grave? Maybe, but it wasn't even that he knew and didn't say anything. That I could have forgiven. But Luke had used his secret knowledge and preyed on his brother's guilt to manipulate Logan to do his bidding. For a good cause, but still….

The man I'd believed he was wouldn't have done that. Almost seven years in and I knew Luke less today than the day we'd married. He'd always been my safe haven, the person who gave me comfort, but those days were over. I felt duped and I'd been keeping him at a distance because of it. Would he use that as an excuse to have an affair?

I didn't want to think the worst of him, but I couldn't seem to help my wayward thoughts. My white knight had fallen off his charger, the illusion of the perfect man, the perfect husband, was shattered. Had he been faithful to me for all the time we'd been apart the same way I was to him? Or was a little something on the side just the way he did things whether we were together or not?

I didn't know. What was worse, I didn't know how to ask or if he'd even tell me the truth.

If I'd believe him if he said he had forsaken all others.

And that scared the hell out of me.

―――

Though the air conditioning was on, my bedroom felt close and stuffy. I shoved the windows up to let the night air remove some of the staleness and shut off the light to keep the bugs from bee-lining to the tear in the screen. My alcohol induced buzz was gone and though my body was tired, my mind processed the day's events, trying to formulate a plan of attack.

In the morning, I'd gather information on the beachfront property. Find out who exactly had given Big Joey the phony lease. He was a nice enough guy, and maybe I could find him someplace else to live if he couldn't pay the market value rent. I also needed to dig out Celeste's rental agreement and probe to find what the terms of her eviction had been. My blood pressure was still up that I hadn't found out what was going on until after she'd been evicted.

Evicting a tenant is a long and arduous undertaking. A company like Damaged Goods can streamline the process, but there are still certain steps that must be followed to the letter of the law. A tenant must be given proper notice of a breach of rental agreement and provided with a clear amount of time to fix that breach. If they don't comply, paperwork has to be filed by the court and the property owner serves the tenant with the notice of the lawsuit via a certified process server, like myself. Five days after the tenant has been notified, more paperwork has to be filed on behalf of the plaintiff at the court and a judge will pass a judgment of possession to remove the tenant from the property. At that point the property owner can have the sheriff forcibly remove the tenant from the property, if necessary.

She must have been notified at least *twice* that this was coming before the sheriff padlocked her out of her trailer. Yet she'd said nothing to me. Served me right for not checking on her, but really, there was only so much drama a girl could be expected to put up with in a day. Though we'd been getting along better, my history with my mother was complicated and fraught with emotional landmines.

And now she was living with me.

With a grunt, I flipped onto my side and gave Luke's pillow a good whack. I'd read somewhere that hitting a pillow was supposed to be therapeutic so I sat up and did it again. And again. I put more and more force behind each blow, slamming my fists down hard, imaging my husband's handsome face. Was it wrong that I wanted to inflict some of the hurt I was feeling on him? Maybe so, but if that was wrong, I didn't want to be right.

Out of breath, I flopped onto my back and stared at the ceiling, panting. I wouldn't cry. I *refused* to cry. Crying was not productive. Putting sugar in his gas tank was productive. Though it was my gas tank too and we needed the truck for work....

My thoughts of childish pranks ground to a halt when I heard the murmur of male voices outside.

"Where the hell have you been?" Logan snarled. I wondered the same thing about him. I'd thought he'd headed home over an hour ago.

I closed my eyes and slid off the mattress to the floor to creep closer to the window, fully intending to eavesdrop. I needn't have bothered because Luke's voice carried through the still night. "What's it to you?"

"Are you cheating on Jackie?" Logan asked point blank. I held my breath though blood pounded in my ears as my heart raced.

"What? Of course not," his denial was vehement, almost insulted.

"She thinks you are and after that scene at the animal shelter with Jasmine—"

"Justine," Luke corrected, promptly losing any points he'd scored.

Logan's tone dropped to a warning growl. "Do not fuck this up, Luke."

"Damaged Goods is fine."

"I'm not talking about the damn company! I'm talking about your marriage, jackass."

It took a lot to anger Luke but when he went, he went big. "What gives you the right to have any say in what goes on in my marriage?"

I peeked out the window. They stood not even ten yards away, toe to toe and looking like they were ready to kill each other. I opened my mouth to call out and tell them to knock it off but to my surprise, Logan glanced away.

"Don't do this, Luke. She's the best thing that ever happened to you. Don't shut her out."

Luke shoved his brother, not hard, but with enough force to make his point. "Don't tell me what to do."

"Look, I know you're pissed at yourself because you weren't the one to save her—"

Luke swung and his fist connected with the side of Logan's face. Logan went down to one knee, Luke standing over him, seething. "Shut up."

But Logan didn't. He spat, then turned to look up at his brother. "It's not your fault, man."

Luke's tone shook. "She could have died. I was stuck in fucking traffic and my wife could have died. If you hadn't bugged her bag…"

My heart was lodged in my esophagus, neatly cutting off my air supply. The incident. They were talking about the incident. I gripped the windowsill so I didn't slide to the floor in a puddle of useless Jackie goo.

"But I *did* bug her bag because I'm a paranoid SOB and she *didn't* die. She's right inside. And yet you're acting like she's gone. Like you want her gone."

"She blames me." Luke's voice was thick as he said those words.

No I don't, I thought at the same time Logan said, "Bull. She blames herself."

Luke sat down on the ground next to his brother, all the fight leeched out of him. "She has nightmares. She won't talk to me about them. Won't talk to me about anything. What am I supposed to do?"

"Anything except what you've been doing. This isn't like your time in the military. You can't just go off and do your own thing and let her handle it on her own. You're here and she needs you, man. So I'm asking you again. Where *the hell* have you been?"

There was silence and I watched them, the two dark forms sitting side by side facing away from the house, knees drawn up as they stared at the darkened neighborhood.

Luke spoke first. "I like it there. At the shelter. And before you say it, it wasn't the flirting with Justine."

"So what was it?"

"The dogs," Luke said simply. "I like being around them, like helping them. They're always so glad to see me and I know what I can do for them. It's easy. Being married...isn't."

Being married or being married to me? The good side of this eavesdropping thing, I wasn't worried about Luke cheating on me. Now, I was worried that he resented me. Had we only stayed together so long because we'd been living separate lives? Or was I just impossible to be with?

"I wouldn't know," Logan lowered his voice, though I could still hear every word. "Mom and Dad make it look easy, but then again, they have their own way of doing things and to hell with everyone else. You guys have been married for seven years, but at the same time you haven't been. You have to find your own way of doing things."

"Yeah," Luke rose and I ducked down so they wouldn't catch me in the act. "You want to come in for a beer?"

"No, I'm gonna go crash. By the way, Celeste is in your guestroom."

There was a hint of a smile in Logan's voice and I bit my lip as I remembered the time he'd been sleeping in the guest room and I'd inadvertently tripped over him. Stark naked.

Ah, memories.

"Thanks for the heads up." Luke said. "And the kick in the ass."

"Anytime, my brother." Logan said. "And Luke?"

"Yeah?"

"Just so you know, not fighting for her is the biggest regret of my life. Don't make the same mistake I did."

I listened to his motorcycle start, then rumble off into the night. After shutting the window, I slunk back into bed. Moments later, the door to our bedroom opened. Luke didn't say anything as he undressed and climbed into bed, but when he pulled me into his arms, I went willingly.

CHAPTER 4

I woke to the feeling of fingers in my hair and the sound of Luke's steady heartbeat beneath my ear.

"You awake?" His voice was gruffer than usual, thick with sleep.

A crash emanated from the direction of the kitchen. "No," I groaned and covered my face with my hands. The memories from the day before were not welcome in my head prior to a vat of morning coffee.

My pillow, which was really Luke's bare chest, shook in silent mirth. "I heard we had an overnight guest."

"An uninvited one," I groused and rolled onto my back.

Luke propped himself up on an elbow and looked down at me. Dark stubble covered his strong chin and there were bags under his eyes. "About yesterday—"

Another crash from the kitchen. I threw the covers back and reached for my bathrobe. "We need to get out there before she kills herself."

He gripped the arm I wasn't trying to stuff into a terrycloth sleeve. "Jackie, we need to talk."

I paused, robe hanging off one shoulder and looked him square in the face. "You're right, we do. And we will. Just not right now, because I'm serious when I say she'll die if she keeps it up. The kitchen curse is not forgiving."

Thud, thud, smash. "It sounds like she's giving the Incredible Hulk a prostate exam." Luke grumbled, but he threw back the covers, too.

"More likely she's trying to make coffee. Wait here, I'll let you know when it's safe."

"My hero," the words were mocking but his expression was sincere right before he pulled me into an unexpected hug. "Are we all right?"

My hands slid up his back. "I think we will be." Eventually.

"You know there was nothing going on with Justine."

I did. But the temptation was there and he'd been flirting with it, hardcore. Plus, I still had doubts about the years we'd been apart. I'd never asked, never thought I *had* to ask him not to sleep around. We were married and not in a swingers kinda way. To me, fidelity was a hard and fast rule, no matter how often temptation gave you a lap dance. But I really was worried Celeste would inadvertently invoke the kitchen curse and manage to decapitate herself so all I said was, "I believe you."

Luke kissed the top of my head. "Good. Let's get your mom out of here so we can make some noise."

How like a man to think that one quick conversational Band-Aid and some sex would fix all that ailed our marriage. Eh, he'd figure it out soon enough when I made him swear on his left testicle that he'd never go back to that particular animal shelter or see Justine again.

Celeste had every cabinet door flung open and was crawling across the kitchen floor on her hands and knees, sweeping spilled coffee grounds into a pile and cursing under her breath. "I couldn't find a broom," she explained.

"The back of the pantry door." I retrieved the broom and gave her a hand up. "I'll get this cleaned up."

She snatched the broom out of my hands, steely determination glinting in her red-rimmed eyes. "It's my mess, I'll clean it up."

I was fairly sure she was talking about more than just the coffee. What the hell was it with everyone wanting me to tackle the big issues right when I rolled out of bed? A girl needed a moment to gather her thoughts, to stick her head in the fridge and stare blankly so her brain didn't melt from the friction.

"Celeste," I began but she held up a hand to stop me.

"I'm sorry I came here last night. I should have gone somewhere else. Silly me, to think my only child would show a little compassion for her mother." Her shoulders squared off and her voice had a little wiggle in it, classic drama mama in a bid for sympathy.

If she was gonna poke the sleeping bear, she deserved to have her head bitten off. "Oh yeah, like where? If I recall correctly, your last boyfriend is wearing a toe tag."

"You don't have to be so hateful," she sniffed.

"You made me carry his dead body across the trailer park!" It was not my proudest moment, discovering that my mother had literally screwed a man to death and agreeing to help her move his corpse back to his own home. I'd done it to avoid this exact scenario, having my mom living with me.

The irony was not lost on me.

"Look," I said as I moved to the coffee pot. "I don't want to fight with you about this. I'm upset because you knew what was going on and didn't bother to tell me. Did you ever think I could have stopped the eviction if I'd known about it sooner?"

Celeste swept the coffee grounds into a dustpan and dumped them into the trash before she turned to face me.

"Did you ever think I was embarrassed that I couldn't handle it on my own? That I have to come to my daughter every time life decides to kick me. I have my pride, Jackie."

"And it's made you homeless." The second I said it, I wished I could call the words back, even before I saw her wounded expression. Damn it, I really needed to look into having the filter between my brain and my mouth repaired. "Mom, I'm sorry."

Pivoting on her heel, Celeste marched back to the third bedroom and slammed the door.

"Batting a thousand," I mumbled and trudged to the coffee pot. Talking to Celeste had me on edge and knowing more conversations like the one we'd just had were in store made it even worse. I had to dive into the files today, find her stinking rental agreement and figure out just what had gone wrong.

Luke joined me in the kitchen and poured himself a cup of coffee. "Logan called, he's gonna be late."

"Perfect. You can help me do some digging in the office. We need to find Celeste's lease."

Luke made a face, he hated paperwork. "Can she really be evicted, even though she owns the trailer outright?"

"Unfortunately, yes. As long as the trailer sits on rented land, she's subject to the same property owner-tenant relationship as a regular renter. Throw in the HOA and we've got ourselves a big old mess."

"Can you get her back in?" Luke popped two slices of oatmeal bread into the toaster, one for me and one for him. I knew that without asking, he'd bring me the honey jar to slather on my breakfast instead of butter. The little things, we had down to a science.

"I doubt it, not now that the eviction has been finalized. We'll need to see about getting her stuff moved into storage and selling the place. That's why I need the rental agreement, so we know exactly what her options are."

Luke scratched his stubble and lowered his voice. "How long is she going to be here?"

"I wish I knew." I frowned as I added a level teaspoon of sugar to my coffee. "Does it bother you that she's here?"

He gave me a half shrug. "It's a little awkward. She's never liked me."

"She doesn't know you." Which was partly my fault, though I didn't say it out loud. With Luke gone so often I'd kept him all to myself when he was home. And I hadn't felt the need to invite Celeste and her low rent drama into our limited time together. Other than the passing glance at a holiday party they were practically strangers. "Look, if you want me to find other accommodations for her, I will. Our marriage doesn't need her baggage right now anyway. And she always travels with the full matching designer knock-off set."

Luke sighed. "I can't kick her out, she's your mom. And you were so great when we had Logan and my mom here... No, it's fine. I just want some down time with you."

"We'll make the time," I promised him and promised myself. "Come on, we have paperwork to tackle."

Logan showed up mid-morning, though he stayed out on the verandah with Celeste.

"What are we paying him for again?" I grumbled to Luke as the sound of my mother's laughter carried through the screen door. "Entertainment director? Gigolo?"

"We're not paying him at all." Luke said. "Or getting paid, for that matter. Face facts, Jackie. Her lease isn't here."

I ran a hand through my hair as I stared at the mess

around us. He was right, we'd been tearing through the boxes for hours but found no trace of Celeste's rental agreement. "Damn it. I know I had it. I remember putting it away about a week after she moved in."

"Can you get another copy?" Luke asked hopefully.

My shoulders sagged. "I'll have to. As well as the deed to her trailer. Enough for today, we need to focus on work."

Luke rose and stretched his back. "Okay. What's first?"

I stacked the piles of paperwork, vowing I'd spend some time setting up a valid filing system at the first opportunity. "Get Logan in here and I'll bring you both up to speed at once."

A few minutes later the Dark Prince lounged against the doorframe while Luke studied the computer screen from behind me. I couldn't look into Logan's eyes directly, not with the memory of his words from the night before ringing in my ears.

Not fighting for her is the biggest regret of my life.

Yeah, I wasn't about to touch that with a ten foot salami.

"Nice of you to join us," I sniped instead and tried not to wonder if he'd sat in the truck watching over me while we both waited for Luke to show up. Wouldn't have been the first time he'd lurked outside of the house without my knowledge. That should have been creepy, but instead it reassured me to know he was looking out for me.

"What did you unearth?" Logan, in total badass mode, folded his arms across his chest, raised a brow and waited.

"There are no realtors in the greater Miami area named Marlena Cruz. The number on the card Big Joey slipped me was disconnected and his lease itself is a standard document with phony info typed in."

"So, in other words, zilch," the Dark Prince muttered.

"Did you contact Mrs. Pomeroy?" Luke asked, referring to the client who'd hired us.

"Yes, and she wants Big Joey gone, pronto. I asked her if we could offer him a real lease for the same apartment, but she just wants him out, do not pass go, do not collect a two hundred dollar deposit."

"And she didn't even see the elephant." Logan said.

"So we should go talk to him again," Luke circled around the desk. "Maybe he'll cooperate and leave without a problem."

Logan's snort was just a smidge faster than mine.

Luke shrugged. "Well, we can hope for the best, right?"

"As long as we plan for the worst," I said.

Leaving Celeste at our house was tough but I pointed to the stack of take-out menus and made her swear not to cook anything, not even boil water for tea. It was ninety-five degrees out and barely noon, no sane person drank tea in this weather.

"I feel like I'm leaving a teenage girl home alone for the first time," I said as I climbed into the back of the big black truck. "It'll be a miracle if the place is still standing when we get back."

"Does your insurance cover the kitchen curse?" Logan smirked as he merged with traffic heading east.

I bit my lip, pretty sure that it didn't.

The town of Surfside is sandwiched between the village of Bal Harbor and the City of Miami Beach. It stretches from 87th Terrace to 96th Street and with its tidy public beaches, boutiques, and plethora of parks, it is the very definition of a picturesque seaside community. Big Joey and his elephant trunks really didn't blend.

"So how are we gonna handle this?" I asked my fellow passengers as the ocean grew closer through the front windshield.

"He's a squatter and he's got to leave," Logan said. "We'll call the cops if we have to."

Lease on the Beach

I really hoped it wouldn't come to that. Hideous as he might be, I kinda liked Big Joey, just not his taste in swimwear.

"You'll never guess what I saw this morning." Joey greeted us like old friends when we knocked on the door. Thankfully, he wore board shorts and a button down shirt, though it hung open over his beer gut. "A freaking turtle! He was right there on the sand. Is that cool or what? Yous guys want some coffee or a calzone or anything?"

"Uh no, thanks." Logan was closest to me and I elbowed him in the ribs.

"What?" he hissed irritably.

I made a face that clearly said, *don't you feel like a heel for doing this*? He turned away without answering. Maybe it was just me.

"I mean he must have been, whatchamacallit," Big Joey snapped his fingers as though commanding the word that eluded him to come. His dark brown eyes lit up with triumph as he said, "Nesting. Do you think he's gonna have babies? That would be so cute, little baby turtles all flapping around. I've never seen nothin' like that. Do you know when they hatch?"

Maybe it was because Celeste had been evicted yesterday or maybe just Big Joey's enthusiasm over seeing the baby turtles but I didn't want to say what came next. "No, I don't. Listen Mr. Santino, I looked into your lease and it's not valid. Marlena Cruz had no right to show you this house, never mind rent it to you. You're going to have to vacate."

The smile slid off Big Joey's face. "What do you mean?"

"You've been trespassing on this property," Luke stepped forward. "I'm sorry, but you need to leave immediately."

Big Joey shook his head, back and forth, the very image of denial. "This can't be right," he said.

"Do you have someplace else to go?" I asked. I had

connections all over Miami, I was sure I could find him temporary lodgings while he looked for a new place.

"This ain't right." Joey focused on me. "I pay my rent every month on time."

"To the wrong person," Logan said, not unkindly. "It was a scam, Mr. Santino. Whoever you've been paying has conned you out of your money and our client out of her property."

"And she's just gonna get away with it?" His eyes were sad, his expression crestfallen, probably thinking of the baby turtles he'd never see hatch.

"No," I said before I realized what I meant to do. "No, she sure isn't. We're going to find out who conned you and we'll make them pay."

CHAPTER 5

"What the hell do you think you're doing?" Logan snarled at me when the three members of Damaged Goods were alone outside the apartment complex. Big Joey had gone inside to pack his meager belongings and Logan had worked himself up to DEFCON 2. "Promising that guy justice like you're some sort of vigilante?"

"He's been conned," I folded my arms across my chest. I'd taken a psychology course when I'd worked for the sheriff's department. Body language sent out messages the same way words did and some people responded to physical cues better than verbal ones. I wanted to make sure the Dark Prince understood I wouldn't budge on this. "It's not right."

"No," Luke said. "It's not right, but it's not our job to make it right, either. We work for the property owner, not Mr. Santino."

"The only thing necessary for the triumph of evil is for good men to do nothing." I recited the Edmund Burke quote, a personal favorite of mine, and lifted my chin. "Nobody's forcing you two to do anything, but I want to try and find out who conned this tenant out of almost five grand."

"Five?" Luke frowned. "How do you figure that?"

"He put down a two thousand dollar security deposit, plus first and last month's rent. And he just made this month's payment. If I can follow the money transfer, I'll find out who's benefited from this scam. I'll do it all on my own time, it has nothing to do with Damaged Goods."

Logan cast me a black look. "Don't you think you have enough on your plate?"

He was nonspecific about what I had on my plate, but I saw the way his gaze slid to Luke, almost as though he was issuing me a warning.

Since when did I take warnings from Logan Parker?

I faced Luke and went against the company protocol I'd set up about no PDA's on the job. I took his hand in mine. "I need to try and help him. I'll take care of the Celeste thing too and this won't interfere with company time, but it's something I need to do."

Luke's lips thinned but he nodded once. We both turned to face the bigger obstacle, A.K.A. The Dark Prince.

He took his sunglasses off and pinched the bridge of his nose. "Okay. I still say it's a mistake, but I can see I'm outnumbered. If you can dig up the financials, that's something he can take to the cops. But we're not P.I.'s here, Jackie. You can't just go loaning out your resources to anyone who tugs at your heartstrings."

"Sure," I chirped, the word entirely non-committal. Logan's eyes narrowed as though he knew I hadn't just agreed with him but he couldn't prove it.

I made a few phone calls while the guys helped Big Joey and found an apartment for rent a few miles inland for the same price he'd been paying for his non-lease. It wasn't on the beach, but he could afford it and it offered immediate occupancy. And Mrs. Pomeroy had offered to cover the cost of relocation for our displaced squatter.

Big Joey cast one more longing glance at the beach while the movers loaded his stuff onto a truck. "It was nice while it lasted."

"Hey, you'll be just like the rest of us locals who have to schlep to the beach by car, hunt for hours for a parking spot, walk miles across burning hot sand all in the name of a little R&R." I told him.

"This was my dream, you know? Retire on the beach."

"Retire?" I frowned. Joey Santino didn't look any older than Logan, who was in his late thirties. "Aren't you a little young to think about retirement? What did you retire from, anyway?"

He shrugged his massive shoulders. "I invested in a fleet of food trucks my brother Donny owns and operates in Manhattan, the boroughs, Long Island and Jersey. You wouldn't believe what those trucks are worth. As for the retirement, it was a health based decision. My doc told me I needed less stress in my life."

I made a face as we watched his furniture packed in bubble wrap. So much for less stress.

"I'll keep my ear to the ground on another beach rental nearby and let you know if anything pops up." I slipped him my card.

"Thanks Jackie. You're a good egg, and don't let anyone tell you otherwise." He raised his hand and I gave him a fist bump.

After he left, Luke, Logan, and I went through room by room, looking for damage or anything that would need to be repaired before the owner could re-rent the apartment. There wasn't much, some carpet that needed to be tacked down, the small dining area needed new light bulbs in the hanging fixture and the wall in the living room was scuffed and should probably be sanded down and repainted. Otherwise the place was in move-in condition.

"I don't get it," I said to Logan as we secured the small deck that led down to the beach. A storm was rolling in, the clouds scudding swiftly overhead. "How did Marlena Cruz access this place to begin with?"

He could have pointed out that he'd washed his hands of the investigation, but he didn't. "You should probably start off with a list of anyone who had access to a key. Call the owner and let her know we're done here and find out the last time she changed the locks and find out who had keys."

I recalled his mutterings from the day before about owning a house and wondered if he'd been serious. "Are you really looking to buy a place?" I asked as he shut and locked the door and closed the vertical blinds on the excellent view.

A shrug. "Makes more sense than renting, especially since I'm going to be sticking around town."

While Luke was in the military, Logan disappeared for months on end. If Luke knew where his brother went during his sojourns, he'd never told me and I didn't want to pry. Much. A little while back, Logan had mentioned he'd once been a sous chef at an Irish pub, though I was still wrestling with that mental picture. The man could cook like nobody's business.

I wanted to ask if Marcy factored into his decision at all, or if it was just because his brother was back in town for good. Picturing Logan as a homeowner was messing with my mind a little. Though I'd only been in his personal space once, the décor had been sparse. Blank walls, standard drapes, black satin sheets…yeah not gonna think about his sheets.

Any questions seemed too invasive though, like I was overly concerned with his movements. Which I wasn't. It was just natural curiosity about a member of my extended family who seemed to spend his every waking moment at my house.

Lease on the Beach

"Well, good luck with the house hunt." I just refrained from slapping him on the back in a show of coworker solidarity. Cripes, that would have been embarrassing.

"Actually, I already have my eye on a place."

"Really?" My teeth sank into my lower lip as I fought the urge to crowbar him open like a locked trunk. Okay, the curiosity was eating me alive, so sue me.

He grunted. "If you want to know, just ask me outright."

"Okay, so where's this terrific house, Logan?"

He flashed me a smirk. "None of your business, Jackie."

Oh he was evil. Temptation, wrapped in sin and coated in malevolence. "Fine, don't tell me. I'll just bug your personal property so I can keep tabs on you." Of course unlike him, I didn't have easy access to cool tech gismos, even if I knew how to work them. It was an empty threat and we both knew it.

Luke came out of the single bedroom holding the little thing he used to check the outlets. "Everything's fine there. What are you two bickering about now?"

"Nothing," I said at the same time Logan muttered, "Your wife is a busybody."

"Am not."

"Are too."

"That's mature," Luke shook his head. "Come on, we better head out."

Back in the truck, I called Mrs. Pomeroy to let her know the apartment was clear. Her voicemail picked up immediately, so I left a detailed message and requested she return my call at her earliest convenience.

The storm broke just as we hit the interstate and the snarl of traffic slowed to a hogtied belly crawl. My knee bounced and I tried to pinpoint why I felt so restless all of a sudden. The guys were tense too, not talking, just staring out the windshield. To distract myself from the unexplained anxiety, I made a mental task list of things I needed to take care of in order of priority. Check our bank balance and make sure Mrs. Pomeroy paid up, tout suite. Obtain another copy of Celeste's rental agreement and get her trailer cleaned out and her belongings put into storage. That one made me flinch.

Accepting that I had a mother who'd played fast-and-loose with the eviction process was a bitter pill to swallow. Decent folks didn't typically get evicted and I'd worked hard to leave the PWT—poor white trash— label behind me. The system was set up to protect tenants first and foremost because only a real bastard would enjoy seeing someone kicked out of their home. Many times property owners and tenants could take less drastic measures to stave off eviction. It was less hassle for everyone involved if disputes could be solved without legal intervention. Most cases I'd dealt with during my tenure as a certified process server were more like Big Joey's, where the party in the wrong made reparations and moved on with their lives, instead of more dramatic scenes. Like Celeste being padlocked out of her trailer so her dupe of a daughter had to slink back to the trailer park, hat in hand, and ask to get her stuff back.

"Damn it," I mumbled.

"Something wrong?" Luke asked from the front seat.

Almost everything, I thought. "I'm just trying to sort out Celeste's situation. There's something hinky going on there, something she won't tell me."

"Do you think it has something to do with how the old landlord died?" Logan glanced at me over his shoulder.

Mental forehead smack. Hadn't I just been ruminating about Richard Stanley's death earlier? "If someone found out that Stanley didn't die peacefully in his sleep, that he was with Celeste, maybe they had an ax to grind with her."

"Wait a minute," Luke said as traffic crawled along. "What do you mean, he was with Celeste?"

"He was in her trailer when he died." Ahead of us a blue hair in a Cadillac DeVille was in the right-hand lane with her right blinker on. I frowned as she stood on her brakes and six cars merged between her and the tractor trailer in front of her.

"So how did he get back to his own place?" Luke asked. There was a dangerous note in his voice, one of menace with an underlying warning.

Uh oh. I'd never mentioned the corpse carrying to my husband, but Logan had caught me off guard. "We sort of carried him."

"You helped her with this?" Luke asked Logan.

"Don't look at me. That was all her crazy. She just told me about it after." Logan cheerfully threw me under the bus.

There was utter silence. Then, Luke maneuvered the truck until we rode up on the shoulder to pass the DeVille and take the next exit.

I kicked the back of Logan's seat like a petulant eight year old. *That* could have gone better.

"LOGAN, could you make sure Celeste is okay?" I asked when Luke parked in front of our bungalow, but made no move to get out. There was no way we could have the knock-down drag out screaming match that had been building since yesterday afternoon with my mother and his brother listening in. The truck was a good secondary option but I needed the Dark Prince to am-scray before Luke hit critical mass.

Logan glanced between the two of us and then sighed. "Not a problem."

JENNIFER L HART

Luke waited until his brother was secured in the house.

"Let me explain," I started as I climbed over the gearshift to take Logan's vacated seat. Luke didn't move a muscle, his jaw clenched tight as he stared out the windshield. "Celeste called me—"

"When?" he interrupted.

"A few weeks ago. During the Gomez thing."

I could hear his molars grinding together. "Yet another situation you inserted yourself into regardless of the consequences. Do you do this all the time?"

His tone bugged me. "Help people? Try to do what's right? Yeah, Luke, I do."

He snorted.

"I *was* helping Celeste, whether you want to believe it or not. Her reputation couldn't have born that kind of hit. She would have lost her station at the beauty parlor and all of her friends as well as her trailer if they knew she'd literally screwed her landlord to death."

"So you thought the best move was to risk *your* reputation and help her stage a crime scene?"

"There was no crime! He was an older man who ate bacon at every meal and he had a heart attack. I was only protecting my mother from a scandal. Do you think I go out looking for trouble like that? No, but I've been protecting her my whole life. You can't ask me to just stop."

"And then the first thing you do is tell my brother about it, yet you neglected to mention it to me? Was that protecting your mother, too?" He made a sound of disgust.

I hated him a little bit in that moment. "No, jackass, that was me protecting *you* and Damaged Goods because I didn't want to drag us both down if word did get out. You could get another process server on board but I didn't want to tank both our careers in one fell swoop."

He was fuming, but so was I and I sucked in just enough air to keep going. "What's it to you all of a sudden what I do when I'm not with you? I didn't question what you were up to when we weren't together, even though I probably should have."

"I knew it. I knew you thought I was cheating." He pointed an accusing finger in my face.

I knocked it aside. "No, damn you, I didn't because I trust you. I'm not going to pretend it didn't hurt me to see you there with her, to see her flirting shamelessly with you and you not setting her straight about the fact that , oh yeah, by the way I'm freaking married, but I trust you. Even though I'm not sure that I should."

His eyebrows drew down furiously. "And what's that supposed to mean?"

"I've told you multiple times that I've been faithful to you, but it dawned on me yesterday that you've never once said that to me. Not one single time since we've been married."

"No, I haven't." his voice was low, dangerous, like a lion crouched in the tall grass, ready to spring. "I didn't think I needed to say it. I thought you understood that I didn't want anyone else, would *never* want anyone else the way I want you." He shouted the words at me as though he could hurt me with their impact when the opposite was true.

I sucked in a sharp breath. Blinked as all the fight went out of me. "Luke—"

"Tell me how to fix it, Jackie," he said, his gaze pleading. "Tell me how to be with you without all this insanity coming between us. It never used to be this way. What changed?"

"I don't know," I whispered.

Luke inhaled and held the breath as he uttered, "Tell me the truth, are you sick of me?"

What? "No, Luke. I—"

Someone knocked on the window behind me. I jumped, Luke cursed but he lowered the window.

"Sorry to interrupt," Logan did look genuinely sorry, but he pushed on. "One of Celeste's neighbors just called. The landlord is putting all her stuff out on the street."

CHAPTER 6

"You can't do that," I said to Barry Stanley, the new owner of Celeste's trailer park. "The trailer itself is still legally hers, as is everything inside it." I held the copy of her deed up in front of his face.

We'd arrived onsite at Summer's Meadow mobile home park to find another property management team dumping my mother's possessions in the storm water runoff ditch outside the trailer park. I was livid, both at the unprofessionalism of the thoughtless team and at the dumbass landlord who'd sanctioned their actions.

"Celeste Drummond vacated her residence, which sits atop my property and is connected to my utilities. The writ of possession grants me the right to remove her personal belongings." Barry was a squat man in his late fifties with severe male pattern baldness except for a tuft of curly gray and black hair that grew dead center on his shiny pink scalp. If I were him I would have done the Bruce Willis thing and just shaved it all instead of looking like I had a Brillo pad stuck to my head, but he hadn't asked my advice.

"Right," I agreed. "But not to *enter* the unit. Tell your team of thugs to stand down, or I'll call the sheriff out here to charge you with breaking and entering." I was bluffing, no way did I want my name associated with this clusterfuck in official police circles, but Barry the Toad didn't know that.

"Your mother abandoned her property. I have several potential tenants interested in that lot." He made it sound like Celeste had flitted off to Vegas instead of being forcibly evicted. I glanced to where Luke and Logan loaded overflowing boxes of my mother's life into the bed of the big black truck and my hands curled into fists.

"Understood. But the trailer is still her property and I will see to it that it's removed from your lot as soon as possible. Also, I require a copy of her original property agreement as well as a record of any of the park rules to facilitate the sale of the trailer."

There are four ways the property owner of a mobile home park in the state of Florida can evict a tenant who owns her trailer outright. If she doesn't pay her lot rent or utilities. If the trailer owner is convicted of violating federal, state, or local law and her actions threaten the well-being of the other park residents. If she violates her rental agreement or the stated mobile home park, or MPH, rules. And lastly, if the MHP owner wants to change the way his land is being used.

As far as I knew, Celeste hadn't been convicted of any crimes, did pay her rent and since no one else in the Summer's Meadow mobile home park was affected, Celeste must have violated her rental agreement or the park rules somehow. It was important to figure out exactly what had happened because with a court ordered eviction on her rental history, finding a new place for her to live wasn't going to be easy.

Barry crossed his stocky arms over his barrel chest, the

same closed for business body language as I'd used on Logan earlier. He wore a wife beater with a short sleeved plaid button down over the top and a pair of cutoff cargo pants. "I'm not going to waste another second on you or your white trash mother." He shuffled off across the lot.

"Smarmy little troll," I muttered and stalked back to the trailer to help pack up whatever the goon squad hadn't tossed into the gutter.

The place was a wreck, every cabinet open, the contents littered across the narrow counters and floor. A box of cereal had been upended over the floor and then walked through so that every step involved a crunching sound. Her curtains were torn down and draped haphazardly over her floral sofa. The television was hanging crookedly on the wall.

"Hey," Logan came up the steps, hooking one arm of his sunglasses in his black crewneck tee as he maneuvered inside the cramped space.

"Hey," I answered as I tried to unhook the dangling flat screen. I'd bought it for her five years ago during a black Friday sale and had the scars to prove it. "Can you give me a hand with this?"

I needn't have asked. Logan hefted the thirty six inch contraption with ease as I disconnected the cables. I offered him a smile of thanks and rose to stretch my back as he placed the set carefully against the wall. Where's Luke?"

His eyes locked on my breasts as he spoke. Nope, definitely not batting for the home team. "The truck was full so he's taking it back to your house. He's going to see about renting a U-haul. I volunteered to stay and help you pack up."

He may have his faults, but deep down Logan Parker had a soft heart. "Thanks. God, this is so depressing."

"What is?" Logan looked around. "I'm sure it looked

better before those asswipes trampled through here like a herd of impotent wildebeests."

I smiled a little at the image and knelt to collect Celeste's photos. The Popsicle stick frame I'd given her for mother's day in third grade was trashed. "No, it's not the mess, though I do plan to burn their asses in a Yelp review. No, the trailer is fine. Hell, this is freaking millionaire's row compared to the places we lived in while I was growing up."

"Is this you?" Logan carefully shook glass from the photo that had been in the frame.

I glanced over his shoulder at the shot. "In all my glory. I was probably about nine there."

"An obvious hell-raiser even then."

I frowned when he tucked the small photograph carefully in his wallet, but didn't comment. To distract myself, I started folding the curtains. "It's ironic, you know? You being here now. I never wanted you or Luke to see my humble beginnings. To see how I used to live. "

Logan frowned. "Why not?"

I shrugged, feeling like a moron for bringing it up.

He stopped me from where I stacked magazines into a box. "Talk to me, Jackie."

I blew out a breath. "It's embarrassing, to come from this. I've worked really hard to put it all behind me, but Celeste just can't keep her shit together and I get sucked down with her. That's what you interrupted before, Luke railing on me about getting pulled into her drama. Like I even have a choice."

Logan crouched beside me and started on the books. He frowned at the cover of *No Mercy*, probably not pegging my mother as a science fiction erotic romance fan. "Maybe it's not her fault, did you ever think of that?"

I snorted and turned back to the magazines. "Trust me, it's *always* her fault. She could have come to me and maybe I could have stopped this. Instead, she kicked it under the rug and left me dealing with her big old bag of crazy. Now, I've got to find her a new place to live, just like the good old days."

Logan frowned. "Has this happened before?"

"No. We always left when things got too rocky, before the paperwork went through."

"Jesus," Logan looked like he wanted to say something more but didn't know what.

I shrugged and turned back to what I was doing. "It's part of why I do what I do. The rules only work when everyone plays by them. People who don't, deserve to get thrown out on their freeloading asses."

"I never knew you had such a personal reason."

"It's not something I like to talk about. Ever since I was eleven—"

Shit, that was not a memory I wanted to drag out under the spotlight. I turned back to clearing off the built-in shelving over her entertainment center. "Never mind. See if you can locate the vacuum. We have to get the crumbs up or this place will be infested with bugs."

"What happened when you were eleven?" Logan moved around me until he was blocking the hall. His big broad shoulders filled the entire width of the narrow space.

"Are you my therapist all of a sudden? I gotta tell you, it's not a well-paying gig." I strove to hit our usual banter but missed the mark.

"Jackie, tell me what happened."

I tried to blow it off. "It's really not that big a deal."

He gave me a look that clearly said, *let me be the judge of that*.

I threw my hands up in the air. "Fine, but you have to tell me what house you intend to buy. Tit for tat."

Again his gaze dropped to my chest and I snapped my

fingers at my face to snag his attention back from where it didn't belong. He shrugged, as though even the mention of the word tit was too much for him to handle.

"Deal." He stuck out his hand and I shook. His palms were rough and calloused, a real working man's hands. I shivered and pulled my own sweaty mitt back.

"You first," he prompted.

I shot a nervous glance at the open door. Logan followed my gaze, then pulled me down the pokey hall and through the hanging strands of seashells that acted as her bedroom door. They clicked softly at the disturbance. "Okay, no one will overhear."

I sighed, tempted to sit down onto the unmade bed, but not comfortable with the idea of Logan reclining beside me. "Okay, well you've met Celeste and just to be clear, age has mellowed her drama. She used to search out the party scene a lot of times, leaving me home alone at night and asking a neighbor to keep an ear out for me."

His eyebrows drew down. "Nobody ever reported her leaving you alone like that?"

"Logan, in places like where I grew up nobody cared about much beyond the next fix from their drug of choice." Emotion clogged my voice and I had to swallow past the lump of remembered fear.

"How old were you, the first time she left you?" He asked quietly.

"Seven, I think. At least the first time I was aware she was gone. She always waited until after I went to bed. That night I'd had a nightmare." My heart pounded and I vividly recalled the sensation of waking from dreams of monsters and screaming her name. The trailer was dark and wind blew forcefully outside, causing the cheap siding to flap and bang. Though I hadn't wanted to get out of bed, my mother wasn't in it beside me. "I thought maybe she'd fallen asleep watching T.V. but all the lights were off, so I hid in the closet until I heard her come in. It was scary at first, but I got used to it."

He swore low. "You shouldn't have had to get used to something like that."

I shrugged because he was right. I knew it then too, but I'd been powerless. "It was what it was. You can get used to anything you need to and at the time, there wasn't anything else I could do. So like I said, I got used to it. By the time I was eleven, I was pretty self-sufficient and I was typically the one who put her to bed. So one night she went out and locked the door behind her. I was up past my bedtime watching T.V. This was a different place, and she had one of those small TV VCR combos in her bedroom. I remember I was watching *Designing Women* of all things. I heard keys in the lock. I figured it was Celeste, so I didn't think anything of it until the landlord walked into the bedroom.

"He was drunk as hell and angry. Apparently Mommy Dearest had fallen behind on the rent again. And they had a standing arrangement that if she didn't pay in one way, she'd pay in another." I held Logan's bright blue gaze so I wouldn't be drawn too far back into the memory, of the way the light from the television flickered over the stranger's stubble coated face. The stink of unwashed male and booze that wafted from him.

"I'm not sure if he knew I wasn't Celeste, I looked a lot like her and he obviously wasn't seeing too clearly, but I was sort of stunned stupid. Didn't know what to say, what to do, just frozen. Until he unbuckled his belt."

"God, Jackie. You were just a baby," Logan's voice was thick with emotion.

"Nothing happened," I was quick to assure him. "I locked myself in the bathroom and climbed out the window. I went and hid at the neighbor's, an older woman with like thirty-seven cats. Celeste got back and found him passed out on the bed and me missing and she freaked the hell out. We moved out that very day. So, yeah, it could have been worse."

"It was bad enough," Logan's tone was low. "What was his name?"

"Never mind," I said sharply, afraid at what he might do. "It's over and done with."

"Is he still around? The man who tried to molest you?" His tone was low and dangerous.

"I'm not sure."

"Does Luke know about this?" His whole demeanor was dark and threatening, like the storm clouds we'd seen earlier.

"No, and I don't want you to tell him either." That was the last thing I needed, the two of them bent on vengeance, banding together and shutting out reason and probably doing something epically stupid because they were big damn hero types with more testosterone than sense. "Don't make me regret telling you about this, Logan."

He was shaking visibly, seething with impotent fury. Damn it all, what had I been thinking? He stood there like a bomb and there was no one else to diffuse him.

I did the one thing I always avoided, something I hadn't done since the night he'd saved my life. I reached out and touched him. Just my hands on his bare forearms, but he jolted as though I'd pushed him into an electric fence.

"Hey. Just say no to the crazy trailer park drama, Logan. It'll suck you down if you let it. I got out, built a good life. I don't even remember his name. He's not worth another thought, okay?"

Hot blue eyes met mine and I felt a little dizzy as the small room closed in around us. The intensity threatened to take us both under. I wanted to pull away, wanted to pretend it didn't exist because it held all the destructive force of a category five hurricane, but some things were true whether or not you wanted them to be real or not.

He pulled me roughly against him and buried his face in my hair. In some distant part of my brain warning claxons blared, but remembering that night had shaken me too and I let him hold me, glad of the comfort.

"It's okay," I told him, told myself. My palms pressed into his back, holding him to me. They itched to move, to explore and stroke him, but I willed them to stillness. This was enough. It had to be. I turned my ear and lost myself in the steady, reassuring thump of his heartbeat. "It's over."

Gradually we both stopped shaking and sounds from outside penetrated, the laughter of children, a dog barking, an old man coughing up a lung. Logan was the first to pull back, his head turned. "We should finish up. Luke will be back soon."

"Right." Now that the contact was broken, shame burned deep inside me. Damn it, I didn't want to react to Logan that way. And playing this f-ed up version of truth or dare with him was asking for trouble. I turned around and yanked out a dresser drawer, praying it wouldn't be filled with Celeste's porn stash, or worse, her personal massager. There are some things are girl just shouldn't know about her mom. It overflowed with underwear, thongs in every color of the rainbow, thank goodness. "I'll take this room if you finish up out front."

Heavy footsteps retreated to the front of the trailer. I let out a sigh and dropped my head in my hands. The absolute last thing I needed was to let my tender feelings for Logan out of the box I'd buried them in years before. It was wrong, so wrong, not just because he was my coworker or my husband's brother. I was committed to Luke, had promised to love, honor, and cherish him and him alone. That vow had not been made lightly. Hell, it had barely been made at all.

Luke and I had so much crap to sort through and the past needed to just freaking lie down and die already.

Determined to force the thoughts back into their hidey hole, I did what I did best. Put my head down and got to work.

CHAPTER 7

Though I worried about nightmares after my acid trip down memory lane, the taxing mental and physical day rewarded me with a dreamless night's sleep. Luke's lumberjack snoring woke me the next morning before dawn, and after using the bathroom, I shuffled out to the kitchen to brew a pot of coffee.

I took my steaming mug out front and sat on the steps to watch the sun rise. The colors were particularly splendid that morning, the distant red glow gradually lightening until the entire eastern sky turned orange, then gold and the fluffy clouds stacked like layers on a multi-hued cake. A storm was brewing.

"Pretty, isn't it?"

I turned to find Celeste in the doorway, her eyes on the heaven sent display.

I shrugged. "I bet it looks spectacular over the water."

She frowned. "You always do that, you know. Take something nice and put it down because you think it's not good enough."

I snorted. "Wow, Mom. Real subtle-like."

Her gaze shifted from the line above the trees to my face.

"That wasn't me trying to make a point, Jackie. I know your childhood wasn't perfect, but I did the best I could."

She'd shattered my peace, which was just what she did. Irritated, I rose and turned to face her. "The fact that you can actually believe that staggers me. Leaving me home alone starting at age seven while you went out to get high as a freaking kite was not doing your best. It was a selfish choice."

She'd wrapped her arms around herself. "I know that."

"Do you, Celeste? Do you really? God, why did you even keep me anyway? Just to torture me?"

A single tear, too perfectly timed to be genuine, slid down her face. "If you're telling me you think you would have been better off if I'd had an abortion—."

"I wasn't saying that." Damn it, I knew better than to engage with her, because she was unable to take it down a notch. "Look, I really don't want to talk about this okay? The past is the past, let's just leave it there to rot. Are you working today?"

She looked at me and I gritted my teeth, waiting for her to pick up the conversational ball and drop the grenade we'd been passing back and forth in an emotional game of hot potato.

"Yeah," she said at last. "I need to be in by nine. Do you mind giving me a ride?"

Celeste worked at Curly Q's a kitschy little salon not too far from the University of Miami. Unfortunately, the dated hair shop with its psychedelic swirl wallpaper failed to draw any of the college students. Instead they specialized in wash and sets for seniors, who were meager tippers, but still loyal customers.

"You can take my car." I told her, not wanting to play chauffeur. She was already living with me, and the more time we spent in each other's company, the deeper down the rabbit hole we'd go. Celeste had a license, though she never had money for a vehicle of her own. She was perfectly capable of driving herself to work and back. "My day is shaping up to be a little scattered."

I still hadn't heard back from Mrs. Pomeroy and she hadn't paid us for evicting Big Joey. Call me kooky, but if I was going to feel like crap for evicting that nice, albeit fashion-challenged guy, I wanted to get paid for it. Then there were our new cases, all of which came in in a big, overwhelming rush this morning when Pauly Cavell, our jerkoff IT guy, finally got the website and email up and running and had called me at oh dark hundred to tell me that we were officially back online. And, of course there were my side projects of tracking down the phony realtor Marlena Cruz, fixing my marriage and finding my mother the hair dresser a permanent home, no pun intended.

Celeste looked like she wanted to argue with my plan to hand her Bessie Mae's keys and scoot, but thankfully the roar of a motorcycle interrupted our strained conversation. Logan turned the corner onto our street, pulled into the driveway and stopped in his customary parking spot to the right of Bessie Mae. He removed his helmet, revealing damp black hair and his rogue's smile. He wore a leather jacket over a white t-shirt and jeans, though how anyone could wear leather in this heat was beyond me. Still, he cut a lusty picture.

"What's he doing here so early?" I still had bed head for crying out loud.

"Lord, have mercy," Celeste breathed. "Is there anything as sexy as a man on a motorcycle?"

"And I'm out." I rose, waved to Logan, and turned to go back inside. There was something really icky about my mother lusting over my brother-in-law. It could have been worse, she could have been all hormonally hot-n-bothered for Luke. Yet the thought didn't make me feel any better.

I pulled a yogurt from the fridge and a spoon from the drawer and tried not to stare out the window where Celeste and Logan were chatting like bosom buddies. My stomach sank as he withdrew his wallet and handed something to her. Crap, was he giving her money? If it was for sexual favors, I was just going to go ahead and kill myself now.

Strong arms wrapped around me from behind.

I jumped, startled. "You scared me."

Luke's breath was warm and minty fresh as he said, "Penny for your thoughts?"

"You'd get change back." I turned and smiled up at him, dismissing the weirdness out front. "Did you sleep well?"

He made a sort of humming sound in the back of his throat. "Mmmmm, except that I woke up alone."

"Your snoring drove me to the coffee pot." Setting my now empty yogurt container on the table I turned to face him fully.

"Let me make it up to you." His melted chocolate eyes were hot with desire. Luke had always been a morning person, in every sense of the word.

"This is so not the time or the place—" My words cut off abruptly as he did something wicked with his hands. "Logan's here and Celeste…oh, Luke… don't…."

"Don't stop you mean?" His grin was triumphant.

The ability to make sense faded fast as what I wanted and what I should do collided. He pressed me up against the fridge and the stainless steel was cool against my back. His big body blocked the windows so no one looking in would see what he was doing, though we'd get busted if either my mom or Logan walked through the door.

He knew it too, I saw the exhilaration in his eyes, the thrill of the gamble. That was his plan, I realized with a jolt. He wanted to roll the dice, to risk us getting caught like a couple of horny teenagers who didn't have the control to keep our hands to ourselves. An illicit thrill shot through me, knowing we could be discovered any moment, recognizing that he knew it too.

"Because I'll stop if you really want me to…." The manipulative bastard smirked.

"Don't you dare." I shook my head, then nodded, gasped again as I clung to him, thoughts scattering. "God—,"

"You can just call me Luke." He kissed me then, a hot possessive kiss. The kind of kiss he hadn't given me for a long time, not since the early days of our marriage. It was a kiss with attitude. It said, I know what I want and I'm going to get it, so you can just deal with it.

I'd forgotten how it could be between us. How he focused on me so intently that he trapped me in the moment, kept my wandering mind firmly in the here and now. Luke could take me out of myself, overwhelming my every sense when he fixed all his intensity on me. When he took charge I stopped thinking, stopped worrying, and enjoyed him and what he made me feel. The entire universe shrank down until it was just the two of us locked together.

He knew my body well, knew me, carnally at least. I gasped for breath as his lips traveled down the side of my neck, then up to my ear. "Now, Ace. Right now."

I bit my lip to keep from crying out. My vision wavered in and out for a second and I clung to him so I wouldn't collapse onto the floor.

"Thanks," I wheezed as I struggled for breath. "I needed that."

"I'm not done with you yet." He took my hand and led me into the bedroom.

The front door opened and I heard Celeste's laughter. I ran, barely stifling a squeak. Luke made sure to lock the bedroom door.

"Where'd they go?" I asked Luke as we reemerged into the living room an hour later. We were freshly showered and ready to get on with the business at hand, but there was no sign of Logan or Celeste.

"Maybe they took the hint." Luke slapped my backside playfully as he made his way to the coffee pot.

I checked the driveway from the front window. "Well, Bessie Mae is gone, so I'm guessing Celeste went to work. Logan's bike is still here though."

"Maybe he's in the office?" Luke raised his voice and shouted his brother's name. No answer. He shrugged to me. "I'm out of ideas here."

Sure, I was grateful that Logan wasn't in the other room while I had my wicked way with his brother, but his disappearing act was a little too weird. "Do you suppose he went with Celeste?"

"Somehow I can't picture him at the Curly Q."

I worried my lower lip as the rabid thoughts in my head ran amuck. The scene on the porch earlier played through my mind. No, no way would Logan really be doing my mom. He was dating Marcy for the love of grief. Marcy, who he wasn't sexually involved with. And a man like Logan didn't abstain for long.

It made a sick sort of sense, why he'd been so decent about helping unscrew Celeste's screw up. Men did all sorts of idiotic things they wouldn't normally do for the women they were sleeping with and Celeste was Logan's type, namely easy pickings. And he was hers, because he had a pulse.

"Jackie?" Luke's voice sounded far away.

Damn it, this was bad. Crap, was Mom actually nailing my former lover? Did she think he'd marry her? Did he want

Lease on the Beach

to marry her? Was that why he was all hush-hush about his sudden interest in being a homeowner.

"Ace, you okay?" Luke's tone was filled with concern.

"No." I staggered to the nearest chair and put my head between my knees.

Brother–in–law or not, if he hurt her I'd skin him alive. Hell, I might do it anyway since he was messing with my best friend and my mom. A Dark Prince throw rug would look good in front of the TV.

Luke grasped my chin, his eyes filled with concern. "What's the matter?"

I couldn't tell him about my suspicions. First of all because that's all they were, suspicions. It was entirely possible that I was wrong, that Logan had only chatted with Celeste, spotted her five bucks for lunch and then gone for a stroll around the block, not to the nearest cheap motel for a quickie.

Somehow, I forced a smile. "Sorry, just got a little dizzy. I'm good now."

I tried to stand up, but Luke held me in place. "Do you need to go to the doctor? Or maybe the ER?"

"No, Luke, I'm fine." Again I tried to stand up and again my big strong husband held me in place.

Heavy footsteps thudded on the planks of the verandah. The door opened and Logan came in, took in the scene, me held in place and Luke doing the holding. Logan frowned. "What's wrong?"

"I don't know. She got really pale all of a sudden and she says she's dizzy."

"Was dizzy. It passed. Probably just the heat." I said, trying to wave it off.

Logan knelt on my other side and took my left hand, turning it over so he could take my pulse. I tried to pull away, still protesting that I was all right, but both of the big strong dumbasses ignored me.

"Your heart rate is elevated," Logan said.

"How would you know? What, are you a doctor now?"

"I was a hospital corpsman during my enlistment in the Navy. A medic, remember?"

I hadn't. Logan was a chameleon, a real jack of all trades. It was hard to keep track. "My pulse is probably fast because the two of you are aggravating me."

"Should we take her to the hospital?" Luke asked.

Logan stared into my eyes, his gaze assessing and maybe it was just my imagination but almost a little bit wistful. "Is there any chance you could be pregnant?"

Luke looked from his brother to me and back, his expression shocked. "Pregnant." He whispered the word with awe, the way a five year old girl would say "unicorn."

I shook my head. "No."

"Are you sure?" Logan pressed. "Accidents happen, birth control fails some times. Maybe you should make an appointment with your doctor—"

They had relaxed their various holds on me and I stood up quickly, needing to get away. "I will if we can stop talking about this and get to work, all right? We've got landlords and tenants aplenty waiting on us."

My heart pounded like crazy and I didn't wait for them as I made my way into the office.

That could have gone better.

CHAPTER 8

"Stay in the truck, Jackie." Luke turned around in his seat to stare at me over the tops of his sunglasses.

We were parked in front of a conch house in the Overtown neighborhood, northwest of downtown Miami. Luke and I had stayed in a conch rental during our brief honeymoon in Key West. That one had been adorable, a single story with gingerbread trim, situated right on the beach. This one was in a serious state of disrepair, with visible dents in the tin roof, and huge holes in the lattice work that covered the posts propping the house up off the ground. One of the double hung sash windows had been broken and was boarded up with plywood.

"No can do," I unbuckled my seatbelt. "The tenant needs to be served a seven day notice to cure or quit."

I was the certified process server for Damaged Goods. Anytime a tenant was in violation of his or her lease, I was responsible for delivering legal notices. Procedure dictated that I be on-site whenever official notice had to be given.

"Quit with what?" Logan asked. "What's the complaint?"

"Pets," I told them. "According to his lease, he stated that he didn't have pets, yet the neighbors have complained of animal noises coming from the house. There've also been reports of excessive foot traffic at night."

"Could be anything," Luke said. "Guns, drugs, human trafficking. Stay here, I'll text you if we need you."

It was ridiculous, both of the big, strong dumbasses had gone into serious overprotective mode at the mention of a baby on board. "Why stop there?" I grumped, "Why not just put me in a hermetically sealed bubble?"

"Still wouldn't stop stray bullets," Logan offered.

I rolled my eyes. "For the hundredth time, I. Am. Not. Pregnant." Damn it, if I knew they were going to be this stubborn I would have made them stop at a CVS and pick up a home pregnancy test, even if I had to take it during the car ride over.

"You don't know that for sure." Luke said quietly, his eyes intense. "Not until your doctor's appointment. Is it really worth the risk?"

I thought so, but it was obvious they didn't give a fig what I thought. I opened my mouth to argue more, then shut it. They were both cranked up to full steam testosterone and if the tenant even looked at me sideways, they'd probably overreact, cross a line and then we'd be up the creek with a turd for a paddle. I didn't like it, but I had to stay out of sight and let them do their jobs, for the sake of Damaged Goods. "Fine, but call me on your cell. I want to hear everything that's going on."

"I can do you one better." Logan reached into the back seat, into the Rubbermaid bin full of gear he'd placed there last week. We'd learned the hard way to prepare for anything in this business, or at least bring as much as we could carry. I had to press myself back against the door to get out of his way and tried to ignore the crisp clean scent of him, the way his white t-shirt clung to well-defined shoulders.

Stupid hormones. Cripes, why couldn't I just tell them

both that my wooziness earlier was from the thought of Logan banging my mom? Then maybe they'd stop with all the *you might be pregnant* garbage and let me do my freaking job.

But I held my tongue because I didn't want either of the Parker brothers to know I cared who Logan was shagging. Sure, I could have gone all high and mighty, claimed I was worried about Celeste or Marcy or even Logan getting hurt. But that wasn't the whole truth, not by a long shot.

"Here," Logan handed me a headset, which as little more than an earbud with a microphone attached. "You'll be in constant contact so you can come to our rescue at a moment's notice."

I glowered at him but he had the world's best poker face and I really couldn't tell if he was serious. "Okay, thanks."

He handed another headset to Luke and then inserted the last one in his own ear.

"Can you hear me?" I asked.

Luke grinned. "You're two feet away, Ace."

I rolled my eyes. "Fine, get out of the truck so we can make sure this works."

They disembarked and I scrambled into the front seat. "So? How now brown cow."

"Really?" Logan slid his sunglasses into place but one raised eyebrow conveyed his derision. "That's the best you've got?"

I shrugged. "Short notice. Now stop screwing around and find out what this tenant is doing."

"Yes, Ma'am." Luke nodded once and the two of them crossed the street.

The file on the tenant was wedged between the passenger's seat and the armrest. I plucked it out, opened it and read aloud to the guys. "Tenant is Jamel Smith, age twenty eight. Two priors for assault and battery, one with six months of hard time. He's out on parole, works nights at the stop-n-rob on the corner. No vehicle registered."

"Any details on the assault cases?" Logan muttered.

"No." I frowned. "That's weird."

"What?" I could see Luke hesitate, hand raised to knock on the door.

"His rental agreement states that he lives alone. If he works nights, what's with all the foot traffic?"

"Only one way to find out," Logan muttered.

Luke knocked. Some of the ambient noise filtered through the headset. I could hear traffic passing on the street as an eighteen wheeler drove past and Luke's sharp raps.

"I heard something," Luke muttered. "Footsteps maybe."

A minute passed and Logan pounded on the door. "Mr. Smith? We represent your landlord. Please answer the door, sir."

I shifted my gaze upward to the second story. "I can't see anyone moving around in there."

"I'll check around back." Luke said and made his way to the other side of the porch, to peer in the non-broken window.

"I hear barking," Logan said and sure enough, I could hear a deep woofing through the headset.

"What the hell…?" Luke had pressed his face to the front window. "Logan, Ace, you are not going to believe this."

I was already filling out the notice to cure or quit. "What is it? A Rottweiler? A Pit bull?"

Logan had leapt over the railing to stand beside his brother. He swore long and low.

I hated waiting in the car. "What? What the hell is going on? Is it a puppy mill? Is he breeding these animals?" That would explain the noise and the excessive traffic.

"It's a guy in a dog costume," Logan said.

"Huh?" I wasn't sure I'd heard that right. Luke was

making choking sounds, trying not to laugh. "Are you guys screwing with me?"

"I shit you not, there's a guy in a dog costume barking at us." Logan stood, hands on hips looking in the window.

"Is it the tenant?" I asked. "He's African American, about six two, 180 pounds."

Logan turned toward the truck and I could feel his glower across the distance. "Uh, did you miss the part where I said he's wearing a damn dog costume? He could be purple for all I know."

Luke had doubled over, either vomiting or laughing. I was going to go with laughing. Some things a girl just needed to see for herself. "I'm getting out of the truck now."

Neither of them protested or reacted as I slithered out of the truck and bee-lined for where they stood. Sure enough, a human sized canine was poised on the other side of the window, barking like mad.

"Oh my God." I breathed. "He's a furry."

"A what?" Luke had straightened up.

"A furry is a person who role-plays, pretending to be an animal, it's an offshoot of cos-play."

Both Parker brothers stared at me as though they'd never seen me before.

"I read," I said with a shrug.

"Why," Logan began, his tone deceptively mild, "the fuck would anyone want to do that?"

"Um, different strokes for different folks?" I suggested with a helpless palms up.

"What do we do, Jackie?" Luke cut to the chase.

"Speak!" I said to the man-dog.

"Woof," he replied with gusto.

"It was worth a shot." I was out of ideas, having never come up against this particular issue before. The plush canine certainly wasn't breaking character. Of course not, standing up on two legs and talking to us like rational human beings would have made our lives much simpler. We'd just file that one under, snowball's chance in hell.

"Well technically," I said staring in at the dog, "he hasn't broken his lease. There's nothing on the rental agreement about a guy *pretending* to be a dog. And we can't just go in and see if he's peeing on the rug or chewing up the linoleum."

Logan grimaced and Luke was turning red, his shoulders shaking as he fought his laughter yet again.

We had a couple of choices. Either we could post a 24 hour inspection notice and then go in and see what state the place was in or… "Let's come back tonight, around the time when Jamel Smith goes to work. If the dog is still there, we know it's someone else and we can investigate the foot traffic complaint."

We returned to the truck and Luke cranked the AC, then slumped over the wheel, wheezing with laughter. "That's the most awesome thing I've ever seen."

"You don't get out enough," the Dark Prince intoned.

Luke's giddiness was contagious, for me at least. The memory of the big plush dog barking at us through the window had my eyes filling with tears, gasping as I struggled to catch my breath.

Logan glowered back at me. "You two are messed up, you know that?"

"Pot," I said gesturing to him, then waving to Luke. "Meet kettle. Sorry to tell you, but you're both black."

"Get out," Logan said to his brother. "I'm driving you two weirdoes to the nearest looney bin."

"Hey, we're not too far from Mrs. Pomeroy's office," I said as we drove through downtown on our way to the next rental.

"Let's stop in, shake the old money tree and see what falls out."

The corner of Luke's mouth kicked up. "What do you want us to do, dangle her out of the window?"

"That'll be plan B for Bottoms Up."

Logan couldn't find a decent parking spot near the high rise so he let us out in front of the building's entrance. "I'll circle the block. Call me when you want to rendezvous."

"There are times I wish I'd been in the military," I told Luke as we entered the air conditioned lobby. "So I could use words like rendezvous without sounding like a big tool."

He grinned down at me. "Do you know which floor she's on?"

"Not a clue." There was a directory though, to the right of the elevator and I scanned the names until I saw E. Pomeroy. "Sixth floor, suite F for flakey owner. Remember that."

"You make it hard to forget."

I pushed the up button and turned to survey the lobby while we waited. Other than Luke and myself everyone wore business suits, complete with jackets and ties for the men and nylons for the women.

"I can't imagine getting dressed in a suit every day," I whispered. "Pantyhose in Miami seems like cruel and unusual punishment."

"Tell me about it." Luke deadpanned.

My Luke was back, smiling and joking and a sheer pleasure to be around. Whether it was our illicit *rendezvous* in the kitchen, or the thought of a nonexistent rug rat, he seemed more at ease than he had since "the incident."

"It's nice to see you happy." I told him. "Even though I'm not pregnant."

Luke just smiled.

The elevator doors opened and we exited onto the sixth floor. Large offices sat on either side of the aisle. The entire floor was composed of glass and chrome, allowing us to see the people working diligently in all their type A glory. It felt more like being in a human aquarium than an office building, a study on the human condition. No one turned a hair as we approached suite F, the corner office at the end of the hall.

"The blinds are closed." I stated the obvious.

"Maybe she's out to lunch?" Luke suggested.

I crossed my arms. "We'll wait."

There was no receptionist so Luke rapped softly on the door. It was light, and swung open under the force, revealing the horror within.

"Shit," Luke sprinted into the room, to where Mrs. Pomeroy lay on her side on her formerly pristine white carpet, which was now soaked through with what appeared to be blood. It was everywhere I looked, sprayed across the blinds, the glass, soaked through her pink linen suit. Luke reached down to check for a pulse, though it was obvious she was already dead. "Jackie, call 911."

My hands shook as I turned my back on the woman's sightless eyes. "I'm calling Sergeant Vasquez."

Dollars to doughnuts, he was not going to be happy to hear from me again.

CHAPTER 9

Sergeant Vasquez was in his late thirties, a handsome man with mysterious dark eyes that missed nothing. He hadn't said a word to us when he'd arrived twenty minutes ago, just lifted the crime scene tape and entered the room. I shifted my weight from foot to foot and rubbed Luke's back in a soothing motion. Damn it all, I really hated when we found dead people. And I hated it more when those people had obviously been murdered. I was no forensics expert, but no natural death I could think of would result in that much blood spatter.

"You shouldn't have entered the room." One of the uniformed officers, a stern faced woman who looked like she wrestled alligators in her spare time, lectured Luke. "You contaminated the crime scene."

"He was trying to help her." I didn't mention that it was obvious from the moment the door swung open that Mrs. Pomeroy had been beyond all earthly help.

Luke's hands and the knees of his jeans were drenched in blood. Officer Grim informed him he'd have to be cleared by the crime scene unit before he could leave. We agreed and stood off to the side to let the police work. I'd texted Logan to let him know he should find a parking space and wait for us, though I hadn't taken the time to explain why. He'd find out soon enough.

"Can I wash my hands?" Luke seemed to shake himself free of the fugue state he'd been in and I breathed in relief.

"Wait until they tell you it's okay." I murmured under my breath.

As though he'd heard me, Vasquez turned his head sharply and looked directly at me. As I'd predicted he wasn't happy to see me again.

"Mr. Parker, a tech will see to you in a minute. Jackie, will you come with me." He didn't phrase it as a request.

"How come he's Mr. Parker and I'm Jackie?" I asked as Vasquez led me into an empty office down the hall. All the drones had abandoned the hive for the duration of the investigation.

Vasquez narrowed his eyes, as though he was assessing whether or not I was being a smartass. Though that was usually a safe bet, I genuinely wanted to know.

"I don't think of you as Mrs. Parker, I suppose. Would you like me to call you that?"

I shook my head. "Not necessary. Do I get to call you Enrique?"

"No." His face didn't show even an ounce of humor. Understandable under the circumstances. "Now explain to me exactly what happened."

I took a deep breath and related the situation with the beach cottage and Big Joey Santino.

"So you're saying Mr. Santino had beef with Mrs. Pomeroy?"

I shook my head. "I didn't say that."

"You just told me she insisted you remove him from her

property without even offering him a legitimate lease. I would think that would make him angry."

"He left peaceably though," I argued, sorry to bring Big Joey into this mess. "We've run across plenty of tenants and landlords predisposed to violence and I know the type. Big Joey was a pussy cat. Well, not literally a pussy cat," I tagged on, remembering the furry who may or may not be Jamel Smith.

Vasquez didn't roll his eyes at me but I could tell he wanted to. "Do you know where I can find, Mr. Santino now?"

I rattled off the address of the short term apartment where I'd stashed Big Joey and his elephant trunks. "How did she die?"

Vasquez met my gaze. "She was beaten to death, bludgeoned by a blunt instrument. It's not a nice way to go."

I shivered. Having seen the aftermath was bad enough but thinking about someone beating on Mrs. Pomeroy had my gorge rising. "How come no one heard that going on? This building is packed with worker bees."

"M.E. estimates time of death between nine and eleven PM. So it happened late last night, before anyone else came in. No one even knew she was here."

"Sounds like someone -knew her schedule."

"Could be. Or it could be a message. Do you know if Mr. Santino has any Mob affiliations?"

I blinked. "You think this was a hit?"

"We can't rule anything out at this point."

My legs gave out and I sank into the nearest office chair. Big Joey and his love for the freaking sea turtles couldn't possibly be a wise guy. Wouldn't he have gone all batshit crazy when we evicted him? "Holy green guacamole."

Vasquez squatted in front of me. "Do yourself a favor and stay out of this one, Jackie."

I frowned. "You make it sound like I try to get into trouble."

"Try or not, you always manage it. Last time you were lucky to escape with your life, the last thing you want to do is put yourself on the radar for some organized crime family. ¿Entiendes?"

His soft Hispanic accent drove the question home better than loudly shouted English ever could. Did I understand?

"Sí," I answered him with the itty bit of Spanish I had on tap. I could also ask him where the bathroom was and say I needed a towel but after that, I was SOL. So much for four years of high school Spanish.

He patted my knee, then rose. "You wait here. Your husband should be ready soon."

For once I didn't argue.

"SHE'S DEAD?" Logan asked for the third time.

"Do you think I'm making this up?"

The Dark Prince glowered. "Why the hell didn't you tell me what was up?"

"We didn't need you," Luke said coolly. It was the first time he'd spoken since we'd left the crime scene. His tone was even but there was another layer buried beneath the words.

Logan flinched as if his brother had struck him.

I blew out an exasperated breath. "If you two make me be the voice of reason in this little trio of mayhem, I promise you will regret it. Now, who's next on the list?"

Luke turned around in the seat leveling his glare at me. "Finding a dead body means we're done for the day."

"Bull." I glared back. "We're way behind and we're not

getting paid from Mrs. Pomeroy's estate anytime soon. We need to get back to work."

"These are extenuating circumstances," Luke grumbled.

I wasn't about to back down, though part of me wanted to climb back into bed and comfort my husband, whose cage had been visibly rattled. "If we quit doing our job every time we had to contend with extenuating circumstances, we'd never accomplish a damn thing."

"Jackie's right," Logan spoke up, surprising us both because he never agreed with me. "We're still building this business and our reputation matters. We have to show that we'll stay on task no matter what."

Luke turned his head away, staring out the window. I heard his knuckles crack, could see the agitation in the tense set of his shoulders. Logan met my eyes in the rearview mirror for a moment before refocusing on the road. "Where to next?"

Right, I had the files. After a few minutes of rooting around in my bag, I came up with the most pressing case. "Place in Silver Bluffs, rental duplex house converted into four apartments. Downstairs neighbors have called the cops a couple of times because of excessive foot traffic at all hours of the night. We have to find out what the heck is going on and serve them a cure or quit."

Neither of the Parker brothers answered me as Logan cut west through downtown. Something was eating at Luke and I had a feeling it was more than his inability to keep me out of harm's way. He hadn't been acting like himself and I needed to get to the bottom of it, ASAP.

The sub neighborhood of Silver Bluff is located directly below Coral Gate and is part of the larger Coral Way neighborhood. Originally part of the City of Silver Bluff, it was annexed into the City of Miami in the 1920's. Much like our development, the neighborhood was a melting pot of white, black, Hispanic and "other", all of whom stretched every dime to make ends meet.

Logan parked the truck almost a block from the duplex apartments. "Who's the tenant?"

"Arlene Lipinski, thirty-four. Says on her rental agreement she works at the Port and has two sons, fourteen and seventeen. No priors on any of them."

"Has the rent been paid?" Luke asked.

"Like clockwork the first of every month."

"Then why are we here?" Logan turned in the seat to look at me.

"There's been a complaint of a chemical smell in the building. Neighbors say it's coming from her place. Landlord has checked out all the other apartments but found nothing. How do you want to play this?"

"Let's keep vigil for a bit, see if there's anything interesting happening."

We sat in silence for about twenty minutes. My bladder was uncomfortably full. I regretted not using the nice, clean office facilities downtown but after finding Mrs. Pomeroy, I hadn't been thinking about my bodily functions. Damn it, what was it about surveillance that made me have to pee?

Another five minutes with the Parker brothers and their caste iron bladders not budging and I couldn't take it anymore. "Guys?"

"Do you see what I see?" Logan murmured.

Luke had the door open already. "Jackie, for the love of all that is holy, stay in the damn car."

"But—"

He turned to face me. "No buts this time. I think we're dealing with a meth lab. Stay put." He shut the door firmly.

Guess I wasn't using their bathroom.

Logan was already halfway down the block with Luke in hot pursuit so I scrambled in front to get a better view. Two

Lease on the Beach

people stood on the miniscule front porch, one a younger man with a shaved head and full tattoo sleeves of some intricate pattern. From my vantage point he could have been any ethnicity from a well-tanned Caucasian to a very light skinned African American. He wore a wife beater and low rise jeans with half of his blue and yellow checked boxer shorts on display. His sneakers probably cost more than my car.

The other person was a woman, one of those not quite fat and not quiet thin women built like a fireplug, though her face was hollow. I couldn't tell what age she might be, her skin was horrible, even worse than a lifelong sunbather. Her hair was stringy and her hands moved frantically as she talked through what I guessed were cracked lips to Mr. Half Moon Rising. Yeah, they weren't even subtle about the fact that there was a drug deal going down in broad daylight.

She's a junkie, I thought. Or, if Luke was right in his assessment of meth being cooked up, a tweaker. Shit. No wonder the guys had taken off like their asses were on fire.

Okay, this one time I'd stay in the car. I dug out my brand spanking new cell phone, punched in 91 and let my finger hover over the other 1, ready to make the call and praying neither of the people pulled a weapon on the Parker brothers.

The woman was so lost in her frantic explanation that she didn't notice Logan coming. Not so for Mr. Half Moon. He jumped the steps, his pants jarred even lower by the motion, but he hiked them up and booked around the corner of the house, fleeing for all he was worth.

Luke made shooing gestures at the woman who started screaming at him. His voice rose and I heard him shout though I couldn't tell what he said. The woman had an iota of self-preservation because she finally retreated. I expected him to follow Logan at that point but he stood sentry on the porch. Maybe in case the guy came back?

My bladder screamed, of course at the worst possible moment. I was playing Lt. Uhura, needed to keep hailing frequencies open. No way could I bail on the guys and find the nearest convenience store and I'd promised to stay in the truck.

THERE WAS AN ALMOST empty paper cup in the cup holder. Logan must have hit a Starbucks drive thru while he was waiting on us. I thought about it for half a second, then checked the street. Only Luke still holding vigil. Okay, so the cup it would be. Desperate times and all.

The logistics took a little thought. Finally, I pushed the passenger's seat as far back as it would go before scooting my ass to the edge of the seat and kicking one leg free of my capris and underwear and tucking them safely out of the way. I moved the cup into place and then, ah… sweet relief.

I glanced around for napkins or tissues but the guys kept the truck way too tidy for any fast food flotsam to accumulate. Of course my bag was in the back but it kind of defeated the purpose to redress and undress again so I'd make do.

Shoot, my pants had been turned inside out. I'd have to do some impressive contortionist work to get them back on. I was just about to set the almost full cup down when the driver's side door was flung open.

"Out, bitch." Mr. Half Moon scrambled inside before I could say a word. The midday sun glinted off a sharp edged switchblade.

I made a halfhearted choking noise, dropping the cup in my lap in my haste to reach the handle.

"Get out!" he roared. I turned my back on him, heart

hammering, hands shaking. Finally the door gave way and I fell on my bare ass onto the hot pavement.

Luke and Logan reached me just as the truck peeled away from the curb.

"I really tried," I said glancing up at them. "To stay in the car."

CHAPTER 10

"Okay." I squared my shoulders, trying to muster as much dignity as possible when I'd just mooned the neighborhood. Surprising that these people weren't used to it by now. "In hindsight, we should have gone home after we found the body."

"Ya think?" Luke was starting to sound more and more like the Dark Prince and I didn't like it.

I threw my hands in the air. "How was I supposed to know we'd get carjacked?"

"Guys, this isn't helping." Logan's expression was grim. "We need a ride home. Jackie, do you have any emergency favors you could call in."

I gnawed my lip. Considering I'd doused myself with a pee pee latte and Luke still sported bloodstains on his pants, this wasn't a spot me a fiver for lunch kinda favor. "I'll try Marcy first."

The guys waited.

"My phone is still in the truck." I pointed out.

Logan heaved a sigh and dug out his cell.

But Marcy was in a deposition and the woman at the County Clerk's office was supremely unhelpful as to when she'd be back. Her sister Gertie didn't drive and all my other friends had normal jobs, they couldn't exactly drop work to chauffeur our rolling biohazard.

As a last ditch effort I dialed Celeste and was relieved to see Logan didn't have her already programed into his phone. She picked up on the first ring. "I need a favor."

"Really?" My mother sounded supremely skeptical. Well, considering the way we'd left things this morning, I didn't really blame her.

"So if you could give us a ride, that would be great."

"I have a client coming in twenty minutes." Celeste said. "Wouldn't it be irresponsible of me to just blow off work to go gallivanting with you?"

"There will be no gallivanting." It was hot and I smelled like I'd wet my pants even after I'd taken great pains *not* to. Nothing irritated me like wasted effort. Plus Luke's gaze was boring holes through the back of my skull. "For crying out loud, Mom. We were just carjacked. This is, by its very definition, an emergency and you have my freaking car!" *And you're staying at my house and slowly driving me insane.* I kept the last bit to myself since I doubted it would help.

"Fine. I'll be there soon." She hung up the way she did everything else, dramatically.

Logan took his phone back to call the local five-os and alert them to the carjacking. "Too bad we don't have OnStar. Make the whole thing easier," I said to Luke in a pitiable attempt at conversation.

"Since when is anything easy." He rubbed his forehead as though his head hurt. I would have hugged him, but that wouldn't be doing him any favors. And even if I hadn't been covered in filth, I was afraid he'd reject me.

Instead I squared my shoulders and faced him. "We have a few minutes here. Want to tell me what's eating at you?"

He dropped his hand. "Other than my wife doesn't listen to me anymore?"

What? "Luke, I tried. Did you want me to fight the guy just to stay in the car?"

"This isn't about you staying in the damn car!" he shouted.

"Then what the hell is it about?" I shouted back. We were drawing a crowd along with several flies. "What exactly has crawled up your ass and died, Luke? I really want to know."

He laughed but there was no humor in it. "*Now*? Now you want to talk, in the middle of the street after we've been carjacked? That figures. If it's not a big public scene it's not worth doing. Like mother like daughter, huh?"

My head snapped back as though he'd struck out with his fists instead of words. "I can't believe you just said that to me," I whispered.

"Knock it off, both of you." Logan's tone was a low, warning growl. "Separate work and personal space."

Luke opened his mouth, ready to argue but the police showed up. I stalked off, not too far in case they needed my statement but I needed to put some distance between myself and Luke before I lost it.

Settling myself on the curb, I leaned back and looked up at the gathering clouds, watched the palm fronds pulled over in the wind. A storm was heading our way. I bit my lip and wondered if Celeste would mind making two trips back and forth so I didn't have to spend another second with Mr. Fire and Ice. What the hell was his damage anyway? His mood changed faster than the weather and was just as destructive as a category five hurricane. In that moment I hated him a little bit because no one has the ability to cut you like someone you've let see the real you.

To think, a few weeks ago my greatest fear had been losing Luke because of a secret I'd kept from him. But now,

now I was afraid he'd walk because he knew it all, the real me. Maybe it was two sides of the same irrational fear coin but come heads or tails, I'd still lose.

"You okay?" Logan kicked the toe of my sneaker gently. A brotherly tap.

"Fine," I said because really, what else could I do? Sob on his shoulder? That was wrong for so many reasons.

"Bull," Logan lowered himself to a section of curb, upwind, I noticed with a small smile.

"That bad is it?"

His lips twitched. "You've smelled better."

I raised a brow. "Like when I was drunk and throwing up on you?"

He grimaced. "No that was definitely worse."

"If I remember right, you were stoic about the entire episode."

"Sorry to burst your bubble, but I was a Corpsman. I've had plenty of people blow chunks on me. You've seen one Technicolor yawn, you've seen them all."

I closed my eyes and leaned my face up to the sun. "He hates me."

"He doesn't. He hates himself."

That made no sense and I turned to face him full on. "Why?"

"Think about it, Jackie."

I did. A minute later, "I got nothin'."

Logan uttered a particularly salty epithet. "Your latest client was found dead and the prime suspect is the guy you helped to forcibly relocate. He's worried about you."

I shook my head. "That makes absolutely zero sense. If he's so worried about me then why is he picking a fight?"

"Because," Logan spoke with measured patience. "He doesn't know what else to do and he needs an outlet for all that frustration and worry."

I stared at him. "And you know this why?"

He just shrugged.

Though I intended to question him further, Celeste turned the corner in Bessie Mae. I rose and looked for Luke, who was still talking to the officers. Turning back to Logan I said, "Thanks, Dr. Phil."

"You can thank me by never calling me that again."

Luke was waiting for me when I got out of the shower. Though I was clean and sweet smelling once more, I felt like I was at a serious disadvantage wearing only a towel. Since it was closing in on five PM and I was in no mood to go out again, I decided to forgo looking awesome and just be comfortable. Though normally I'd dress right in front of my husband, a feeling of unease and vulnerability had crept in and taken root. I turned my back on Luke and pulled on a set of white knit shorts beneath the towel.

"Jackie, I didn't mean what I said."

"Which part?" Half the towel tucked itself inside my shorts and I dropped it so it hung like a terrycloth tail. "Accusing me of not listening to you or accusing me of being *just like my mother*?" Venom coated my words.

He didn't say anything for a minute and instead of pulling on my bra and shirt, I whirled to face him, still topless. "What the hell is going on with you, Luke? I feel like I don't know you at all."

"You don't." His tone was soft but definite.

That stung. "Maybe not, but whose fault is that?"

He shrugged helplessly. "It was the situation, with me enlisted we've been apart more than we've been together. I just thought things would be different when I got back. No one's to blame."

Lease on the Beach

"Except you're blaming me. For what, not living up to your expectations? How is that right or fair?"

"It's not. Rationally I know it's not but I can't let go of this picture I had in my head."

I knew what he was talking about. The mental picture of us living happily ever after had been my constant companion during the long lonely hours when he'd been deployed. The reality of the two of us looked nothing like that image. I kept telling myself that we were going through an adjustment period, that it would all smooth itself out, but the mantra was ringing hollow in my ears.

Ripping the towel free, I flung it across the room. His lips twitched at my topless rage but I was too wound up to find anything funny at the moment.

"I don't know what to do," I said helplessly. Tears threatened and I closed my eyes. "It's like one minute everything's fine and the next it falls to pieces. Tell me how to fix this."

Luke rose and pulled me into his arms. A sob escaped and he made small, soothing noises until I quieted. "Some things you can't fix, Ace."

I froze. "Does that mean you don't want to fix this, fix us?"

He brushed my hair back out of my face. "We're not broken, Jackie. We're just…out of sync. Not with work, but I'm not satisfied putting our marriage second to Damaged Goods anymore."

Big. Handsome. Idiot. "Luke, the only reason I joined Damaged Goods was to be with you. If you think it's a problem I'll quit right now."

I would, wouldn't I? Of course I would. If it came between the job that had me seeing horrific things and being covered in muck on a regular basis and my marriage, I would absolutely pick my relationship with Luke. So why did I hold my breath while I waited for him to respond?

Luke met and held my gaze. "No, Jackie, I told you, it isn't just one thing that needs to change. We need to find a way to mesh our lives together because we've never had to do it before."

Relief coursed through me until a new thought popped into view. "When you say our lives, you really mean my life, right? You made a comment not so long ago about how you felt like this was more my place than yours. Do you think I don't want to make room for you here?"

"I think you're trying. I also think you're an independent woman and you're not used to having someone around to explain yourself to."

I narrowed my eyes at him. "*Explain* myself?"

Luke raised his hands as if to ward me off. "That came out wrong."

"Boy did it ever."

A genuine smile appeared. "You make it hard to think when you're topless like that."

I rolled my eyes. "Sure, blame the ta-tas. They just keep eye-humping you."

"I think it's the other way around." He pulled me in for a fast kiss. I tried to deepen it but he pulled back, his gaze serious. "Promise me you're not going to try to help Big Joey Santino anymore."

I threw my hands up. "Why does everyone think I have this pathological need to dig into murder investigations? It was a onetime thing. Believe me, I've learned my lesson."

Luke just looked at me.

"Okay, a two time thing, but it was the same killer so it only counts as one."

"Mrs. Pomeroy today makes three. That's three dead bodies we've come across in two months. If anything ever happened to you...."

Damn it all, Logan was right, Luke was frantic over my

safety. Stupid Dark Prince and his mind reading abilities. "Luke, I promise I won't intentionally involve myself in a situation I can't handle."

"That's not exactly reassuring," he growled. "What about what happened earlier?"

"The carjacking was a fluke thing, nothing either of us could control. Maybe if Logan ran faster he would have caught that guy. Maybe if I'd thought to lock the truck doors it wouldn't have happened. But people get carjacked every day in this city, it's a miracle it hasn't happened sooner." It was also why I continued to drive Bessie Mae, the POS. No one would bother to carjack her.

"You'll stay away from Santino?"

I put my hands on his chest, "Luke, trust me to make the right call. I can't have you hawking my every move, okay? Maybe I read Big Joey wrong. Anyone who could do that to Mrs. Pomeroy is seriously disturbed. But guilty or innocent, I have no reason to go near him again. Now, I'm starving, let's get some dinner."

"You in the mood for *Frankie's Pizza*?"

I grinned. "Always."

"As much as I enjoy the view you better put a top on. Logan and your mom are still hanging around. "

I reached for the door knob. "Why bother? They've both seen the goods before."

Luke's jaw dropped.

I raised a brow, surprised he hadn't called my bluff. "Too soon?"

Luke laughed and thrust the tank top at me. "Jackie, you're too much."

I pulled the shirt on. "And here I thought I was just right."

CHAPTER 11

"So, what about Jamel Smith?" Logan asked as he snagged the last slice of pizza.

"What about him?" I pushed my plate away and leaned back in my chair. Mercifully, Celeste was absent. After dropping us off, she went back to Curly Q's to tend to the client she'd left high and dry.

"We were going to go back and see if the furry is still there when Smith was supposed to be at work." Luke reminded me.

What did it say about my day that I'd forgotten about a man dressed in a dog costume? "Right. But we don't have a vehicle or our paperwork." I really hoped the cops found the Big Black Truck all in one piece because getting a replacement vehicle through insurance could take weeks. And somehow I couldn't see the three of us squished inside Bessie Mae like a Parker family clown car. Oh and my brand new frigging phone with the devil's own two year contract that was also MIA…the fun never ended.

Logan and Luke exchanged glances. "Well, you can print the paperwork again, right?"

"Yeah," I said slowly. Something was up, the itching at the

back of my neck warned me I wouldn't like whatever the brothers were scheming. "But Celeste has Bessie Mae so what's the plan for transportation?"

Luke and Logan exchanged anther indecipherable glance.

"Spit it out already guys because my imagination is going into overtime here."

"Rebecca has a car. A van actually. She said we could use it." Luke drained his soda.

"Rebecca?"

"Rebecca Murphy? She's selling the house next door." Logan reminded me as though I were senile.

Oh, that Rebecca. I'd made a habit of checking in on her father until he'd been unable to maintain living on his own and had been moved to a retirement community a little while back. "So, Rebecca is just going to loan us her van for the duration? Doesn't she need it?"

Logan shook his head. "She has her father's car and says she'd be happy to let us use the van, if...."

And there's the rub. "If what?"

"She needs a babysitter."

I frowned. "Not following."

The Dark Prince blew out a sigh. "I said you'd watch her twins whenever she wanted and in exchange we get to use the van."

I stared at him, wondering, no, *praying* he was joking. When it became obvious he wasn't I slammed my palms down on the table. "You *volunteered* me as a babysitter without asking me?"

One sardonic eyebrow went up. "When you put it that way it sounds bad."

My head whipped around to face Luke. "Did you agree to this?"

Luke didn't answer directly, which said it all. "I don't think it's a big deal, you do favors for people all the time."

"Yeah, favors *I* offer. That's worlds away from you two loaning me out like the village goat!"

Logan barked out a laugh and I focused my wrath on him. "Why the hell can't the two of you babysit?"

Luke put a soothing hand on my shoulder. "We can't all watch the kids and keep working at the same time."

His reasonable tone chafed like a sandpaper thong, especially because what he was asking was completely unreasonable. "So how come I've been elected to hold down the flipping fort, because I have *ovaries?*"

They were smart enough to hold their piece and it clicked. My molars ground against each other as though I could pulverize this crazy idea to powder. "I told you both already. I. Am. Not. Pregnant."

The guys exchanged a look that clearly said, beware of irrational females. "It's too late to cancel, now." Logan said finally.

The doorbell rang. Celeste would just walk in. "That's her?" I squeaked.

Logan pushed his chair back, obviously eager to flee my wrath. "I'll get it."

A choked noise escaped as I studied our disaster area home. Power tools, uncovered electrical sockets, glass end tables. It was a kiddie death trap.

I glared at my husband. "Really, Luke?"

He knit his fingers through mine. "I'd stay with you but I don't feel right sending Logan out alone, not with the way our luck's run lately. And this way I'll know you're home safe and sound. Can you do this for me?"

"I don't know." I answered honestly. "My experience with children is limited to when I was one, and that wasn't so hot."

Luke gave my hand a squeeze. "One night, Jackie, just see how it goes. If you hate it, I'll stay with them next time. It's good practice."

"Good practice for what?" I asked but we were interrupted by Rebecca. She had one of her twins in her arms, the little girl's hand clamped on to a hank of her hair. Logan carried the other who looked up at him with enormous blue eyes. Yet another female fallen under the Dark Prince's spell.

"Thanks so much for this, Jackie." Rebecca Murphy was a plump woman a few years my senior. She appeared more harried every time I saw her, and I was betting the twin terrors had something to do with it.

"No problem," I forced a smile. "How's your dad?"

Mr. Murphy had been my neighbor since I moved in. The lonely widower suffered from Alzheimer's and had been unable to continue living by himself. I didn't envy Rebecca's position, having to relocate her father for his own good while being a single mom to her twins. The woman did need help, I just wasn't sure I could offer much.

Rebecca shifted Thing 1 to her left side and tried to free her hair. "Well enough, considering. It'll help when we close on the house."

"You have a buyer?" The bungalow next door was a showpiece and Rebecca was asking top dollar for it. "I wasn't even aware it had been listed yet."

Rebecca frowned and looked to Logan. "It's not but—"

"We should really get going," Logan said.

Thing 2 chose that moment to start squirming in Logan's grip and shrieking, "Down, down down!"

Her sister picked up the battle cry, their cherubic faces twisting.

"Luke, are we good?" I asked, panicking.

The door to the office closed with a thump. "All the power tools are locked up."

Rebecca set her burden down and the toddler dashed for the kitchen. Rebecca snagged her by the back of her pink overalls and strapped the child into the double stroller as she told me, "The girls have already been fed and had their baths. Sammy's allergic to peanuts, bees, shellfish and a few other things, there's a complete list in the diaper bag. I packed an Epi-pen and the pediatrician's phone number just in case. Kasey is doing well with potty training, but still wears a diaper at night. There are animal crackers and juice boxes here. Bedtime is 8:30. I'll be just up the road at the office catching up on paperwork until about ten."

Without further ado Logan plopped Thing 2 in my lap. The girl started to bawl instantly. "Good luck."

"Wait," I called but all three of them made for the door as though the hounds of hell were on their heels.

Thing 1 screamed unintelligibly from the stroller.

"Shit." I grumbled and hefted the squirming child.

"Shit," Kacey, or maybe it was Sammy, repeated. "Shit, shit shit!"

Thing 1 was turning beet red and Thing 2 repeated the four letter curse at ear -splitting levels.

"Who wants ice cream?" I asked a bit desperately.

That got their attention, if only for a moment. I strapped Thing 2 into the stroller beside her sister. Neither of them liked that and the screaming grew more desperate. My blood pressure spiked as I dug frantically for the list of allergies Rebecca had mentioned and checked the ingredients on the container of fudge ripple twice because I couldn't hear myself think over the caterwauling. When I was sure I wouldn't inadvertently poison them, I grabbed two spoons and dragged a chair over to them.

They opened their little mouths like baby birds and I shoveled the sweet treat inside simultaneously. Then, blessed silence.

"Aunt Jackie's survival tip number one, girls, it tastes better when eaten directly from the carton. Plus, no dishes."

There was some drooling and blinking as they ate and I

watched for signs of hives or choking but they were good for the moment. Eventually though, I was going to run out of ice cream. Then what?

I DECIDED it would be easiest to contain the girls in my bedroom. Nothing sharp or breakable for them to get into and they had a blast playing dress up in my clothes and shoes.

"Aw, who's styling?" I asked Sammy as she clomped about in my wedges.

She grinned at me then pitched forward, but I managed to catch her before she face planted into the rug. She came up laughing like walking in heels was the greatest thing ever.

Over by the closet, Kacey shrieked, this time in delight as she discovered yet another purse to drag out of the closet. The girl had a serious jones for handbags and didn't give a fig that mine were all off the truck specials.

The fashion show went on for a bit before the girls started to wear off their ice cream high. Thank God, because I was completely exhausted.

After changing them into diapers, washing sticky faces and hands, and cajoling them into pajamas, I snuggled beneath the covers as they drifted off to sleep. Despite my fatigue I was wide awake when a car pulled up into the driveway.

Carefully, I extracted myself from the covers and moved to the window to see who it was, expecting either Luke and Logan or Celeste. Instead, an unfamiliar blue Honda Civic had taken the Big Black truck's usual parking space.

I frowned when a woman climbed out and frowned harder when I recognized her—the blonde from the shelter. Justine, the one Luke had been flirt-mancing.

The last thing I wanted was to talk to her but I couldn't have her ringing the doorbell and waking up the girls. So I opened the window and popped out the screen instead. "Luke isn't here." I called to her, my tone tinged with bitterness.

She'd been heading for the front door but jumped at the sound of my voice. "Oh, okay. Um, actually I came here to talk to you. Do you have a minute?"

I turned back to look at my bed, at the sleeping children my husband and his brother had foisted on me. If I could survive them, I could handle Justine. "I'll meet you out front in a minute."

"Okay."

No way was I letting that slag into my home to see its state of barely leashed chaos. Whatever she had to say to me, she could say on the porch. I popped the screen back in but left the window open so I could hear the girls. I slid my feet into flip flops and headed out front, reminding myself that I couldn't rant and rave the way I wanted to because I had innocent children within earshot. Who I'd already taught to cuss like a sailor on leave.

"About the other day," Justine began but I held up a hand.

"Have you slept with my husband?"

"No," she said right away and then added on. "And I didn't know he was married. If I had, I never would have said that, about seeing his place. I'm not a home wrecker."

I had to give her credit, it took guts to come face the other woman. "I believe you."

She nodded and shifted from foot to foot. "Look, I don't know what the deal is with you two and it's probably not my place to say, but it was obvious to me that Luke is lonely."

So am I, I thought but kept my mouth shut.

There was an awkward pause and I could tell she was groping around for something else to say, some way to leave on a better note than she'd come. "How long have you two been together?" She asked finally.

"Seven years." Off and on.

That took her back a minute. "That's awhile."

I bristled and my insides churned unpleasantly. I despised this feeling, and Justine by proxy, because she had no idea what the inside of my marriage looked like, how happy Luke and I were.

Or were we?

Damn it, maybe I had been happy and he was miserable and all this time I didn't know because I hadn't been paying attention.

"Okay, well this is awkward now so I'm just going to go." Justine chucked her thumb at the Civic. "Tell Luke I'll see him at the shelter."

The hell you will. I thought and went back into the sanctuary of my house.

CHAPTER 12

The next morning Logan occupied the kitchen when I stumbled to the coffee pot.

"Good morning, Sunshine," the Dark Prince intoned. "Want some breakfast?"

"Cooking bacon will not save your bacon," I growled at him. "How could you just stick me with those kids like that?"

Logan smirked as he cracked eggs into a bowl. "Always the drama queen. You made it through relatively unscathed, better than when we're on the job. Sit and have some coffee."

He may be a jerk but I knew good advice when I heard it. After a few sips of a truly excellent French roast I felt a little less like bathing in his entrails. "So, how did it go?"

"It didn't. No sign of Jamel Smith or the furry." Logan added things to the egg mixture then dipped bread into it. I zoned out for a while and then snapped back to reality when he served me bacon and French toast along with fresh squeezed orange juice. As far as peace offerings went I approved, though I was already making plans to get even with him and Luke for their high-handedness and duplicity.

The food smelled divine and even though I wanted to hold a grudge a little bit longer, my will power was sadly lacking. Apparently, I could be bought with bacon. Plus the sly devil had used cinnamon raisin bread and topped it with what tasted like apple pie filling. I groaned around the first bite. Dear sweet God in heaven, the man knew how to cook. From his satisfied expression, he was obviously way too pleased with himself.

"I'm still mad at you." The words lacked the proper vitriol with a mouth full of cinnamon raisin goodness.

"Something new and different." Logan brought his own plate to the table, tossed me a wink and tucked in.

We ate in silence for a spell, me gathering my thoughts, the Dark Prince not courting my wrath for once. No doubt it had been one severely screwed-up week. The business was spinning its wheels at every turn and we were no closer to getting paid. We needed to buckle down to get the personal crap squared away so we could function as a team again.

"Where's your mom?" Logan asked, breaking into my thoughts.

"Sleeping, I think." Celeste had never been an early bird, even when she didn't spend all night partying.

But Logan shook his head. "Your rattletrap car isn't here."

I blinked. "You mean she never came home last night?"

Logan didn't say anything, he didn't have to. The concern on his face mirrored my own. I uttered a quiet oath. Celeste staying out all night wasn't exactly a novel experience but things had been rough on her lately, and she had a nasty habit of getting into more trouble while trying to drown her sorrows.

I reached for the portable phone. "I have a bad feeling about this."

I called Celeste first and when she didn't pick up I tromped down the hall into the office to boot up the computer. Having a smartphone on hand had made me technologically dependent and I didn't have Curly Q's phone number written down anywhere.

Of course, the salon didn't open until nine. I drummed my fingers on the desk, trying to figure out where she would have gone. Her trailer was no longer an option and if she had any friends to stay with she would have gone to them before me. Had she hooked up with some random barfly?

Luke came in to the office, his hair damp from a shower. He looked particularly scrumptious in a pair of faded blue jeans and a green t-shirt that molded to him like a second skin. I of course looked like hell, since I'd stumbled out of bed to the coffee pot and had been shanghaied into dealing with the next frigging crisis before I could put myself together. Insecurity and worry over my foolhardy mother made me snappish. "Justine stopped by last night."

Luke, who had been bending down to give me a kiss, froze in place. "She did? Why?"

The fact that he was clearly mystified over why she'd decided to show up at our home made me feel a little better. "Apparently she felt she owed me an apology. How did she know where we lived?"

"I wrote our address down on the volunteer paperwork." My husband leaned back against the desk and crossed one ankle over the other. His hands wrapped around the lip of the desk, knuckles turning white. "Did you bite her head off?"

"No." I'd wanted to, but Justine wasn't the person I was upset with, not really. I sat back in my chair to study my husband's face while I murmured. "It's not her fault you didn't tell her you were married."

He looked directly at me, his gaze unflinching. "I was going to tell her…but…"

Though I wanted to jump out of my chair, grab onto his

muscular shoulders and shake him until his teeth rattled, I held myself perfectly still and prompted, "But what?"

He met my gaze, held it. "But, I really don't have a good reason why I didn't say anything to her. I know that I should have set her straight but I just… didn't. I'm sorry, Jackie."

I respected him for not making an excuse but somehow that made it worse. Luke had known what he was doing was out of line, known it would hurt me. And he'd done it anyway. Maybe to hurt me? That didn't bode well for the future of our marriage. I had enough passive-aggression to deal with from Celeste, I didn't need it from my significant other, too. "What would have happened if I hadn't stopped by there the other day? How far would it have gone?"

He shifted, obviously uncomfortable. "Nothing happened. Isn't that the important thing?"

Bile churned in my stomach. If he really believed that he was dumber than a box of hair. "No, Luke it isn't. Getting called on your bullshit means that I stopped you this time. It gives me no assurances that you'll be faithful moving forward. I need to be able to trust you. And right now I can't even stand looking at you."

Luke's expression was pained. "Don't do this, Ace."

"I didn't do anything. Maybe that's the problem, I don't know what you need so you went looking elsewhere for it."

"Jackie, I love you."

"You're not acting like it." I said flatly. Slowly, so as not to upset the delicious breakfast I rose out of the chair.

"Jackie." He reached for me, but I shrugged out of his grip.

"I need space right now, Luke."

His expression clouded over. "Seven goddamn years apart wasn't enough space for you?"

I didn't answer, knowing I'd scream and possibly upchuck if we kept at each other.

Logan hovered in the hallway just outside the door. From

the concern on his face I knew he'd overheard our conversation. "You okay?" he whispered.

For an insane moment, I wanted to fling myself at him, to let Logan hold me while I sobbed my broken heart out. Instead I shook my head. "No, I'm not. Please keep him away from me for the day. I just need a little time to decompress."

Logan nodded. "You got it."

He meant it, too. Even if he had to hogtie the brother he loved more than anyone, Logan would keep his promise. Satisfied if not happy, I shuffled into the bedroom and locked the door, then leaned against it and closed my eyes. Why was it that the Parker brother I could count on wasn't the one I was married to?

"The pregnancy test was negative." Dr. Lin told me.

I breathed in relief even as I shivered in the paper hospital gown. The last thing my family circus needed right now was a new addition. As much as I'd enjoyed hanging out with Things 1 and 2 last night, there was something to be said for giving them back after a few hours. Plus, nine months without a cocktail sounded like cruel and unusual punishment at this juncture. "Can I get a copy of that in writing?"

Dr. Lin studied my face through the thick, square glasses that emphasized her keen intelligence. "Is this good news?"

"Very good news. My husband and brother-in-law want to encase me in bubble wrap and they didn't believe me when I said I wasn't pregnant. Having it in writing will help." Maybe.

In spite of my odd request the doctor only nodded. "I'll have the receptionist make you a copy."

"Thanks." Eager to get back into my street clothes, I

reached for my drawstring pants but paused when the doctor didn't leave right away. "Is there anything else?"

"Keep in mind that pregnancy complications go up as you get older. If you and your husband want a family, you should discuss it sooner rather than later."

"It's just not a good time for us." Jackie Parker—Mistress of the Understatement.

"Do you have any other concerns? You look fatigued." She probed.

"Just overworked." I forced a smile.

She nodded, her stick straight black ponytail swishing with the movement. "Try to take a couple days to rest. Even though you're not pregnant, it's a good idea to give your body a break. Maybe a long weekend vacation?"

"I'll keep it in mind." And I would because taking a mental health break was about as close to a vacation as I was gonna get.

Marcy, who was acting as my chauffeur for the day, rose when I entered the lobby, pregnancy test results in hand. "Well? Are you eating for two?"

I shook my head. "Nope."

Her shoulders sagged. "That's a relief."

Her reaction had me raising a brow. "Why were you so worried?"

"Because I don't have the time or money to throw you a decent baby shower. Besides, it would be nice if I was at least engaged before you start spawning."

"You make me sound like a frigging salmon," I groused as we left the medical complex.

"Sorry," Marcy said as she unlocked her Impala.

I could tell she meant it. Though I really didn't want to know, I asked, "Things any better with Logan?"

"Haven't heard from him but I'm pretty sure it's a lost cause." She turned the engine over and cranked the AC. The temperature was in the upper eighties and humid as a wet dishtowel for the second day in a row. Storm season was closing in fast.

"Sorry, doll. He's a dumbass if he doesn't recognize how awesome you are." My comment lacked its usual barbs because the Dark Prince was doing me a solid and keeping Luke off my case.

"Would you…?" Marcy paused and then shook her head. "Never mind."

"You want me to talk to him?" I guessed, a knot forming in my midsection.

"I can't ask you to do that, you have enough on your plate."

"Yeah, but it's always easier tackling someone else's problems. What is it you want me to say?"

"Just find out if he's even interested in me."

"I'll pass him a note in study hall." The car had cooled off and we both climbed inside.

"Where to now, smartass?"

"Unfortunately, to get yet another phone. I can't do business without it. Do you have to get back to work right away?"

"Nah, I have court this afternoon, so I'm free until one."

"Good, I'm taking you to lunch, anywhere you want, my treat." Knowing Marcy, the only place she'd want to go for lunch was to the nearest ice cream parlor anyway. Woman after my own heart.

An hour later, my credit card wheezed from the exorbitant transfer fees and replacement phone cost, but as soon as the phone charged, I'd be set to go back to work.

"Any apps you purchased will have to be downloaded again. Your contacts are still on file here and I was able to download them into the new phone. You really should get a warranty this time, in case anything else happens." Adam's

Adam's apple bobbed in a hypnotizing rhythm as he lectured me.

"If I find the other phone can I return this one?" Not that there was much hope of that but still.

"All sales are final." Adam swiped my credit card again and I swear a puff of smoke emanated from the magnetic strip.

I really needed to get paid. "Thanks a bunch."

He didn't respond to my sarcasm as he handed me the receipt.

Since Bessie Mae and Celeste were still MIA I had to wait until I got home to charge my phone. Marcy drove us to the nearest ice cream parlor.

"What's up with you?" She asked as she mushed rainbow sprinkles into her chocolate ice cream. "You're acting weird. Stuff still off with you and Luke?"

I watched as the hot fudge melted my vanilla ice cream. "Like alternate dimension kind of off. We've fought more this week than we have in our whole marriage. I feel like I don't know him and that he doesn't know me. He was so excited and neurotic at the idea I might be pregnant, but all I could think was how could we bring a baby into our disaster of a life?"

"What do you want from him?"

I thought about it as I swirled my spoon around the perimeter of the little plastic dish. What did I expect from my husband? Faithfulness obviously. Devotion. A sense of security and not just obnoxious overprotectiveness. More than anything else though, I wanted to feel like he understood me or at the very least, accepted and appreciated me as I was—not as his wife, but as Jackie the woman.

The way Logan did.

I flinched and stuffed that thought back in the crevice it'd escaped from. "It's complicated."

"Unfortunately, I don't have time for complicated." Marcy rose. "Let's go out tomorrow night, have a few drinks just the two of us."

We hadn't done that in months, not since I'd started at Damaged Goods. "Sounds like a plan."

We tossed our empty ice cream bowls and Marcy drove me home. I plugged in my new phone and went to the office to tackle some filing. A few hours later I emerged with a crick in my neck and a sense of accomplishment. Hopefully, the guys had a productive day.

The light was blinking on my new cell phone indicating a voicemail. That was weird, I hadn't heard it ring. Then again, I'd had my iPod in the dock blaring my angry chick playlist. After punching in my code to access my messages, I held my breath. This was probably the first time in my adult life that I was actually hoping to hear from Celeste.

"Jackie?" That was Celeste's voice all right. She sounded off though, upset. I prayed she hadn't been in an accident.

There was a scuffle and an obviously distorted voice on the other end took the phone, though I could still hear Celeste in the background. The words made my blood run cold.

"We have your mother. You will help us or she dies."

CHAPTER 13

"What do they mean by "help us"? What is it they want?" Logan asked as I finished playing the voicemail message for him and Luke. "There's got to be more to it than that."

I disconnected the call to my voicemail. "There isn't. From the time stamp, the message came in last night around ten p.m. I didn't get it because my phone was in the hijacked vehicle, which is still MIA."

"Call the police," Logan suggested. "Kidnapping is a felony."

I shook my head. "You heard the message. I have a feeling that bringing the authorities into this would be very bad for Celeste. Deadly even. The last thing we want to do is upset these people when they have her at their mercy."

Logan pushed out of his chair and started pacing. "Okay, then we'll look into it ourselves. Luke and I can go to the salon, find out what time Celeste left. See if we can track down your car. Chances are good that whoever grabbed her abandoned it somewhere."

I wrung my hands. "But that's not going to bring us any

closer to finding out who grabbed her or what they want from me."

It made no sense, I didn't have money or influence in the kind of circles that would provoke a kidnapper. What the hell did they want from me?

"Can we get a tie-breaker here?" Logan scowled at his brother.

Luke had been quiet, his gazed fixed on the desk, expression blank. At Logan's words he looked up. "Jackie's right, we should wait for them to call back and get a list of their demands. They could be watching and if we do anything out of the ordinary they might hurt Celeste."

Logan didn't like that, his distaste was written clearly across his features. Even more than his brother, the Dark Prince was a man of action, an Alpha who fought for the people he called his own. "So what then, business as usual?"

His question was meant sarcastically but Luke nodded. "Exactly. If Jackie doesn't want to call the police, then we've got nothing to do but act like everything's normal." He rose from his seat without looking at me, hugging me or offering sympathy in any way. My heart hurt when he left the room.

Logan put a hand over his eyes, his posture radiating frustration. Though I'd meant to be more subtle about it I blurted out, "Are you sleeping with my mother?"

His hand dropped from his face. "Are you serious?"

"Well, I know you aren't sleeping with Marcy and you and Celeste were acting chummy the other day. I promise I won't think less of you—"

"*Won't think less of me?*" He rose, knocking over the office chair he'd been sitting on. Hands clenched at his sides, he shook visibly, his rage barely contained. "Is it even fucking *possible* for you to think less of me?"

"I didn't mean it like that, I just need to know you won't go off halfcocked to play hero."

Lease on the Beach

"So what, if I'm not sleeping with her does that mean I don't give a rat's hairy ass about getting her back? Enlighten me, Jackie. Is that how it works in your head?"

I pushed up out of the chair and went toe to toe with him. "This is my mother's life on the line! Damn it, Logan, I need to know that I can count on you!"

He was breathing hard, puffing like a locomotive tackling a steep incline. There were tight lines around his mouth and I knew he was furious and wanted to take my head off.

Before I knew what he was doing, Logan had pulled me into a tight embrace, squeezing me for all I was worth. Stunned, I stood still, hands still balled into fists at my side. Slowly, the heat of his body seeped into me and I gradually relaxed into his embrace. It was more than a hug, more than comfort.

He leaned his whiskered cheek against the top of my hair. His voice was low, almost a growl when he spoke. "You can always count on me, Jackie. Always. Doesn't matter who I'm fucking—I'll still be here for you."

Sudden tears clogged my throat and it took a few tries to swallow past them. "Is that a yes or a no?" I croaked.

I half expected him to get angry again but when he pulled away I saw only steely determination. "No, I'm not sleeping with your mother. Happy?"

Relieved was more like it. I closed my eyes, fighting the fatigue that had set in. These last few days had been hell and I was more mixed than ever. "I need to be able to count on you, Logan. Luke's... his temper is volatile and changes like the weather. I don't know where his head is at, but he feels like a stranger all of a sudden. I don't trust that he has my back. And we don't have time to work out our issues, not with Celeste's life hanging in the balance. I *need* you on my side." There was no way to overstate the significance.

His finger hooked beneath my chin, forcing me to look up at him. To meet his steady, blue gaze. "I've got your back."

I let out a shaky breath. Part of me wanted to ask Logan to talk to Luke for me again. Two things stopped me. One, that the last conversation they'd had about me hadn't gone very well. But more importantly, it wasn't fair to Logan, asking him to put himself in the middle again. "Okay, so I've got the phone, we have Rebecca's car. Let's go manage some property."

Since Jamel Smith worked nights and we hadn't gotten anywhere close to the furry and the Parker brothers didn't want me going anywhere near the meth house, I plucked a new file from my bag and directed Luke out into the boonies. "This is a new one. Gary Markov, age twenty-five. Lives in an RV which his uncle cosigned for him but Good old Gary hasn't made a payment. Uncle Osgood wants us to serve a cure or quit and get the eviction process started so his credit rating doesn't get tanked."

Focusing on work was good, gave me something to do other than fret over Celeste. How was it possible that I was worried about her and at the same time guilt-stricken because I wasn't doing more to find her? She had to be all right, must be because there was so much unsettled between us. I needed to mend our relationship. Silently, I beseeched the universe that I'd never ignore another of her phone calls as long as she came home alive and unhurt.

"A mobile home, huh?" Luke said. His tone was neutral, mild even. "Do we really have jurisdiction for this?"

"According to Osgood, he didn't know about the nonpayment and he's paid for the vehicle. Sent me a copy of the lean. So yes, technically he's the owner and he has the right to evict Gary."

Logan rubbed his chin. "Does he know where Gary's been keeping the RV? He'd need a hookup for electricity and sewer."

I checked my phone to reassure myself that I still had a signal in case the kidnapper called. "I've got an address for an RV park he frequents."

I rattled it off and Logan plugged it into the GPS. After a moment a light started blinking on the two dimensional map. "That's practically in the Everglades," Logan murmured.

I almost asked him if he had something better to do, then flinched when I remembered about Celeste. "I'm up for a ride if you guys are good."

Luke gave a curt nod and Logan clapped him on the shoulder. "Let's go."

Logan flipped through radio stations as Luke drove. I stared out the window, watching as the scenery changed from suburban to rural. I saw none of it, my mind otherwise occupied. The initial panic over my mother being abducted had worn off and now I was trying to pin down the why of it.

God and Elvis knew, Celeste Drummond had made her share of enemies over the years, most recently the folks at the trailer park. Somehow though, I thought that this latest incident had more to do with me than her. She'd been driving my car a few hours after Luke and I had found Mrs. Pomeroy. Perhaps it was just the timetable but the two events were linked in my mind.

"Uh oh," Luke said, breaking me out of my reverie. "The Garrison crew is here."

I frowned as I took in the dirt parking area. Rusted-out pickups, windowless vans, beat-up sedans and campers were clustered together in the lot. "Where exactly is here, and why are there so many people?"

Logan swore softly. "I think it's Amnesty Day."

I blanched. Amnesty Day was Florida's pet trade. People who wanted to give up their current pets came to a location to swap out the old and maybe bring home a new one. And we're not talking about cats and dogs here. The majority of the animals swapped on amnesty day were reptiles, often poisonous snakes or constrictors. It was probably better that people who'd realized the error of their ways had someplace to leave the creatures instead of setting them loose in the swamp, but it was nowhere I wanted to hang out.

"Do you see the motorhome?" Luke craned his neck around the lot. "I don't want to get into it with John here if I can help it."

John Garrison was the smarmy SOB who ran Garrison Property Management, the eviction specialists who'd taken such care cleaning out Celeste's trailer.

We were double parked behind a minibus that looked like a silver Twinkie on wheels. From my position in the back, I couldn't see anything past it.

Logan turned around in his seat. "Jackie, hand me that blue duffel bag."

I gripped the handles and did as he asked. "You're not going to shoot John, are you?"

The Dark Prince glared at me over the tops of his sunglasses. "Not unless I have to. I want to bug the motorhome. Won't do us much good to post notice on it if we can't find it again and something tells me our guy is going to book when he finds out what's doing."

"Good plan," Luke said. "Jackie, you want to look for the tenant or find out what John is up to?"

"You're giving me a choice between a snake and a whole bunch of them, you realize?"

"Pick your poison," Luke deadpanned.

"I'll take John. At least he's charmed by my assets and not

Lease on the Beach

liable to swallow me whole." I tugged my tank top a fraction lower, glad I'd put on a terrific bra that hefted the girls up to epic proportions.

It was gratifying that my husband's gaze stayed on me as I climbed out of the car.

Logan hefted the duffel and I gave him the file on the RV we were looking for. He thumbed through it. "Make sure your phones are on. I'll text you if our guy is in his camper. Otherwise we'll meet back here."

Luke nodded. "No shouting. You don't want to upset the animals."

A shudder rolled through me. "I'll keep it in mind."

The Dark Prince moved off toward the rows of campers at the back end of the lot. To my surprise, Luke grabbed my hand and led me toward the knot of people clustered in front of a white canopy.

"Relax," Luke murmured. "We're just a normal couple out pet shopping for pythons."

A breathy laugh escaped. "Puts my fear of canines into perspective. Did you see where John and his goons went?"

"Over there," he pointed to a line off to the right. From our place I could see a long line of people holding cages, sacks that wriggled in a highly disturbing way and even a glass aquarium that contained what I thought was an iguana.

"Maybe he's here looking for a girlfriend," I suggested, only half kidding. "It could have nothing to do with our guy."

"Speak of the devil," Luke breathed and dropped my hand.

"Where?" I shaded my eyes and tried to follow his gaze, but there were too many people and pets milling around.

"The guy with the monkey on his shoulder. Two o'clock."

The monkey in question was one of those adorable little ones with the white ruff around his humanoid face. I could easily picture him wearing a little fez and a vest like Abu from the animated movie *Aladdin*. "Oh, shoot, I want to switch and cover the monkey."

"If you really want to. I'll distract John, you go feel out our guy. Don't let him know who you are, we don't want him to rabbit before Logan's got the bug in place. Follow him back to the RV if you can. And be careful." He kissed me on my forehead then turned away.

The sun was halfway to the horizon and Amnesty Day was winding down. I slid my sunglasses onto my head as I approached Gary and his monkey. His t-shirt was ripped and dirty, his jeans several sizes too loose. His hands shook like he was going through withdrawal. The monkey chittered, wrapping its tail around Gary's thin neck.

There was a tiny woman in line ahead of him with a giant Boa Constrictor wrapped around her. "I don't understand it," she said. "Lulu must be sick or something. She hasn't eaten in days."

Lulu hissed, wriggled and looked straight at me with horrible eyes. Then her beady glare turned to Gary's companion.

The monkey screeched.

It took two of the veterinary assistants to get the heavy snake off the woman and onto the table. The thing hissed at them and one of them stepped back quickly. It's flat evil eyes turned back to the monkey.

Gary stepped back, his companion chittered. I got a really bad feeling and judged the distance back to the car.

"Has Lulu been sleeping all right?" The vet, a braver man than I, nudged the snake's midsection. "Any other symptoms?"

"She's been grumpy." The woman was oblivious to the scene, too worked up over her pet's health. "And she sleeps in bed with me."

The vet's eyes rounded, judged the size of the woman and

the size of the snake. "Well," he said cautiously. "She's, uh, probably making room."

"Over here!" Another worker bee waved Gary over.

Gary shuffled off. I followed as though I were with him, relieved to get away from Lulu.

"What can I do for you?" The harried Amnesty worker asked. He had the look of a man who'd been on his feet all day and was eyeballing the clock, eager for quitting time.

"I wanna sell this." Gary took the monkey off his shoulder and put him on the table.

The man frowned. "We don't exactly pay for them. Has he had his shots?"

"What shots?" Gary was clueless.

"Rabies and the like."

Gary shrugged. "He belonged to my ex-girlfriend, but she couldn't keep him in her apartment. Then she dumped me and left me with him. He's a pain in my ass."

The man made a note on the clipboard he held. "Do you know where she got him from?"

Gary shrugged again.

The man waved to a vet tech. "We'll vaccinate him and you can try selling him to a pet store or a private owner."

The vet tech approached, holding a syringe in one gloved hand. The monkey took one look at the needle, let out an earsplitting screech, and bolted down the table.

Straight for where Lulu lay coiled. The snake's eyes narrowed to evil slits. The monkey screamed again and leapt off into the air. The constrictor lunged, uncoiling her massive bulk. Her appetite was obviously back up to speed.

She missed by half a tail's length, but now that she'd set her sights on dinner, she was ready to run it down. Thankfully the monkey was fast and motivated to move at top speed.

Panicked screams rent the air as the terrified monkey and giant snake wove through the crowd.

"Lulu!" The idiot woman, who was obviously too stupid to draw breath, chased after her precious reptile.

"Fuck," Gary grumbled as he watched the huge snake chase down his profit margin. "I think the snake wants to eat him."

"You're an asshole," I said to Gary.

"Like you're the first person to tell me that."

I had my phone out and was busy texting Luke with one word. *Incoming!* I hoped he could save Abu, but at the very least I didn't want him set on by Lulu.

When I looked up, Gary had disappeared.

CHAPTER 14

"A snake, a monkey, and a douchecanoe walk into a bar," I muttered and scanned the melee for any sign of my quarry. Guessing from the screams to the left, that's the direction Lulu had gone. I made my way back to the parking lot, hoping Logan had enough time to place the bug.

"I thought I recognized that fine ass." Someone slurred behind me.

A beefy hand landed on my shoulder. From the sour armpit smell wafting from him, I knew exactly who it belonged to. "Get your hands off of me, John."

"Or what?" he asked, though he did let go. "What you gonna do?"

I narrowed my eyes on him. "Watch your step. The last SOB who put his hands on me without my permission lived to regret it." Though Luke and Logan hadn't laid hands on Stan Cunningham, the ass grabbing lawyer had nearly wet himself in fear.

"Oh, I'm so scared." John smirked at me, the sarcasm dripping. He was one of those no neck bruisers that crushed beer cans on his head for sport. "By the way, I've gotta say how much I enjoyed tossin' your white trash momma out on her freeloadin' caboose. If it was up to me, I would have offered to exchange favors. I heard tell that's how she does."

The man was obviously trying to get under my skin. Whipping out the "yo' mama' bait was *so* 1990's. I ignored him, instead looking for any hint of Luke or Gary.

Standard issue bully, John didn't like being ignored. "What you doing here anyway, Parker?"

"None of your damn business," I answered and headed back to the row of motorhomes.

"It is, if you be goin' after that little worm, Markov. He's mine."

Shoot, Luke was right, he was horning in on our client list. I played dumb, something men like John Garrison fell for because I had a big rack. "Markov? Never heard of him. I'm just looking for a monkey. See ya. "

My phone rang and I answered it as I walked away, glad I wasn't wearing open toed shoes with all the slithery things about. "Hello?"

"Where are you?" Logan asked.

"Heading into the parking area by the RV's. Did you finish?"

"I didn't even start. The one we're looking for isn't here."

I frowned. "You sure?"

"I went through the lot twice before all hell broke loose. What happened over there anyhow?"

"The food chain happened. I'll meet you back at the car as soon as I find Luke." I hit the end button and tried to think.

Crap. Maybe Gary had traded the RV to someone for drugs. If he was trying to pedal a monkey on Amnesty Day, he was in bad financial straits and all his jitters made me think tweaker looking for his next fix. Well, there was no need to evict him from a place where he wasn't currently living and with the place in question being mobile, all we could do was report it to the police and hope it turned up.

Someone should make an app for reporting stolen vehicles. I could have used it three times already this week.

A fresh wave of screaming came from a cluster of people. My heart rate kicked up and I bolted, knowing instinctively that the eye of this shitstorm was where I'd find Luke. He'd been tailing John and wouldn't have abandoned him unless something more pressing had come up. I pressed my way through the flow of people, searching for my big, strong, dumbass of a husband.

The sight that greeted me froze my blood. Lulu had abandoned her mad chase of the monkey and gone after an easier target. She'd wrapped her powerful body around a little blonde cherub of a girl, who couldn't have been more than six years old. The child was wailing, her frantic mother pleaded for someone to help them. Lulu's idiot owner was shrieking too. And my personal hero was there, holding what looked like a broom handle, intermittently poking at the snake. Even from a distance I could tell he was doing his level best to distract Lulu and keep the creature from squeezing the life out of the girl.

One of the Amnesty Day workers had leveled a pistol at the snake and yelled at Luke to get out of the way so he could take a shot. Surprising that no one else was armed—this was Florida after all.

Luke didn't so much as blink. "You could hit the girl."

"She's dead either way," the man's voice was steady, but his hands shook. "At least this way she's got a chance."

"Please," the mother sobbed. "Somebody help her."

I stood, frozen to the spot, utterly hypnotized by the scene. I wanted to tell Luke to hurry, to be careful that the creature didn't go after him. But the words were stuck in my throat, cutting off my air supply.

Luke walloped the Boa again. She hissed at him. The girl's wailing cut off, her head falling limp.

"Luke!" Logan had appeared at the other side of the circle.

"Stand clear," the man with the gun shouted. "I'm taking the shot!"

"Give me that before you kill someone." Logan lunged for guy, blocking his line of sight.

Luke danced closer to the snake, striking out with the broom handle. From my periphery I could see Logan and the Amnesty worker struggling with the weapon. The snake's eyes narrowed, but she showed no sign of releasing her captive. My heart nearly stopped as time ground to a screeching halt.

Then everything happened at once, as though someone had hit fast forward on the scene. The gun went off, the snake loosened its hold, lunging for something other than Luke. The little girl crumpled to the ground and Luke was there, catching her before her head hit the ground and shouting for a medic.

The monkey, I realized. Abu streaked across the ground, headed straight for me. He climbed me like a tree, chattering and I froze as I realized Lulu was still in hot pursuit, headed directly for the two of us.

Another round of gunfire and the snake's body jerked, then went still. My gaze lifted to see Logan in possession of the firearm. His expression was locked down, his hands steady. He plugged the snake again but it didn't move.

"Lulu!" The snake's owner fell to her knees.

"Are you all right?" Logan put a hand on my shoulder.

I cuddled the monkey, it's tiny body shaking in my arms. Or hell, maybe that was me.

"Jackie, blink if you're okay."

I blinked and managed to exhale. God, that scene would haunt me for years. "I'm okay," I croaked.

Lease on the Beach

Logan took off to see if he could help with the child. All around me people had their cell phones out, photographing the destruction. It had probably gone viral already.

"Jesus, Mary, and a holy bag of chips," I wheezed, unable to tear my gaze from the dead snake.

Abu scrambled up my arm to perch on my shoulder, chittering a little, almost like monkey nervous babble. His tail curled around my neck like a scarf.

"You did that on purpose. Distracted the snake," I realized. "I wished you'd left me out of it, though."

More chittering as he climbed to my other shoulder, snagging my sunglasses off the top of my head.

"Hey now Abu, those are designer lenses!" I made a grab for my shades.

Abu jumped up and down, screeching with exuberance and putting them on his face. He was too damn cute for words.

"Oh, all right. But if you lose them, hero or not, I'll sell you on Craigslist."

"Where'd the monkey come from?" Luke asked me as we walked back to the car.

His shirt was ripped and dirty and he looked tired. I wasn't faring much better, what with Abu practicing his mad social grooming skills and using me for his personal jungle gym. "Markov was trying to sell him here. I think he's got a pretty severe pharmaceutical habit, he looked strung out and desperate."

"Where'd we park?" Luke glanced around the lot, keys in hand.

"We have Rebecca's car, remember? Here, take Abu. I'll

drive." I plucked the monkey from my rat's nest and urged him into Luke's arms.

Luke handed over the key ring, his gaze unfocussed.

His thousand-yard-stare and lifeless tone had me worried. "Luke, are you okay?"

His gaze shifted to meet mine, then darted away. "Sure."

"Liar," I said.

He just shook his head.

Whatever, I couldn't force the man to talk to me. He'd scared a decade off my life and that was before Lulu had zeroed in on me. Hot, sweaty, and irritated, I climbed into the car and turned it on, cranked the AC as high as it would go and buckled myself in, more than ready to make tracks for civilization.

A moment later, Luke climbed in next to me. He slipped his fingers through mine and squeezed. I hesitated, then squeezed back.

"He saved you again," Luke muttered.

"What?" I lifted my head and turned to face him.

"Logan, he saved your life again."

I frowned. "You don't know that. Lulu was after Abu, not me, I was just in the wrong place at the wrong time." Again. So didn't want to dwell on that.

"Look me in the eye and tell me you weren't scared to death."

I couldn't. The way my body shook after the fight or flight response screamed through my central nervous system told me my fear had been very real. "It's more complicated than that. I was scared for you, and for that little girl, too. Why does this even matter?"

A muscle jumped in Luke's jaw. "Do you ever feel like you made the wrong choice by picking me?"

My mouth fell open. How exactly was I supposed to respond to that? I struggled for words but none came.

Luke looked out the window. "I wouldn't blame you for it. I see the two of you together, I know there's still something there."

"I thought we were past this," I whispered. "I thought you understood—"

Logan opened the back door and slid in behind Luke. "What a fricking nightmare."

He wasn't kidding. I shook myself when I realized he was talking about the scene with the snake and not the highly unsettling conversation Luke and I had been having. I cleared my throat and shifted around to face him. "Is the girl going to be okay?"

"I think so. She's stable and I wouldn't be surprised if she has a few cracked ribs, but she's a fighter. The EMTs were loading her into the ambulance when I left. What are you two doing?"

Hell if I knew. "Waiting on you. Have you met Abu yet?"

One sardonic eyebrow lifted. "Abu, really? Of course what could I expect from the mastermind that came up with Bessie Mae?"

"Don't listen to him, Abu," I said to the monkey. "He's just jealous."

Logan snorted. "That'll be the day."

Abu cocked his head and then scrambled between the seats to get to the Dark Prince. I cringed, afraid he was going to attack Logan but instead he circled the man's lap and then curled up, looking for all the world like he was about to take a nap.

Luke barked out a hollow laugh. "It figures."

"What?" Logan's face held shock and a healthy helping of *what the hell do I do now?*

"Relax," I said to all of them and turned the engine over. "It'll be fine."

Night had fallen and the stars were out. I turned on the

car's high beams since we were in the middle of BFE Nowhere so I didn't crash into a deer or a gator or something. There was only so much wildlife I could deal with in a given twenty four hour period.

I'd clicked on the radio to an alternative rock station and was glad for the fast paced music to help drown out my thoughts. I didn't look at Luke or engage Logan in conversation, couldn't deal with the stress of them right now. The only thing I had going for me was my steely determination to keep moving forward.

Traffic had started to increase along with the speed limit as we headed west. I needed a bath and a glass of wine. No, make that a bottle of wine. And sleep if I could manage it. I was tired enough but there was so much to deal with.

"Stop!" Luke shouted.

Reflexively both feet went to the brakes and the car skidded to a stop. Behind me angry horns blared as motorists circumnavigated the car.

"What?" I asked. "What's wrong?"

But Luke had thrown open the car door and was running down the road, back in the direction we'd passed.

Abu screeched at ear-splitting decibels.

"What the hell?" the Dark Prince growled.

In the rearview mirror I watched as Luke jumped down into the gutter alongside of the road. "Oh hell, I think he just found a body."

CHAPTER 15

"Well at least it wasn't a dead body," Logan said as we helped Joseph Santino into the car. "This time anyway."

I crouched down in front of Big Joey. "What happened to you?"

He was a mass of bruises, one eye swollen shut, lip split and blood dripping down onto his white wife beater. He spat a mouthful of blood and what might have been a tooth out of the open door, but didn't answer my question.

"Stay with him, Abu." I said.

The monkey scrambled up Big Joey's arm and onto his head like a furry little hat.

I rose and motioned to the Parker brothers to follow me. When we were out of hearing range I asked "What happened to him?"

"My guess is someone beat him to hell then dropped him off." Luke kept his voice low as he spoke. "Just dumped him along the side of the road."

That sounded utterly horrific. "Why though? Why would someone do that to him?"

Logan looked back to the car. "A better question is why was he left here? Is it a message for us to find?"

Despite the humidity, a chill shot through me. "Do you think it has something to do with Celeste's abduction? Or Mrs. Pomeroy's death?"

"All I know," Luke murmured, "is that Sargent Vasquez is looking for Santino in connection to Mrs. Pomeroy's murder. If we don't call him, we're officially interfering with a police investigation."

"But what about Celeste?" Logan asked. "What if the kidnappers grabbed Big Joey and left him here for us to find and hide. It's too much of a coincidence that he was abandoned right where we would find him. If we turn him over to the police, they might kill her."

I was too wrung out to deal with this. I checked my phone, even dialed in my voicemail to see if there had been any new contact from the kidnappers. Not so much as a peep.

"We can't risk it," I said to Luke. "We can always turn Santino in to Vasquez later, but if we're supposed to hide him instead, the mistake could cost my mother her life."

Luke's hands were on his hips, staring at the ground. Mr. *I Always Play By the Rules* didn't like it. I didn't blame him, but what choice did we have?

"Logan, you okay to drive? I want to sit in back with Joey. Maybe he'll talk to me."

"Absolutely not," Luke's eyes turned hard. "Jackie, the man could be a killer."

"You evicted him from his beach house," the Dark Prince pointed out. "I doubt you're his favorite person."

The two of them had folded their arms over their chests, bookends of male stubbornness. Going through that wall of muscle wasn't an option, I needed to retrench. I threw my hands up in the air. "Fine, have it your way."

Twin glowers and matching nods of grim satisfaction.

We made our way back to the car. Logan climbed in back and I resumed my position behind the wheel. I reached out and fiddled with the rearview mirror as an excuse to keep an eye on our new passenger. Big Joey had his head back against the seat, one beefy finger clutched in Abu's tiny grip. The monkey stared at him with big eyes as though he'd taken my instructions to watch the man to heart.

Silently, I merged back onto the road. Luke and Logan were silent, though the tension radiating off the big male bodies was thick in the confined space.

"Where am I going?" I asked the car in general, hoping Joey would cough up a clue. No such luck.

"My place," Logan said. "They might be watching your house and I have a med kit there. I think he'll need a few stitches."

"Where is your place?" I asked, glancing at him in the rearview. Luke looked over at me, but didn't comment. Good thing too, I was sick of his attitude and in no mood to put up with more of his passive-aggressive BS.

Logan gave me directions and soon I drove into a small apartment complex parking area. Flagami was a decent neighborhood on the west side of the city, made up of mostly middle class folks who didn't mind a longer commute to downtown. The neighborhood sported its own unique nightlife in the forms of supper clubs and lounges, less flashy than South Beach, but just as popular, especially among locals.

Logan led our motley little crew through a breezeway to a second floor apartment. In spite of my fatigue, I was curious to see what his private space looked like these days. I could easily imagine big leather couches and a massive entertainment system.

As it turned out the one bedroom apartment was

completely devoid of personality. White stucco walls, light gray carpet, non-descript particle board furniture. The television was a flatscreen, though a reasonably sized one for the space. Mini-blinds covered the window but no curtains. The couch was beige fabric, not leather, which was more sensible in Miami. Overall, the apartment was bland and colorless, with no personal touches in sight.

"How long have you lived here?" I asked as I checked around for boxes.

"About three years." Logan dropped his keys on the immaculate kitchen counter.

"Cool," I said because really, what else could I say? Maybe, you ever heard of Pottery Barn or buy some freaking throw pillows already, but both were too rude and totally beside the point.

Maybe I'd suggest to Marcy that she help him decorate. Logan had too much personality to live in such a blah space. I could feel it sucking out my will to live even now.

"Is this okay, Joey?" I asked.

Luke shot me a *what the hell* look, because really, what would we do if Joey said no?

"Yeah," he said and swayed on his feet.

"Jackie, there's a Rubbermaid bin in the bedroom closet. Go grab it and a couple of towels." Logan didn't wait for me to reply as he went to the kitchen and turned on the faucet to scrub his hands.

I went down the short hall. The bathroom was on the right. I took in a pedestal sink and standard issue white tub/shower combo, plus toilet. The space was clean, no drips of toothpaste in the sink or hair in the shower drain. Should I snoop? Well, he'd sent me in here instead of coming himself so why the hell not? I glanced over my shoulder but the coast was clear. I checked the medicine cabinet. Razor, toothbrush, comb, shaving cream, three unopened bars of Ivory soap. No

Lease on the Beach

condoms or antibiotics, not so much as an aspirin. A row of white towels was neatly folded on a wire shelf beside the sink. I snagged two and left, feeling vaguely disappointed.

The bedroom was next. My hand hovered over the doorknob, memories of the last time I'd been in Logan Parker's bedroom swamped me. The feel of his stubble against my bare skin, the heat burning in him, the way his blue eyes turned to cobalt fire. The way he whispered my name as though it tasted good on his tongue.

"Jackie?" he called.

"Oh, for the love of grief," I muttered, gripping the handle tightly. "I need therapy."

I pushed the door open. My jaw dropped.

"Are you finding everything?" Logan called.

It was pink. Not pale pink, nu-uh. The walls of Logan Parker's bedroom were Pepto-Bismol, freaking pink. The unmade king sized bed revealed white linens and there was no other furniture, but I couldn't tear my eyes from the Kill-Me-Now pink walls.

"Is Barbie your decorator?" I called out. "Because I'm getting a low-rent dream house vibe here."

A bark of laughter, though I couldn't tell from who. Then footsteps.

"Smartass," Logan muttered as he pushed past me into the room. "The landlord offered me a deal if I took it as is."

"And you've been sleeping in what looks like a lower intestine for a little bit off your rent for three flipping years?"

Logan didn't answer, just opened his closet door.

"Oh, God," I breathed as the inner closet was revealed. "It's pink in there, too. Come out of the closet, Logan and let me bask in all your pink glory."

Logan retrieved a large Rubbermaid bin, sent me a glower but I didn't think he meant it. "Like you're one to talk, living in an unfinished house."

I was too busy cackling to go on the defensive. "Thank you," I said, meaning it. I'd needed the laugh, which explained why he'd sent me on the supply run.

Logan rolled his eyes, but I didn't miss his upturned lips as he walked away.

Big Joey didn't say a word as Logan patched him up. Luke and I took turns asking him questions about what had happened to him, who'd roughed him up, but every inquiry was met with the same stony silence. I dropped into a chair and put my head in my hands, exhaustion taking hold.

"You should go home." Logan said. "Both of you."

"What about him?" Luke chucked a thumb at Big Joey. "What's to stop him from killing you in your sleep?"

The Dark Prince shrugged. "So I don't sleep."

Luke put his hands on his hips and glared at his brother. "For how long though. You can't stay awake indefinitely."

"If you've got a better plan, I'd love to hear it."

I dragged Luke into the breezeway while Logan was finishing up. "This is getting us nowhere."

My husband ran a hand through his hair. "It's not too late to call Vasquez. Maybe do it through a third party, like Marcy, in case anyone is monitoring your phone calls."

"I don't want to drag Marcy into this if we have any other choice." An idea had rooted itself in my head, like an itch that wouldn't go away. "Let me try and get through to him."

"Isn't that what we've been doing?"

Putting a hand on Luke's arm, I stared into his eyes. "I mean on my own. I think I can get him to talk to me."

Luke scowled. "He could attack you."

Deep in my gut I still believed Big Joey wasn't a violent guy. Maybe it was idiotic to base my measure of a man's character on his delight over baby sea turtles, but the image stayed in my head. There was someone out there who was a bigger threat than him. I felt the certainty of my conviction all the way down to my bones. A soulless monster who would beat Mrs. Pomeroy to death, who had abducted my mother. I'd come face to face with a killer before, I knew for sure that evil existed and it wasn't present in Big Joey. I glanced around to make sure none of Logan's neighbors would overhear, then lowered my voice. "Tie him to the chair. Leave me with your Taser."

Luke opened his mouth to refuse outright but I kept on going, needing to get it all out. "If this doesn't work we'll call Vasquez in. But I have to at least try."

He looked at me for a long moment, then closed his eyes. "Fine, but either Logan or I will stay in the apartment with you in case you need back up. Whichever of us you want."

I thought about what he'd ask me earlier, if I regretted not being with Logan. "It wasn't a choice. What you asked me earlier. Being with Logan was never really an option for me."

He frowned. "Now's not the time—"

Wrapping my hands around the back of his neck, I pulled him down until his lips met mine and kissed the ever-loving shit out of him.

He stood still, utterly stunned for a moment, obviously shocked. Then his arms went around me, and he pulled my body flush against his while his mouth devoured mine.

Eventually we had to come up for air. Reluctantly, I stepped back, struggling to suck in some much needed oxygen.

"Jackie—"

"It's never the right time," I panted, fisting my hands in his shirt. "There's always something else to deal with. But Luke, I will *make* time for you and only for you. So what does that tell you?"

His hands traveled up to my face, his palms rough against my skin, his hold gentle as if he cradled a baby bird. "God, I love you so much."

I kissed him again, needing another taste of him, wanting to drown all my worry, all my fears for Celeste, for our future in the need I had for him. It wasn't just physical—my world had been turned inside out since my near death experience and I drifted, rudderless without him. Luke was just as desperate, shoving me against the stucco wall, angling his mouth for a deeper taste.

Someone cleared their throat. Loudly.

We both turned to face the open doorway. Logan stood there, watching us, his expression carefully blanked. Abu perched on his shoulder, looking as though he belonged there. "Do me a favor before you two take off. Keep an eye on him so I can shower."

Though part of me was embarrassed to have been caught necking like some hormone ridden teenagers out in the breezeway of his apartment complex, I clung to Luke, not wanting to let him go. Everything else was falling to pieces around me but if I had him, I would make it through.

"Jackie wants a little one on one time with our friend," Luke told his brother.

Logan's eyes narrowed but he didn't say anything. He didn't have to, I knew he objected, vehemently. Well, tough tacos.

"I'll get the Taser out of the car." Luke pulled away first. "I'll go grab us some dinner while you guys talk."

I watched him jog down the steps and open the trunk, not wanting to look away.

"Good to see you two getting along again," Logan murmured.

I couldn't tell if he was being sarcastic or not, but I gave him the benefit of the doubt. "Yeah. I never feel quite right when we're at odds."

"Unlike with me. That's how you like it, us squaring off."

I turned to face him. "No, I really don't. I think it's just habit at this point, our default setting, you know? "

His eyes were so blue as he studied me. "Yeah, I do know."

Abu chattered and I put my hand out so the monkey could scramble onto me. "I'm trying to be better."

"And I appreciate that. What I don't appreciate is the fact that you're sexually manipulating my brother to get your own way when it comes to the on the job stuff."

My jaw dropped. Abu screeched as though he was outraged on my behalf.

"I'll be in the shower. Do what you like at your own risk." Logan turned back into the apartment and shut the door in my face.

CHAPTER 16

"I'm going to kill him," I spoke in a low, flat tone as I stared at the closed door. "I'm going to get a gun and shoot him dead."

Sexually manipulate, my pasty white hide. The barb stung, burrowed deep under my skin. Considering my fatigue, the irritant was unbearable and I didn't know whether to laugh or cry. Why could I never manage to get along with more than one Parker brother at a time? What exactly was my damage? Or theirs?

The worse part though, I feared Logan was right. Not that I was sexually manipulating my husband, but that my feminine skill sets played a big part in our group dynamic. But the way he'd said it, like I was some sort of cold-blooded Mata Hari, pissed me right the hell off.

"Jackie?" Luke had returned, Taser in hand. "Is everything okay?"

I took the weapon from him. It wasn't a gun, but it was close enough to make me nervous. The last thing I wanted was to zap the few brain cells that would occasionally bump together in my noggin. Maybe I should test it though, to make sure it worked. "I might have to use this on your brother."

"What's that?" Luke, who had been in the process of opening the apartment door, glanced at me over his shoulder.

"Never mind," I followed him inside.

Logan had handcuffed Big Joey to the chair he sat on. God only knew where the Dark Prince had manifested the hardware from, but I was betting his nightstand. Joey's sweat dampened head was bent at an awkward angle, his bloated body a mass of bandages. He looked sad and sickly, almost half dead. I wanted to ask the guys to move him to somewhere he would be a little more comfortable, but didn't bother wasting my breath. They'd never go for it.

Instead, I went into the kitchen and opened the fridge. Bottled water marched in anal retentive rows on the top shelf. Just to be contrary, I snagged two out of the middle and shoved a few more off-kilter. Then, I tugged open the drawer next to the sink.

"What are you looking for?" Logan growled from the open doorway.

"A knife to geld you with, jackass," I muttered. That drawer was a bust, so I slammed it shut and took a pull off my water bottle. I set it aside and then attacked the next drawer.

"Jackie."

"A frigging straw, okay? I'm crazy thirsty so he's probably dehydrated and with that busted lip, I thought it would be easier for him to drink through a straw. Is that all right with you, or do you think I'll try to *manipulate* him, too?"

Logan's eyes narrowed. He pushed past me and went to a cabinet at the far end of the galley kitchen. Reached up to the top shelf, he extracted a rectangular box and then held it out to me. "Will this suffice?"

"I'll make do." If that was his idea of a peace offering he could go kick rocks.

I snagged the waters and stomped out of the small space.

Luke frowned at his brother but Logan merely pushed past him to that bland bathroom. My shoulders sagged in relief as the door shut.

I'll always be here for you.

What had seemed to be a promise now felt more like a threat. Didn't matter that the intensity in Logan's eyes when he'd spoken those words had reverberated in my soul. Viciously, I stuffed the memory down to deal with later. Much later.

"Are you sure about this, Ace?" Luke was looking down at Big Joey's balding head. "Because I can stay—"

"I'll be just ducky." I covered his lips with my fingertips. I needed the space and freedom to work only his absence could bring.

Luke pulled me in close for a kiss and I let him, though I couldn't lose myself in him the way I had before. Damn Logan Parker straight to hell for ruining everything!

Sexually manipulate, my lily white hide.

Luke pulled back and nodded once before he left. I sagged as I heard the shower come on in the other room, then turned toward Big Joey.

"Alone at last," I said to Big Joey. "Anything you want to confess to me, big guy? Murder, mayhem, any of that ringing a bell?"

He looked uncomfortable with his arms bound behind him, but I knew better than to let him up. Settling one of the dining room chairs at a ninety degree angle, I plopped down next to him and opened the other bottle of water. "Thirsty?"

He didn't answer, his head still lolling towards his lap.

God, what if he needed more medical care? Logan had patched him up to the best of his abilities, but there might be internal damage or something that we couldn't see, didn't know enough to treat. I had my phone in my hand and was prepared to dial when I remembered Celeste, and thought about her tied and beaten the way this man had been.

Abu chittered from his position on the counter and I turned to look at him. When I turned back, Big Joey's brown eyes were looking straight at me.

"Water," he breathed.

I aimed the straw for his lips. "Go slowly."

Just like all the other men in my life, he ignored my advice, and sucked down the water in great, greedy gulps. I pulled the bottle away when he started to choke and pounded on his back.

"Contrary to popular opinion, I really don't enjoy saying, I told you so," I said in a mild voice.

Joey sputtered a bit and I used the hem of his blood-stained wife beater to wipe his chin. "Better?"

He nodded.

"Feel up to answering some questions?"

His gaze shifted to my shirt, to the cleavage peeking out between the stained linen. "What'll you give me for it?"

"Really?" I asked. "Did Logan put you up to this?"

"Who's Logan?"

"The loser with the pink bedroom," I muttered to myself. Then louder. "The guy who patched you up."

Joey just shrugged. "He didn't say nothing."

I stared at him but he seemed to be telling the truth. And honestly it was a little bit flattering that beaten and bleeding he still wanted a peek at the girls.

My gaze swung first to the front door and then to the bathroom. If either of the Parker brothers caught wind of this little game, I'd never live it down. But what else did I have to work with?

"Fine, we'll play strip interrogation. You get a button for every five questions you answer to my satisfaction."

"Every other question. And I get two vetoes." Joey had gone from half dead lowlife to shrewd negotiator.

"Every three questions and one veto." I fired back. "I have a lot more questions than I have buttons."

"Deal," His shoulder shifted as though he was trying to shake on it and then frowned as if he'd forgotten that he was tied up.

"Who hurt you?"

He leaned back in the chair. "A guy by the name of Danny O'Rourke and his crew."

I shifted closer. "Did he leave you for us to find?"

"I really don't know. I'm supposed to send a message to my family he's here in Miami."

"Did Danny O'Rourke kidnap my mother?"

Joey frowned. "If he did, I didn't see her. What's with the monkey?"

"It's a long story." I ignored Abu and popped a button at the bottom of my shirt.

"Hey, that's no fair." Joey said.

"I popped a button, rules are rules."

He looked sullen with his busted lip pouting out like that and I almost reconsidered when he sighed. "Get on with it."

I thought for a moment. "What was the message you were supposed to give your family?"

"Veto." Joey's gaze was glued to my fingers poised over the next button from the bottom.

"Fine. Did O'Rourke have anything to do with Mrs. Pomeroy's death?"

"I couldn't say."

"Can't say or don't know?" I pushed. "Because can't say sounds like a veto and we agreed you'd only get one."

"I don't know."

"Did they know each other?"

"I don't know. And that's another button."

"The veto doesn't count!" I said, outraged.

"I'm not counting the veto. You asked if O'Rourke had anything to do with Mrs. Pomeroy's death, if it was can't say or don't know and if they knew each other. Three questions so one button."

My eyes narrowed. "Have you done this before?"

His bloodied lips twitched. "Maybe once or twice."

Damn it all. I undid the next button. We were getting into dicey territory and I only had a name of another Mob family member, nothing about Celeste or Mrs. Pomeroy. I needed to ask better questions before Luke or Logan returned.

"Have you ever heard the name Celeste Drummond?"

He shook his head violently. "No."

"Who is Marlena Cruz?"

He frowned, his eyes narrowing as though I was trying to trick him. "My real estate agent."

"She doesn't exist though. I checked. Why did Mrs. Pomeroy insist you be removed from her beach house? That isn't protocol."

Big Joey looked away. "She was my biological mother. I came down here to find her."

My lips parted. Shit. Hadn't seen that one coming.

"That's a button," he said, though the light had gone out of his eyes.

I undid the button over my naval, mind whirling.

The bathroom door opened and the Dark Prince emerged on a cloud of steam. He wore one of those white towels around his hips, his hair dripping wet. Those dark blue eyes scanned me up and down, noting the three opened buttons at my midsection. Though I hadn't felt even a tingle revealing that small strip of skin to the man I'd been questioning, Logan's gaze was like a brand, searing my tender skin.

"Learn anything?"

Motive. Big Joey had motive to kill Mrs. Pomeroy who was apparently his long lost mother. Had she truly known who he was when she had us remove him? And how did the mysterious Marlena Cruz fit into the puzzle?

I'd also learned that Logan Parker still looked delicious in a towel. His shoulders were enormous, arms bulging with well-developed muscle. The man had a frigging eight pack of rippling abs and his skin was the most beautiful cast of bronze. A thicket of black hair matted his chest, descending down that perfect trail which disappeared into the towel. I wanted to get up and circle behind him, see those magnificent shoulders from the back, a fact which unnerved me because I had no business looking at him.

"Put some clothes on. You look like an ad for gay porn," I snapped.

Joey barked out a laugh and Abu screeched.

Logan didn't move right away, his gaze trained on my face, lids lowering to shade his expression. I lifted my chin, threw my shoulders back and gave him a nonverbal *up yours* with my rigid posture.

"It's nice to know," he said in a low, satisfied tone. "That two can play this game."

MERCIFULLY, Logan retreated to his pink circle of hell. With Luke due back at any minute and my mind out to sea on what other questions I should be asking Big Joey, I helped him drink more water. Restless, I got up and strode into the living area, which was only about three feet away from the dining room. I paced back again, then into the kitchen to change it up.

Had Big Joey killed his mother? I looked over at him. Abu

Lease on the Beach

was doing a handstand on the table and Big Joey was speaking quietly to the monkey. With his doughy face and body he didn't look like a threat, not the way the Dark Prince did. Sin on a stick and all that jazz.

Stop it, Jackie, I scolded myself. So what if I was still attracted to Logan. I meant every word I'd said to Luke about picking him. He was my choice and I'd promised him faithfulness. Same as he'd promised me.

I flinched as I thought of Justine the animal lover. Was it any wonder I had been eye-humping Logan, especially with him strutting around in a towel like that?

But it had to stop, I was better than this, stronger in both will and character. I was not the girl who slept with her husband's brother.

Well, at least not again.

My cell rang and I answered it. "Hello?"

"If you want to see your mother alive, you'll do exactly as I say," the distorted voice was low but audible.

I raced to the bedroom door and pounded on it madly. Logan must have been holding the knob because he yanked it open right away. He took one look at my face and then crouched low so he could hear the person on the other end.

I gripped the phone so hard my body shook. "Who are you? What do you want? I swear if you hurt one hair on her head, I'll—"

"Go to her trailer at midnight. You'll receive further instructions then. If you call the police, she dies."

The phone clicked in my ear.

I sagged against the wall. "Damn it. What do they want from me?"

"I wish I knew."

"Jackie? Logan?" Luke called from the front of the apartment.

Well at least he was back. I pushed past Logan, needing to feel Luke's arms around me….

And stopped dead when I saw Sargent Enrique Vasquez standing next to my husband.

The man's eyes went from me, to Logan, then to the chair where big Joey was trussed up like a Christmas goose.

"I wanted to let you know we found your car. Looks like you found something I was looking for, too."

CHAPTER 17

"Well, at least he didn't arrest us," Logan grumbled after Vasquez left with Big Joey Santino in tow.

"Yet," I muttered darkly.

"I didn't know he'd followed me here," Luke said for the third time. "I swear I wouldn't have told him without talking to you two first."

I put my head down on the dining room table and Abu climbed on it. "What are we going to do?"

Luke put his hands on my shoulders "What can we do? Other than go to Celeste's trailer at midnight like he said?"

"Jackie, you're sure he didn't say anything about Santino?" Logan asked.

I shook my head and Abu chittered in disapproval. "No, you heard almost all of it. And from what I got out of Big Joey, he didn't have any idea Celeste had been abducted. If the same guy had her, he had her out of sight."

"I don't like this," Logan growled. "There's no way all of this shit is unrelated."

Luke kept up with the neck massage. "You should try to

get some sleep, Ace. Logan and I will head to the impound lot and pick up the truck."

"Here?" I glanced around the apartment, not liking the idea of climbing into Logan's bed. Things were just too weird lately for that to be a viable option.

Luke shook his head. "We can bring you home first. But we better go now, as the impound lot closes at eight."

We trooped down the stairs, two men, a woman and a monkey and back out into Rebecca's POS. The drive back to our bungalow was silent and I was glad it was just me and Abu going inside.

Though I'd intended to go for a shower my bed was too inviting. I kicked off my shoes, put the Taser on the dresser and flopped down onto the mattress, face first. Abu prowled the room for a spell but eventually, he climbed up next to me and curled into a little ball of primate cuteness.

I hadn't even realized I'd intended to sleep until a scratching sound woke me. The clock told me I'd been asleep for under an hour. I sat up, disoriented and almost more tired than when I'd gone to sleep. I looked around for Abu, but he was still curled up on the bed.

The scratching sound came again, louder this time. It sounded like it was coming from the bedroom window. I couldn't see out, all the blinds were pulled. As quietly as I could, I slithered off the bed and reached for the dresser, for the Taser I'd left sitting on top. It wouldn't do me much good through the window though, so I decided to sneak around the side of the house.

If I'd been thinking more clearly, I would have nabbed my cell phone and called 911. But it was the middle of the night, my mother had been abducted, and I had a monkey to protect.

The back door made a slight scraping noise as I let myself out into the sultry night air. The back porch was littered with tools Luke had left out so I picked my way through the construction zone and down to the lawn. We weren't the dump truckloads of money into the lawn kind of people. There were brown patches, and bald spots, not a nice soft cushy landing zone, but I was proud of how steadily I maneuvered around to the side of the house.

A massive black shape was crouched below the pane of glass. A human shape, wearing a hoodie in this heat. Obviously up to no good. I held the Taser with both hands, aiming for center mass. Didn't matter where the damn thing landed, the prongs were designed to go through clothing and send the electrical into the Tas-ee. In theory anyway.

The scratching sound resumed and as I drew closer, I realized the person on the ground had cut the screen and wedged a crowbar into my bedroom window.

"Boy did you pick the wrong place and time." I shot him in the back and pulled the trigger.

The body shook horribly as electrical current raced through it, hunting for a ground. I stopped and the hoodie wearer collapsed in a heap between my hydrangea bushes.

"Who the hell are you?"

No answer. The inert form appeared to be breathing though, so that was a good sign.

"What are you doing here?"

"You stole—," the reedy voice sounded familiar. It was definitely male, broke off in a coughing fit.

A car turned the corner, followed by a truck. A big black truck. The headlights from both vehicles illuminated me and the hoodie wearer, sending towering shadows up against the side of the house.

"Jackie?" Luke called. The sound of a door slamming and then another. "What happened?"

"He was trying to break in," I said.

Suddenly, the lump on the ground rose up and tackled me

around the legs. We went down in a heap and I involuntarily squeezed the Taser trigger again because the body jerked on top of mine obscenely.

"Stop!" the hoodie wearer shrieked. He wet his pants and some of the dampness seeped onto me.

"Seriously?" I dropped the Taser just as the Parker brothers reached us. Logan rolled the guy off of me and Luke helped me to my feet.

"Who the hell are you?"

"It's Markov," I panted.

Not bothering to remove the electrodes, Luke hauled Markov off the ground and shook the smaller man. "Why the hell are you here?"

Markov swung his bloodshot eyes to me. "You stole my monkey."

I put my hands on my hips. It's true what they say, it's better to be pissed off than pissed on. "He almost got eaten by a snake! You were just trying to sell him for drug money."

Logan stepped between us, breaking my eye contact. "Tell us what you did with your RV and we'll give you the monkey back."

"Like hell I will," I snarled. "He'll sell poor Abu to whatever creep pays the most so he can get his next fix."

Logan glanced over his shoulder at me. "We've got a job to do. The monkey is leverage."

My outrage spilled over and I punched Logan in the back. He raised a brow at me and though my knuckles sang, I raised my hand to wallop him again.

"Chill, Ace." Luke grabbed my wrist, preventing me from striking his brother again. "Logan's right."

Markov was shaking a little, whether from withdrawal or the after effects of the Taser, I couldn't tell. He had shifty eyes, no way would I let him take Abu with him. That monkey was a hero.

"What did you do with the RV?" Logan asked again.

"Sold it."

Luke uttered a low oath. "Who bought it?"

"Lipinski. Arlene Lipinski."

I frowned. Where had I heard that name before?

"Son of a bitch," Logan said. "Isn't that the apartment in Silver Bluffs where the car got jacked?"

Luke shook Markov some more. "Is she your dealer?"

"Yeah."

"What's she cooking, Meth?"

Markov shook his head. "Krokodil."

Logan got in the guy's face. "The zombie drug? Man, you must have a death wish."

"Zombie drug?" I frowned, having never heard of the stuff.

"It eats the flesh right off your bones. Life expectancy for your average user is about a year, max. And it's one of the most addictive substances on the planet."

A shiver ripped through me. Sometimes I hated living in the melting pot of Miami. More people meant more crazy ways to kill each other, or abuse themselves into an early grave. "There is no freaking way I'm turning Abu over to this guy."

Markov started cursing, in what I assumed was Russian. He swung in Luke's grip, spittle flying from his mouth.

Logan cleared his throat. "Withdrawal could kill him and the rounds with the Taser can't have done him much good. I'll bring him to the E.R, see if there's anything they can do for him."

"Good, I need a shower anyway." What with the being coated in urine for the second time in a flipping week and all. "When you get back, we'll go to Celeste's trailer park."

Luke flipped the bedroom light on. "Holy shit."

I blinked at the light and my jaw dropped when I saw the carnage. It was a good thing Logan had taken Markov away in a pair of flex cuffs, because at the moment, I was reconsidering returning Abu.

The monkey had torn the bedroom apart in a frenzy. Cosmetics and perfume bottles were strewn everywhere. My honeysuckle scented lotion oozed down the mirror. The stack of magazines I'd left on the bedside table were ripped and shredded, pieces of glossy paper scattered about the room. I'd made the mistake of leaving the bathroom door open and toilet paper was strewn everywhere. The carpet corner that had never been properly tacked down was now ripped up and flopped on its side like a dead trout. The tiffany lamp on my bedside table had been knocked onto the floor, the stained glass broken. The bedding was torn, with stuffing bulging from the mattress and pillows…

I looked around, stunned at the devastation. "We were only outside for a few minutes. How could he have done all this in so little time?"

"Better question is where the hell did he go?"

I followed a streamer of toilet paper into the bathroom. Abu had pulled my purple bathrobe off the back of the door and was crouching on it. When he saw me, he chittered for joy and then scrambled up my leg, leaving a fresh turd on the terrycloth.

"Really?" I said to the monkey. "Really?"

Luke stood behind me, taking in the destruction. "Either he's got multiple personalities or a destructive case of separation anxiety."

We set to work, cleaning up the mess. Thank God the closet door had been shut tight and my clothes were all safe. I had enough trouble keeping up my wardrobe without Abu wigging out all over it.

In the end, we had two bags of trash filled to bursting, including several chunks of carpet that had to be cut out from scent. O.D. We stripped the bed, flipped the mattress to the non-gouged side and remade it with a fresh pair of sheets. I flushed the monkey poop and put my robe in the washing machine. Luke took out the trash while I climbed in the shower. Abu peeked around the corner as if he wanted to climb in under the spray with me.

"I'm mad at you," I told him. I turned away to rinse my hair. "But even if I wasn't, you are not getting in the shower with me. Go find Luke."

He made a sad sound and skulked away.

After I was clean, I toweled myself off and returned to the bedroom

"I'll do the bedroom next," Luke promised. "We can sleep in the spare room until it's done."

But if we moved into that room where would Celeste sleep if we got her back. When, not if, damn it. We would get my mother back alive and unhurt.

I burst into tears. It was a flat out ugly cry, full of fear and heartbreak and exhaustion that rolled through me like tremors.

Like any red blooded male, Luke always appeared terrified when I cried for what he perceived to be no reason. However, I'd trained him well over the last several years and he had enough sense to put his arms around me and say, "It'll be okay. Everything will be fine, I promise."

"It's too much," I sobbed. "I can't handle all of this crap. It's wearing me down. How can anyone live like this?"

"Jackie, look at me." He lifted my chin and looked straight into my eyes. "We are going to get through this. All of it. We'll get your mother back and then—"

"I don't want kids," I blurted.

Luke stepped back, dropping his hands to his side. "What?"

"No children. I know you want that, a baby or babies. I saw it on your face when you thought I might be pregnant. But I just...I can't be responsible for someone else on that level, Luke. I just got you back full time and we have so much to figure out between us. Adding someone else into our crazy lives, an innocent, seems almost cruel. It isn't fair and I won't do it. Not now, maybe not ever."

Can you live with that? The words hung on the tip of my tongue but I bit them back. I didn't want to force a confrontation but the issue had been weighing on me, more than anything. As much as I didn't want to force him into a corner, he needed to know how strongly I felt about this.

Luke turned away, ran a hand through his hair. Started to speak, then stopped. Cleared his throat.

The seconds stretched out like an eternity as questions raced through my mind. Did he still love me? Was my position a deal breaker? Would he run off to be with Justine and have a dozen fat babies, leaving me here in my unfinished home?

"Say something," I whispered.

"Now's not the time to be making any decisions—"

"It's never the time!" My voice sounded shrill in my own ears, sharpened to a knifelike point by the cold stone of desperation in my chest. "We need to make the time."

He gave me that look, the one men get when their women are asking them for something they think is unreasonable. "Jackie, you're under too much stress to make any decisions—"

I held up a hand, cutting him off. "Do not take that tone with me, Luke Parker. I know what I want and what I don't want. I want you, not a baby. You're the one who has to figure out if you want me."

Lease on the Beach

I turned my back on him, and dropped my towel. I'd just bent down to pick up my towel when he gripped my arm and spun me to face him.

"Why are you trying to make me the bad guy here?"

I pulled my arm, trying to break his vice-like hold. "Let go of me."

"Is this about Logan? Are you trying to push me away so you can go to him with a clear conscience?"

"Fuck you," I snarled and shoved him as hard as I could. "I told you before—"

"Those are just words, Jackie. You don't think I see the way he looks at you? The way you look at him when you think I don't notice?"

A fresh batch of tears filled my eyes. "This isn't about Logan, or your insane jealousy. It's about you, running hot and cold on me, about you trying to corner me into agreeing to something that I don't want."

His face turned cold and he dropped my arm. "You don't know what the hell you're talking about."

I moved closer, wagging my finger in his face. "You look me in the eye, Luke Parker, and you tell me that volunteering me to babysit wasn't to get the old biological clock ticking. That knocking me up wouldn't give you the perfect excuse to kick me off of the Damaged Goods team. You thought you wanted me to work with you, but you don't, not really. And instead of manning up and telling me flat out that you don't want to work with me anymore, you're putting all this baby pressure on me."

"You're crazy," Luke said, but he didn't meet my eye.

My heart hurt. He'd needed to hear me say that I picked him. How come he didn't get that I had the same exact need? A need he wasn't meeting.

Out of nowhere I thought of the lyrics to that old Cheap Trick song. *I want you to want me*. That was all I was after, I realized. To know that he wanted me, not just for me to want him. God, I was so tired that nothing made sense anymore, my mind a maze of riddles yet this had all become clear. I was practically begging him to tell me what he wanted and still, crickets.

I thought about telling him to get out, but we still had Celeste's kidnapper to deal with. As much as I craved space, it was one more thing I had to do without.

Instead I turned away, chilled to the bone. "I need to get dressed."

The door to our bedroom shut with a quiet click. When I looked back, Luke was gone.

CHAPTER 18

"What do monkeys eat?" Logan asked out loud.

It was the most anyone had spoken in the half an hour since we'd parked in front of my mother's trailer. The windows were cracked, letting in the sounds of life in the trailer park. Dogs barking, babies crying, glass breaking, drunks shouting. Just like the good old days.

Luke and I were doing our damndest to ignore one another, him looking out one window, surveying the grounds. I stared down at my cell, willing the bugger to ring already. It was ten to twelve and the tension was high, the adrenaline flowing like beer at a frat party. Even Abu seemed tense, hopping from person to person, squeaking low. I hadn't wanted to bring him but didn't dare leave him alone in the house again.

Logan wasn't a chatterer under the best of circumstances so our silence must really be eating at him.

"Bananas," I said.

The Dark Prince turned around in the seat to look at me. "You sure that's not just a stereotype?"

I wasn't, but I'd been a little too busy to call a vet. The last twenty four hours had aged me more than the last thirty two years. "He ate the one I gave him earlier."

"I could call Justine. She might know something," Luke's tone was even and I wanted to eviscerate him for even bringing the hobag's name up, never mind volunteering to contact her as though he was doing me a fricking favor.

"I seriously doubt that," I seethed.

Logan blew out a breath. "Are we all going to have to go to therapy or some shit? 'Cause I gotta tell you, our cheap ass medical plan won't cover it."

"We're fine," Luke said. "Everything's fine."

"Bull. You two are giving me whiplash, you know that? Especially you, Luke."

"Stay out of it," Luke snapped.

"No, because whatever the hell is going on is affecting the job. Am I the only one who noticed that we haven't been paid this month? Not once. We've run down tweakers, battled a giant snake, tied a man to a chair, lost two vehicles and Jackie's mother. One of our employers was beaten to death and after hearing the prognosis for that poor bastard Markov, I'm wondering if this shit is worth it."

I opened my mouth, then shut it again. What could I say, humanity just sucked sometimes.

"You want out?" Luke growled. "There's the door."

Logan shifted to face his brother. "What is wrong with you, Luke? I don't even know you anymore."

Oh, I *so* knew that feeling. I leaned forward, wondering what he would say when my cell rang. Damn it, if my mental train kept getting derailed there would be no escaping the carnage.

With shaking hands, I hit speaker and then cleared my throat. "Hello?"

"Are you in your mother's trailer?"

Lease on the Beach

"No. The landlord padlocked the door after we cleared it out. I want to talk to her."

"You'll talk to her when you give me what I want."

Luke looked ready to say something but I held up a hand. "And what's that?"

"Get inside the trailer, I'll call you back in ten minutes. Be there or you'll never see your mother again." The line went dead.

I let out a string of curses. Great, I had to perform B&E because my life didn't suck enough. What the hell could possibly be inside that trailer that would be worth kidnapping Celeste over?

"Call Vasquez," Luke advised. "It's not too late to involve the cops, but if you start committing crimes you're just digging us all in deeper."

I bit my lip, considering it. We'd been with the man earlier, when he'd taken Big Joey. But involving the police hadn't felt right then. Abu scrambled onto my lap and looked up at me with his big dark eyes. My heart pounded so hard I felt dizzy from all the blood rushing around. If only I could *think*. "It doesn't make any sense. Why do they want me in there?"

"There's not enough time," Logan pointed out. "I can pick the lock, get us in."

He popped the door and as the overhead light came on, I reached out and gripped his arm. "No."

"No?" He turned to look at me as though I was crazy. "They'll kill her."

"There's nothing in there." I said, sure of it. "So the only reason anyone would want me to go inside is to commit a crime."

"Who would want that?" Luke asked.

As I looked up into his puzzled brown gaze it clicked into

place. "Take us to Trade Street. And I want one of you to wait here."

"I will." Luke volunteered. I tried not to be hurt by his obvious relief at getting away from me for a spell. "But what am I waiting for?"

"The police. When the kidnapper calls I'm going to tell him that yes, we're in Celeste's trailer. Call me when they show up for the bust."

Luke nodded and then climbed out of the car. Abu and I moved to the passenger's seat as Logan got behind the wheel.

"Where are we going?" The Dark Prince asked as we left the trailer park behind.

"East end of Trade Street as fast as you can," I inhaled.

"Trade?" Logan asked. "That's a shitty part of town. Why would we go there?"

"Because that's where Celeste is being held." I hoped.

Logan took a hard left and I gripped the *oh shit* bar to keep my ass on the seat. "You better catch me up because I'm not following your thought process."

"Okay, so with a standard kidnapping—"

"Is there such a thing as a standard kidnapping?" The Dark Prince mused.

I ignored him. "Typically, the kidnappers would demand a ransom of some sort. In exchange for which we'd get proof of life. But neither of those things have happened."

Logan hit the brakes as a yellow light turned red. "Still not tracking here, Jackie."

"The only thing this kidnapper asked was that we do something illegal. Like break into the trailer. What would happen if we got caught doing that?"

"Probably get our asses arrested."

I nodded. "I could lose my process serving certificate and Damaged Goods's reputation would be a joke. So who would stand to gain from that?"

The streetlight changed just as the light dawned on Logan. "John Garrison, that smarmy SOB. It makes sense."

"So what I'm going to do is tell him that yes, we broke into the trailer. He'll call the cops and then leave to watch us being dragged off in cuffs and we'll go in and get Celeste."

Logan nodded. "I hope you're right."

"I know I am." That wasn't why I was worried. "You don't think he hurt her do you?"

Logan's hands clenched on the steering wheel. "If he did, he'll have more than a kidnapping charge to deal with."

———

My phone rang as we pulled into a parking space across the street from the shitty building that held Garrison Property Management. If my voice shook as I answered, it was no longer from anxiety. No, now a black fury engulfed me head to foot. I wanted to gut the bastard like a trout. He'd followed me out to the boonies and even talked to me, all the while he'd had my mother locked up in this shithole.

I was going to make sure he was prosecuted to the full extent of the law, then personally see to it that he became someone's prison bitch. And that was if Celeste was completely unharmed.

"Are you inside the trailer?" The warbled voice asked.

My eyes met Logan's and he nodded once.

Taking a deep breath, I lied my ass off. "Yes, we're inside. I want to talk to my mother."

Logan had taken a pair of binoculars out of the glove box and he had them trained across the street. The Garrisons had bragged multiple times that they owned the entire building, operating their property management company out of the first floor storefront and living on the two floors above. In addition to John, he had two hulking sons who aided him with their barely legal form of eviction. If there was a Mrs. Garrison in the picture, she was probably chained to the radiator next to Celeste.

Shaking off the mental image, I focused on keeping my voice level. "If you don't let me talk to my mother right this minute, I'll hang up and call the police."

On the other end of the phone, there was a scuffling sound and then a clang, as though someone had dropped a pot. "Hello?"

"Jackie?" It was Celeste all right. She sounded surprised to hear from me. What the hell had these assholes done to her?

"Mom, are you all right?"

"I'm sorry," Celeste mumbled, her voice sad.

The phone was transferred back to the person with the voice modulator. "Stay where you are. We'll bring her to you."

When the connection broke, I called Luke. "They said they'd bring her to us there. Any sign of the police?"

"Not yet. Want to tell me what's going on?"

When I explained my theory to him there was a pause and then a sigh. "Do you really think the Garrisons would kidnap your mother to put us out of business?"

"It's all I've got to go on."

"What happens next?"

A light came on on the bottom floor of the building across the street. Two men exited through the front door, locking up behind them. From their hulking builds I knew they were part of Team Garrison. They made their way to a windowless van parked a half a block ahead of us.

"It's the sons," Logan confirmed. "No sign of John."

"Luke, John's boys are leaving." I rattled off the license plate to him. "If they show up over there, let the police know what's doing."

From the other end of the phone, I could hear sirens. "What are you going to do?" Luke asked.

My gaze remained fixed on the building. "Go in after Celeste."

"Be careful, Ace," Luke whispered and he disconnected.

"I don't like it." Logan set the binoculars aside. "Let's say John was smart enough to think this up himself. Wouldn't he want to witness our takedown firsthand?"

"Maybe he doesn't trust the boys to keep Celeste secure?"

Logan shook his head. "There's got to be more to it."

I threw my hands up, startling Abu who'd been perched on my shoulder. "If you have a better idea, now's the time to air it out."

A muscle jumped in Logan's jaw, then he turned to face me. "What will it take to keep you in the truck?"

I met and held his gaze. "My mother might be hurt in there. An act of Congress couldn't keep me here."

The Dark Prince blew out a sigh. He removed his sidearm from his holster, checked the clip and then looked at me. "That's what I thought. Just, stay behind me, okay?"

"I will." I was armed with my Taser, hoping to hell I wouldn't have to use it again. "Abu, you stay here and be a good boy, okay? Uncle Logan and I will be right back."

The little primate screamed at me then leapt to the back seat as though I'd hurt his feelings.

"*Uncle* Logan?" the Dark Prince growled. "I know you didn't just turn me into a monkey's uncle."

"You've been called worse." I popped the door and got out, Taser at the ready. "Let's do this."

We scuttled down an alley behind the building, around a few drunks sleeping off their cheap whiskey hangovers, and to the fire escape of the Garrison's building. Going in through the front wasn't an option. The fire escape was ancient, all corroded metal and peeling paint. The bottom rung was about five feet above my head, retracted to keep people from doing exactly what Logan and I planned on doing—using it to break into the building. I had serious doubts about its structural integrity, but it would be a good vantage point to peek in to the rooms on this side.

"You're lighter that I am," Logan pointed out. "I can boost you up there."

"What if it falls?" I squeaked.

"We don't have a lot of options, here, Jackie. Want me to do it?"

I blew out a sigh. "No, I'll go."

Logan surprised me by planting a kiss on my forehead. "Be careful." Then he gripped my hips and heaved me up in what appeared to be an effortless display of masculine strength. His grip was warm and reassuring around my hips, though I felt overbalanced, my double D's not used to fighting gravity this far up.

My heart raced as I reached for the first bar. The thing was folded over so I had to pull it out at an awkward angle.

"Don't drop me," I hissed at Logan.

He grunted something indecipherable in response.

I pulled and yanked with all my upper body strength. Damn it, too bad Abu couldn't talk, he would have been perfect for this recon job. I cursed and repositioned my grip and the ladder came down with an ear splitting clang.

The momentum overbalanced me and for one terrifying moment I thought Logan would drop me face first into the concrete. But his grip shifted and though I landed hard, he managed to keep me upright.

Upright and flush against him.

We froze, our bodies pressed intimately against each other for the first time in a decade. My arms had gone around his neck and my heart was going a mile a minute.

Slowly I raised my gaze from the collar of his black t-shirt to his darkly stubbled jaw, to his bow shaped lips, then finally up to those aqua eyes.

"You okay?" he whispered, making no move to let me go.

One of our hearts was pounding furiously. We were so close, I couldn't tell if it was mine or his. Maybe both at the same galloping rate. It took me a minute to remember how to talk. "Yeah."

He felt good, all warm and solid against me. His scent surrounded me, not a cologne, but just clean, potent male. At this range he was temptation embodied and for a dizzying second I couldn't recall why I should resist.

Above us, an air conditioner cycled on with a chugging sound, breaking our staring contest. As one, we both looked up to see if any of the residents had leaned out the windows to inspect the disturbance in the alley. Nothing.

Sucking in a deep breath of Logan scented air, I willed myself to step away. "Thanks for catching me."

"No problem," Logan said. "But we better get on with it."

Crap, I still had to climb up that death trap, didn't I? Before I could talk myself out of it with thoughts like when was my last tetanus booster and how much did I really weigh, I climbed upward.

The fire escape groaned in protest when I hit the first landing, but it held. Shoving visions of falling to my death out of the way, I pressed my face against the darkened window. The first room was dark but there was a crack of light emanating from under the door. I tried shoving the window up, but it was either locked or painted shut.

"Anything?" Logan called.

Not wanting to alert any of the tenants to my precarious position, I shook my head and then pointed upward to let him know I was going up to the third floor.

The ladders creaked more and my heart was in my throat as I climbed. Before I reached the landing I could see a light was on in the room and some instinct told me that was where I'd find Celeste.

God, he better not have hurt her. Envisioning all the charges that we'd bring up against the Garrisons, I skulked up, curling my body to the left of the window to be as inconspicuous as possible as I peeked inside.

The scene inside was horrific, but nothing like what I'd expected. Across the dimly lit room there was a full sized bed. John Garrison sprawled on it, naked as a newborn and my mother was astride him in reverse cowgirl position. From the expression on her face, I knew that either she had the worst case of Stockholm Syndrome in the history of forcible abductions….

Or she was there of her own free will.

Her eyes opened and she looked straight at me through the grimy pane of glass that separated us. Our gazes locked and the sprout of hope that I'd been clinging too shriveled and died at her guilty expression.

Son of a bitch, my mother had faked her own kidnapping.

CHAPTER 19

"How could you?" I whispered as I stared at the tableau in front of me. The emotions ripping through me like barbed wire were too much to process so I backed away, shaking my head. I couldn't look at her for another minute. Pivoting away, I reached for the ladder to climb down.

"Jackie?" Logan asked. "What is it?"

I didn't have the energy to answer him. It seemed as if I'd aged decades since I'd woken up that morning and my head felt like my jeans did when I'd been pigging out on the Häagen-Dazs— too much crazy, not enough room for it all.

Celeste must have scrambled off her partner-in-crime and lunged for the window because it wrenched up with a loud *thunk* and she called out, "Jackie, wait! I can explain."

Yeah freaking right. I climbed faster, needing away from this building, away from her. Truly, if I could have run away from myself in that moment I would have gone without a backwards glance. I jumped off the ladder, strode past the Dark Prince, uncaring as to whether he would follow.

"What happened?" Logan appeared totally confused. "Is Celeste okay?"

"Celeste is a piece of work," I muttered.

He gripped my arm, holding me in place. "Jackie, what just went down?"

"Interesting choice of words." I tried to tug my arm back, but he held tight. "Let me go."

"Not until you explain what just happened up there."

"My mother was boning our competition, is what. They were in it together."

Logan dropped my arm. "Are you serious?"

"No Logan, I'm screwing with you for shits and giggles. Now can we please get the hell out of here before she tries to chase me down?"

To his credit, Logan didn't say anything else. Unfortunately the holdup was enough for Celeste to throw on a satin robe and some flip flops and come crashing out of the Garrison's building, screeching my name.

Always with the performance, all about her scene, her feelings, her life. What happened to me was just collateral damage. Like a rash from a prescription drug—an unfortunate side effect that just needed to be dealt with.

I gripped Logan's arm and ran for the truck, needing to shut her out. Fiberglass and metal wouldn't be nearly enough of a barrier between me and hurricane drama mama, but it was better than nothing.

We were almost to the truck when Logan pulled free from my grasp, planted the keys in my hand, and rounded on the madwoman chasing after us. He caught her, the impact turning them both in my direction. His grip was true and it kept her from flying past him to get to me. The keys were cold in my hand as I stared, wondering what the hell he was doing.

Our gazes locked. In that moment, there was a communion between us, an understanding that ran deeper than words. He knew I couldn't handle her, knew that I would lose it if I had to stay there and listen to her explain why she thought it was a bright idea to do something as abhorrent as let me believe she'd been kidnapped.

The Dark Prince mouthed one word. *Go.*

I swallowed, humbled by the gesture and whispered, "Way to fall on a grenade, Logan."

The Truck sat under a streetlight, looking for all the world like it had been heaven sent. I climbed into the truck and Abu bounced on the passenger's seat, clearly overjoyed to see me. I locked the doors and cranked the engine over, turning the wheel and hitting the gas. The headlights illuminated them, Celeste fighting to be free and Logan standing strong and solid, acting as a containment bubble and keeping her from wreaking any more havoc.

My hand hovered on the gearshift, ready to burn rubber out of there. Dogs barked and people yelled out of their windows in English and Spanish for them to shut the hell up or get a room already. Farther up the street, I saw John Garrison lumbering out to join the fracas. I looked back at Logan and a calm washed over me. He wanted me to run, expected me to leave him behind to clean up this mess. Like he always did. His dark brows drew down and he jerked his chin toward the highway sign.

I couldn't do it. Couldn't leave him behind, not even for the sake of my sanity.

Uttering an oath, I double parked and, leaving the keys in the ignition, climbed out. Abu screamed in protest but I ignored him.

"Jackie?" Logan's expression was clearly annoyed.

"Let her go and take care of Garrison." The douchecanoe was coming in fast.

Logan nodded and then lowered Celeste's kicking feet to the asphalt and let her go.

She shot forward as though she was a wind up car, beelining straight at me and falling on my feet. "Baby please, give me a chance to—"

"You're drunk, aren't you?" It wasn't a question.

"If you'll let me explain." She looked up at me and I saw her pupils were dilated so small they could have fit in a pinhead. "I can make you see—"

"Make me? I'm not a reluctant ten year old who doesn't want to brush her teeth. You might be my mother but you can't make me do diddly freaking squat."

Her mascara ran down her cheeks. "It was for your own good," she sobbed.

"Yeah, that makes tons of sense, Mom. Helping my business rival, who evicted your ass by the way, blackmail me into breaking the law so I'd get arrested and ruin my company. Brilliant, really."

Her head shook back and forth so hard I thought she might give herself whiplash. "It wasn't like that."

I so didn't give a flying fuck about her skewed version of reality. "Where's my car?"

That stopped her mid sob. "What?"

"My car, the one you were driving. I want it back now."

Her eyes went wide. "That's all you care about, your stupid car?"

I nodded deliberately. "You and me? We're done now. I can't take any more of your crap. It's the same old story every freaking time. So go, get yourself kidnapped for real and maybe you'll come back with a new one. Or don't, either way give me my car and I am out."

Celeste opened her mouth, then shut it again without saying anything. Logan and John Garrison must have been close enough to overhear because John pointed at a public parking area down the road. "It's in there. Key's in it."

I looked him over, head to foot. He had the build of an athlete gone soft around the middle, but he was still attractive, with salt and pepper hair, wide shoulders and muscular arms. He wore only a pair of plaid boxers and moccasins, which looked too weird on him, too civilized. I pictured him more as the hillbilly with the smelly old hound dog and boots covered in pig shit type. It was amazing he had all his own teeth still. He didn't seem drunk either, just pissed off.

"Tell me one thing—was it your idea or hers?"

Garrison folded his arms across his chest. "You best listen to your mama."

"You know what? It doesn't matter. You took her in so she can be your problem from now on." I turned away, headed in the direction of the parking garage.

"Jackie, wait." This from Logan.

"Go pick up your brother."

"Where are you going?" he shouted.

I didn't answer him, just marched off without a backward glance.

BESSIE MAE LOOKED NONE the worse for wear. No missing hubcaps and miracle of miracles, the gas tank was full. I turned the engine over and drove down the snaking ramps to the exit of the parking garage. The thing was unmanned so I paid the full daily rate with the swipe of my credit card and peeled off into the night.

Though I had no destination in mind when I'd left, I wasn't at all surprised when I pulled up in front of the beach house that Joey Santino had rented from Mrs. Pomeroy. I'd always wanted to live at the beach, ever since the first time I'd seen the ocean as a child. The sound of the crashing waves, the crying gulls, the scents of salt and surf, the sun on my face and the wind tugging at my hair, all lulled me into a sense of security I hadn't found anywhere else.

Not until Luke.

Had any of it been real? Our courtship had been a whirlwind thing, going from dating to engaged to married in the blink of an eye. I'd been happy, even with the pall of the Dark Prince hanging over us and my guilt over not telling Luke.

The brass ring in our marriage had been the time when we could truly live together in the way most married couples took for granted. Waking up next to your spouse, sharing breakfast and plans for the day. Luke and I had never had that, not full time, and we'd both longed for a normal life.

It was laughable really. Now that we were "living the dream," we fought like cats and dogs. Luke was stubborn, manipulative, moody, and prone to sulking. Very similar to Celeste. I'd taken off the rose colored hero lenses and gotten a good look at the man my husband was and I didn't like it.

Didn't like him. Even though I loved him.

Was that how it had been for Big Joey meeting his biological mother? Had she let him down when he'd caught a glimpse of the real her? Had it been too much for him to accept?

As I gazed out at the seascape, I wondered if all dreams were better off not realized.

I thought about Logan and how he'd urged me to go and leave him behind. No doubt I'd treated him like crap over the years and he'd done the same for me. Tit for tat, trading quips and veiled insults like a verbal sparring match. But Logan was the one who'd looked after me when his brother had been away. Logan was the one who made me breakfast and helped me clean out my mom's trailer. He'd distracted me and laughed with me and had stayed with me through all of the crap tonight.

One of the Parker brothers was good to me, good *for* me, no matter what. I'd always recognized that truth, deep inside. But I was beginning to understand that maybe it wasn't the brother I had chosen for myself. Maybe, after years of Celeste's manipulations and games, I didn't know how to live any other way.

My phone rang and I ignored it, not ready to talk to anyone yet.

I was running on nerve, past the point of exhaustion. It was no time to make any decisions about my future. Well, not any more, I realized.

The phone rang again. I hit the talk button without looking at the incoming number but didn't say anything, just breathed.

"Are you okay?" Logan asked.

I thought about lying, saying yeah, or I would be. But terror froze my vocal cords.

"Jackie?" he asked. I could hear the concern in his voice. "Do you want me to come get you?"

I thought about Marcy, about how after years of being the caretaker to her sister and giving up her own happiness for someone else's, how she deserved some happiness. The kind of devotion Logan Parker could give to a woman. He'd been carrying a torch for me for a decade and I was selfish to like that. He deserved better, too. The right woman.

My course was set, my bed had been made, and it was past time that I slept in it.

"No," I said. "Tell Luke I'll be home soon. Abu too. And Logan?"

"Yeah?"

"Thanks. For everything."

CHAPTER 20

I'd never intended to get married.

Even though Celeste had never tied the knot, I wasn't jaded on the subject of happily ever after. I'd seen married people before, the kind who clicked and just appeared to belong together. Like low rent Brangelinas, you could never think of one without picturing the other. If I were honest with myself, I even craved that sort of connection with another person. Someone who just got you. Who understood where you were coming from and always made you feel safe.

I just didn't think it was in the hand of cards I'd been dealt. After all, who would ever "get" Celeste and her crazy drama? She was a high-functioning alcoholic drama queen past her prime, and needy as the day was long. She was my white trash cross to bear, the woman who'd given me life and a boatload of insecurities. I would never ask another human being to take her on. Not ever.

Luke and I had met on the beach. He was on leave, visiting his family, and I was taking a much needed day off between final exams and my internship at the sheriff's office. I had hopes that I'd be hired on there after I earned my

Lease on the Beach

process serving certificate and I'd been spending all my free time there, learning all that I could.

Marcy, who'd been my roommate at the time, was going through a rough patch. Her parents had just died and she'd broken up with her boyfriend. Good pal that I was, I dragged both of our pasty, overworked hides to South Beach.

I'd always loved the beach. Even though some people sported bathing suits that cost more than my car, there was something extremely equalizing about everybody being stripped down to very little. The guys ogling my breasts didn't give a rat's ass that I'd bought the blue and pink bathing suit out of a clearance bin at a vintage clothes shop. I could be normal at the beach.

As was our custom, Marcy and I staked out our spot, dropped our beach chairs and towels, and made straight for the nearest hotel tiki bar. I ordered a giant blue margarita, the kind that came with gummy fish in it, and Marcy got her standard strawberry daiquiri.

"You look like a classic movie star," I said to my friend. "Like a blond Audrey Hepburn."

"You are so full of crap." Marcy wore a big white straw hat tied with a black and white polka dot scarf and oversized sunglasses to hide her red rimmed eyes. Her cover up was opaque white and went past her knees.

I stirred my drink so that the gummy fish swam around in their poisonous pond. "You're better off without Victor."

"I know." She picked up her daiquiri and turned to face the water. "I don't really miss him, so much as I miss having someone, you know?"

I didn't. I'd never had someone the way Marcy meant. Sure, I had friends and Celeste but I was like the cheese from the preschool game Farmer in the Dell. Always standing alone. It was better that way.

"God, I can't remember the last time I was at the beach." It was the war cry of the Miami native. With all the beaches to choose from, we didn't tend to spend much time out with the sand and surf.

A memory surfaced, like one of the gummy fish in my rapidly diminishing bowl. The last time I'd been to the beach at night had been with that guy, Logan, the one I'd nailed and bailed.

"What are you thinking about?" Marcy looked over the tops of her humongous sunglasses. "You've got the strangest expression on your face."

"The last time I was at the beach."

"Was it a nude beach?"

I grinned at her. "It wasn't supposed to be."

Her jaw dropped. "Did you, like, do it on the beach?"

"No, I'm teasing you. We went back to his place."

Marcy sucked in a sharp breath. "I've never seen you with a guy. Give me deets! When was this? What did he look like, was he any good and oh, follow up if he was, does he have a brother?"

I threw my head back and laughed. "It was a long time ago, before I met you. And it was just a onetime thing. I was feeling a little down and he was my pick me up."

Marcy tilted her head to the side. "What, wasn't he any good?"

A dreamy smile stole across my face. "No, actually, he was *incredible*."

Marcy picked up a cocktail napkin and began to fan herself. "I've never had incredible. You're giving me a hot flash."

I quirked an eyebrow at her. "That's not me, you're buried in clothes and it's like ninety five degrees out here."

"You know I burn. And don't change the subject, I want to hear about the sex god."

"I didn't say he was a sex god." And I wouldn't say he wasn't either, since I had no frame of reference for comparison.

"So why did you two break up."

I sipped my drink and wondered if she would think less of me if I just blurted out the truth. The margarita helped loosen my tongue. "Technically, we weren't a couple, just a couple of people who collided."

Marcy rested her elbow on the bar top and put her chin in her hand. "So he was a player? A loser? A drug dealing whacko?"

"Not that I know of."

"Did he have mommy issues? I hate it when they have mommy issues."

"No," I laughed. "Have we been scraping scum off the bottom of the dating pool again?"

"I plead the fifth." Marcy suddenly focused on something over my shoulder. "That guy is eye humping you, hardcore. No, don't look, he's with someone."

Of course I'd been in the process of pivoting in my seat to see the guy. "What does he look like?"

"Big, like really big. All muscles. Nice tan. Short dark hair. Green bathing trunks."

My heart started to race. It couldn't be....could it? Miami was huge and it had been years. What were the odds that he would be here at this exact spot at this exact moment? "Does he have blue eyes? Like so bright blue that they can see into your soul?"

Marcy shot me an odd look. "He's wearing sunglasses. And did you miss the part where I said he was with someone?"

"Does she look like his sister?"

"If she is, their family is obviously too close for comfort."

I couldn't stand it anymore. "I'm looking."

"No wait!"

I pivoted on my stool just in time to catch a slender blonde as she slapped the guy in the green trunks across the face.

"Holy crap, what was that?" I looked to Marcy who shrugged.

Even from the distance with his sunglasses on, I knew it wasn't Logan, though there was a resemblance. Or maybe I was just superimposing my memories from that distant night of passion over another built guy with dark hair because he'd been checking me out.

The blonde stood, collected her things and flounced off in a cloud of pissed off. Green bathing trunks got up and for a second I thought he'd chase after her. Instead he made his way across the burning hot sand to where we sat.

"Oh, shit, he's coming over here." Marcy turned away as though he was coming to bust us for doing something bad.

"He probably just wants a drink after getting smacked." So why couldn't I take my eyes off his approach?

He didn't seem to see the bar, or Marcy, his focus was fixed directly on me. "Hey," he offered me his hand. "I'm Luke."

I took it, studying the handprint on his cheek. "Jackie. You okay, Luke? That looked like it stung."

He grinned and I couldn't help grinning back. He had such a contagious smile. "It was worth it."

"WHAT ARE YOU THINKING ABOUT, ACE?" Luke came out onto the verandah, coffee mug in hand. Abu was perched on his shoulder, gnawing on a half-eaten banana.

Lease on the Beach

"When we met."

Luke smiled, but it appeared forced, not the genuine one I had grown addicted to over the years. "That's like a lifetime ago."

No kidding. I patted the step beside me, hoping he would sit next to me and that if I couldn't feel close to him emotionally, maybe I could be close to him in the flesh.

He did but didn't look at me. My heart hurt because I could remember a time when we couldn't keep our eyes, never mind our hands, off each other. He was right—it did feel like a lifetime ago.

I looked down into the dregs of my coffee cup, unsure what to say. Apologizing about the Celeste debacle came to mind. But I was too raw over that betrayal, still not fully accepting that my mother would go to such lengths to test me.

And Luke and I had an ocean of churning feelings separating us. We each stood on our own island, unsure of where or even if we should take the plunge.

"Here," he handed me his coffee cup. "Yours is probably cold."

"Thanks." I cupped the warm mug in my hands and nodded.

Silence.

I couldn't go on like this, not knowing where we stood. "Do you want out?" I whispered.

"Do you?" he shot back, not looking at me.

I didn't need to think about it. "No."

"But you won't quit Damaged Goods," he grumbled.

I wanted to lash out, to ask him why I should be the one to quit when he was the one with the problem. It was ironic, Logan was the one who'd warned Luke about the danger I'd be in with our own property management team. Luke had thought he could handle it, had been glad to have me on board. Somewhere in the last few months, that had changed.

"Does it have to be one or the other?" I asked. My hands were shaking so I set the cup on the step and folded them in my lap. "My job or our marriage?"

His eyebrows pulled together although he was in pain. "I don't know."

"And what about the baby thing? Even if I quit Damaged Goods, I'm not ready for kids." Especially considering I'd just found out that their maternal grandmother was certifiable.

"It doesn't matter now." Luke's tone was flat, lifeless.

I wanted to say I'd quit Damaged Goods, that the only reason I signed on was to spend more time with Luke. To help us reconnect after years of forced separation. Who'd have thought that what had seemed to be the perfect solution would have imploded like this?

It made sense for me to be the one to leave. Property management had been the Parker brothers' idea to begin with. They were big and scary looking. With my process serving certificate, I could get a job somewhere else. Maybe go back to working for the sheriff's office. And maybe distance was what was needed here, not just from Luke, but from Logan, too.

I flushed when I recalled that moment when he'd touched my face last night, when our bodies had been pressed close together. I'd been growing closer to the wrong brother and our messy dynamic was destroying everything I held dear.

My cell rang and I glanced down at the display. "Celeste. Voicemail can deal with her."

"You gonna turn her in for staging the kidnapping?" Luke asked, as though he couldn't care less.

That was the thought that had kept me up all night, in

Lease on the Beach

spite of my exhaustion. I recognized that I should turn her ass over to the D.A. for prosecution. But I'd spent a lifetime protecting her and in spite of my fury, that wasn't a habit I could break on a whim. And I couldn't turn in the Garrisons either without dragging Celeste into it.

"I still don't understand why she did it," Luke said. "Why she would help them hurt us."

"Believe it or not, I don't think she knew what John wanted out of it."

Luke put his head in his hands and Abu chittered, irritated by the shift in his perch. "Maybe I should move out."

Ice formed in my veins at his words. Did he really think more time apart was what we needed? He hadn't said the D word, but it loomed over us like a giant machete, ready to chop our marriage in half.

"Where will you go?" I whispered, praying he didn't say he'd move in with Justine. There'd be no coming back from that.

He didn't look at me, just rose. Abu scurried down him and over to me, as though sensing I needed the comfort. "I'll start looking for a place later today."

Ouch. This was really happening. "If that's what you want."

"Trust me, it isn't, but I don't know what else to do."

"Then do what you have to, because that's what I'm going to do."

I listened to his footsteps retreat into the house.

My cell rang again, this time with an unfamiliar number. Needing the distraction I answered. "Jackie Parker for Damaged Goods Property Management."

"It's me," Sargent Enrique Vasquez said. "We need to talk about the Pomeroy case."

"What do I have to do with it?"

"Joey Santino said he talked to you. "

In all the craziness, I'd forgotten about it. "And?"

"I need to know what he said to you."

I really wasn't in the mood for this. "Why don't you just ask him?"

"Because," Vasquez murmured. "He's bitten off his own tongue."

CHAPTER 21

"This can't be right," I said to Sargent Vasquez as I stared down at the rap sheet for Big Joey Santino. "B&E's? Arson? Assault with a deadly weapon? This isn't the work of a man enamored with baby sea turtles. Are you sure it's the same guy?"

Vasquez leaned forward. "Oh, it's him. DNA analysis found at the crime scene verified it. The fact that he bit off his own tongue to keep from talking to us is just the icing on the corrupt cake."

I drummed my nails on the tabletop. "So you think, what, he came down intentionally to murder his biological mother? Why would he have gone to the trouble of renting that place on the beach? Why not just kill her and go?"

"You ever heard the term *Mens Rea*?" When I shook my head no, he continued. "It's Latin, translating roughly to what's in a man's mind. Basically, what we refer to as motive. The evidence tells us a story and from that story we can extrapolate what happened. But will we ever concretely know why a killer becomes a killer? All I have to go on is the DNA evidence and the facts leading up to the murder. Maybe it took him a while to get up the nerve to see her and renting the condo was his version of testing the waters. Her response was to evict him and when he went to confront her, his anger took over."

It was a neat and tidy explanation and I didn't like it one bit. "So what about Danny O'Rourke? The guy who beat on him and threw him out of a moving car?"

Vasquez leaned back in his chair. "Danny O'Rourke hasn't left New Jersey. I was in contact with the FBI office whose been handling the organized crime in that area and they verified his presence. When I confronted Joey with that little snippet, that's when he went dental on his tongue."

"So how did he end up in the ditch? Who worked him over?"

"Probably his own crew, on his orders."

I shook my head. "That doesn't make any sense. Why involve us?"

Vasquez sighed. "Look, Jackie, you could spend a lifetime looking for a reasonable explanation for illogical actions. Santino looked good for this from the get go, he has the history, the motive, and because he never gave us an alibi, the opportunity."

Shit. "Marlena Cruz. The Realtor with the phony lease. What about her?"

"She doesn't exist. Most likely some woman who worked at a hardware store and obtained access to the vacancy when Mrs. Pomeroy got a spare set of keys made. She took the money Joey was paying toward rent and split."

Damn it. Considering what I'd seen of human nature lately, that explanation made a sick sort of sense. I didn't want Big Joey to be guilty, just like I didn't want to know my mother was capable of staging her own kidnapping, or that Luke was going to move out. But ignoring unpleasant truths didn't make them go away.

Lease on the Beach

"Is there anything else you'd like to know?" Vasquez's dark eyes were kind.

"Just one thing. Why are you bothering to tell me any of this? You don't have to answer my questions the way I have to answer yours. You're well within your rights to be a hardass and tell me to mind my own business."

Vasquez took his time answering. "I like you. I have respect for your team and what it is you do. You have a reputation for following the letter of the law and we've had no complaints about excessive use of force or unethical conduct, like we get with other property management teams. Because of the nature of your job—not to mention your track record—it seems smarter to give you answers so that the next time our paths cross you'll be more cooperative and I don't have to haul you off to jail."

I appreciated his candor, mostly because it felt like everyone in my life had been hiding things from me lately. "You'll get more flies with honey than with vinegar. Just so you know, bullshit attracts the most."

His thin lips twitched as though he were fighting a smile. "If you want to spend your days drowning in shit, yeah maybe. So, is there anything else you can tell me about Joey Santino?"

I held my arms out, palms facing up. "You know everything I do."

Vasquez offered to escort me out, but I waved him off since I knew the layout of the building pretty well by now. Straight through the sea of cluttered desks, bank a right by the vending machines and take the elevator down to the ground floor. Then it was out through the front doors and into the blinding Florida sunshine coating the overflowing parking area.

The Parker brothers waited for me in the big black truck. Luke was behind the wheel and Logan rode shotgun, so I scrambled into the back. Neither asked how it went and I was sick of the pervasive silence. "Why would a man bite his own tongue off?"

"To send a message," the Dark Prince rumbled.

"Kind of a gruesome message." I shuddered, but then frowned. "A message to whom?"

Luke turned the engine over. "To an ally, most likely. It's the most basic way to say *they can't make me talk*."

I leaned back and considered it. "That must mean Joey knows something."

"He's part of an organized crime ring," Logan pointed out. "He probably knows a lot of things that would make lots of people uneasy about him being in police custody."

I said nothing as the downtown urban blight flew by. I needed to stop messing with this case and focus on work. We had three jobs to close out and then figure out who we should send the bill to for the Pomeroy eviction.

Logan turned around in the seat to face me. "Where's Abu?"

"I left him with Marcy for the day." Since the little stinker couldn't be left alone for a minute.

Logan's blue gaze searched my face, his expression full of sympathy. My heart nearly stopped. He knew. Knew that Luke was moving out and that my marriage had gone from rocky to officially on the rocks. It wasn't a surprise that they'd talked about it while I'd been with Vasquez. Something sour twisted in my gut and I wanted to vomit.

I broke his stare by hauling my file folder onto my lap and making a big show of rifling through the paperwork. "Who's up first?"

Luke said, "Two for one. We're going after the Krokodil Lab and Arlene Lipinski first. We'll need to strap you into a vest."

"A vest?" That made no sense, unless…I looked up and

Lease on the Beach

locked stares with the Dark Prince. "You mean a bullet proof vest? Seriously?"

Logan was still studying me. "Drug dealers aren't a joke, Jackie." His tone was flat, brooking no argument. "You were carjacked the last time we were here. We're taking every precaution we can this time out."

It made sense. "Where's the vest?"

Luke said, "In the supply chest, under your seat."

I turned and rifled through the metal box until I found the body armor. The thing weighed a ton.

"Holy frijoles," I said. "How do I do this?"

Logan turned to Luke. "Pull over, and let me help her strap it on."

"That's what he said," I quipped.

It was an asinine thing to say, but Luke actually barked out a laugh, the tension abating a little. It was nice to know that we could still work together, given the circumstances. Luke pulled over into a vacant gas and sip lot and Logan and I got out of the truck.

Logan took the vest from me. "Have you ever worn one of these before? Maybe when you worked at the Sherriff's office?"

I shook my head. "There was never any need. They'd secure the place if the tenant was suspected to be violent."

"Okay, well these are pretty simple, though it's important to get the fit right." He held the body armor up in front of me, measuring where it would fall and then finagling with the Velcro shoulder straps. "It's supposed to come to just above your navel, for maximum comfort and protection."

He stepped back and then undid the Velcro tabs on the side. It proved impossible not to notice how good he smelled as he slipped the body armor over my head. Dark and spicy, the way his pink bedroom had. I wondered what cologne he used.

And then all thought cut off along with my air intake. "Holy crap, is this body armor or a corset?" I wheezed.

"Too tight?" Logan fiddled with the straps. "It's supposed to be even on both sides." He readjusted the Velcro straps and I was able to breathe, even though my boobs were mashed in uncomfortably.

Logan raised an eyebrow. "Good?"

I had a little trouble standing up straight, the jacket dragging me down until all I wanted was to lie on the ground and let gravity win this futile struggle. "It weighs a ton."

"You'll get used to it." Logan had the audacity to chuck me under the chin. "Ready to roll?"

I exhaled deeply and waddled to the truck. Much as I hated to admit it, he was right, I was getting used to the added weight. "Let's roll."

"Yeah, thanks for letting us know." I ended the call and ground my molars together. "Gary Markov is in the ICU."

"From the Taser?" Luke actually turned to look at me.

Once again, we were parked across the street from Arlene Lipinski's rental. The neighborhood looked deserted, all the roaches in their secret dens for the day. At least there weren't any tweakers in sight.

I shook my head. "No, sepsis from all the open sores. They're going to treat him and send him to detox but if he goes back to the Krokodil, he won't make it."

As a unit, the three of us turned to face the apartment, where his dealer lived.

"Do you want me to stay in the car?" I asked, breaking the tense silence. "Or better yet, we could call the cops and let them handle this."

Luke and Logan exchanged a glance I couldn't decipher

and Logan shook his head slightly. "No, if we hand it over to the cops, they'll need to get a warrant. If she thinks we're making a buy, she might let us in."

"A buy?" I asked. "You mean you want to give the tenant a fake identity? Do I need to remind you that the last time we did that I ended up in a kiddie pool full of baby oil?"

"Just to get us in the door," Luke argued. "Do you have a sweatshirt to put on over that vest?"

I frowned. "It's like ninety five degrees out. I'll melt."

"If she sees you in a vest she probably won't let us in," Logan pointed out.

It flipping figured. The one time I actually wanted to wait in the car and the Parker brothers were pushing me out of it into a krokodil den. But I did have a hoodie in back with the Damaged Goods logo which I pulled on top of the body armor. Even with the air conditioning on, I started to sweat. "This," I grumbled, "is gonna suck."

The Parker brothers ignored me. "You going in hot?" Logan asked.

"Yeah. You?"

The Dark Prince nodded and extracted his glock from the glove compartment.

"What about me?" I asked. "Shouldn't I have something?"

They exchanged looks and Luke murmured, "You don't have a concealed carry license."

"What about the Taser?"

"Doesn't always work on addicts," Logan said thoughtfully. "Maybe you should bring some pepper spray."

"Pepper spray?" I was dubious. It seemed so... wimpy. Not that I was eager to shoot anyone, but the Taser was flashy.

Luke got out of the truck and then opened the door and climbed in beside me. "Yeah, that's actually a good idea. Cops have to try out all nonlethal stuff and from what I've heard, most of them would rather be Tasered than take a dose of pepper spray to the face."

He handed me a small cylindrical canister about three inches long with a key chain on the end. "Here."

Our fingers didn't brush as he handed it to me and I tried not to be hurt by the distance he'd so obviously put between us. "Thanks."

"Don't get it on your skin," Logan cautioned. "It burns like a bitch. And aim for the face, eyes, nose, mouth."

"Got it." I put the cylinder in the pocket of my sweatshirt, keeping my palm over it. My cell went into the other pocket and my cure or quit paperwork, all filled out, into my jeans pocket. "I'm ready whenever you guys are."

"Stay behind us," Luke murmured. "If we can confirm she's dealing out of there we call the cops, they get a warrant and bust her."

"Then we have grounds to start the eviction process." I nodded.

We crossed the street and went up the steps. I did my best to slouch over so no one would notice that I was sweating like a pig. The door to the apartment building was closed but unlocked and we let ourselves into the foyer. A nasty chemical smell burned my nose hairs on first contact.

"What the hell is that?"

Logan blew out a breath. "My guess, krokodil. She's not just dealing, she's cooking the shit here."

I bit my lip and tried to breathe through my mouth. This spelled bad news for our property owner with an upper case B. It would take something much stronger than those little tree air fresheners and open windows to get the smell out.

Like a few gallons of gasoline and a book of matches.

Luke looked to Logan, who nodded, then back to me. "You ready, Ace?"

Ace. I smiled a little at the nickname, glad he still believed me to be competent enough to get the job done despite the recent operational hiccups.

I nodded and then hunched over, trying to look like a strung-out tweaker.

Luke raised his knuckles and knocked. The door to the studio apartment slowly swung open.

"Shit," Logan muttered as he surveyed the obviously abandoned space. "She's gone."

CHAPTER 22

"What now?" I asked. It was more of a rhetorical question submitted to the universe in general rather than anything I expected either of the Parker brothers to answer, so I was surprised when Luke answered.

"Let's proceed with the paperwork for evicting Ms. Lipinski."

I wrinkled my nose in distaste. The small space smelled like a combination of rotting mule and hot garbage. The linoleum was peeled up in several spots and the indoor-outdoor carpeting had several stains that could have been anything from Gatorade to urine. All but one of the windows had plywood over it and several of the bare bulbs had been removed. The countertop was scorched in several places. There was shabby and then there was crack den. "The city might condemn this place."

Luke shrugged. "That's between them and the owner."

Not wanting to touch anything, I used the doorjamb for a table to fill out the necessary forms. "Take pictures of everything. This is thousands of dollars of property damage. We'll need documentation for the eviction case."

Logan tucked his sidearm into its holster and took out his smart phone. "Is it any wonder that she traded up to the RV when she had the chance? Even Abu smells better than this heap."

I winced. Bad enough that one of the properties we were responsible for looked like it had been through the Apocalypse. Judging from the smell, it wouldn't be long before Arlene Lipinski's side business trashed the RV as well. "I have calls in to several friends at the Sheriff's office. She doesn't have legitimate paperwork on the RV and we can remove her as a squatter as soon as we find her."

"Yo, bitch, you here?" A low male voice called from out in the hall.

Luke and I exchanged glances. "Get to cover," he mouthed.

Logan—as always—was less subtle. He shoved me behind him, into the corner farthest from the door. I tripped on a filthy mattress and went down hard. That didn't stop me from extracting my tiny vial of pepper spray and shaking the ever-loving shit out of it. It wouldn't do a damn thing against a spray of bullets but it was better than nothing.

Knuckles rapped against the door and then tried the knob. "Arlene? Where you at?"

Luke made a hand signal and Logan backed up until they flanked the door on either side. Luke leaned forward, sidearm still drawn and unlocked the door.

When it opened, the guy who'd carjacked me stood on the other side.

He took one look at the two barrels aimed at his puss and bolted.

Logan had his weapon stowed and was on the guy in three seconds, taking him down to the floor in a flying tackle. The guy struggled, but since he'd carjacked me earlier in the week, I couldn't muster any sympathy for him.

Luke used a set of zip tie cuffs to subdue the newcomer. "Who are you?"

I felt like a weeble, trying to get back to my feet. The restriction of the bulletproof vest made every move more arduous. Finally, Logan offered me a hand up. "That's the guy who carjacked us, right?"

"Yeah."

We looked down at the guy turtled on the floor. "What do we do with him now?" Luke asked.

I bit my lip. Legally speaking, we had no right to hold him. He wasn't a tenant and we weren't cops, but he had shoved a knife in my face. "I could call the cops and have him picked up."

Logan nodded. "Do it. We'll get this place squared away."

I pasted the notice to cure or quit on the door, not that it would matter. Given the damages to the place, the tenant would do better to buy the building from the owner if she had that kind of cash. Of course now that the police knew it had been used to deal out of, they'd be canvasing this street on a regular basis to keep an eye out for illegal activity.

We locked up and waited outside on the front stoop for the local five-oh's. I studied the carjacker. Though he looked plenty pissed off, his hands weren't shaking and his eyes were clear. "Hey, do you use that shit Arlene's been cooking up?"

His lip curled revealing crooked yellowing teeth. "Do I's look stupid to yous?"

I put my hands on my hips. "You really don't want me to answer that."

He lunged for me, but Luke maintained his grip. "Watch it, Ace."

"So you're one of her dealers then?" Passing out that poison to desperate people like candy canes on Christmas. Very costly candy canes. I sort of wanted to knee him in the cojones, just for that. Instead I asked, "Do you know where she'd take off to?"

The guy hocked a lugie at me, hit me right in my bullet-proof vest. We all watched it slime its way down.

"Why do people always spit on her?" Luke asked.

"She's just the lucky one," Logan deadpanned.

"Really?" I asked. "Really? You want to add assault and battery to assault with a deadly weapon?"

"Stupid bitch," the dealer said.

Out on the street, a black and white pulled up to the curb.

"Misogynistic asshat," I retorted as Luke perp-walked the guy down the steps.

"Those cuffs need to come off," the cops said. "We'll recuff him with our set."

The dealer's eyes were fixed on me as Luke cut off the flex cuffs. The female police officer had one bracelet around his wrist when the guy launched himself at me.

One second I was standing, the next I was flat on my back with a lunatic on top of me, trying to get his hands around my throat. He called me bitch and ho and every other name for female anatomy going as he tried to choke me to death.

I didn't think, just swung the hand holding the pepper spray up and hit the depressor, at the last minute flinging my other arm up over my face. Panicked and blinded, I wasn't sure I'd dosed him in the sensitive spots so I swung the little device around, making sure my bases—and his face—were covered.

Male cursing and then the dealer's weight was off of me. Panting, I rolled up onto one elbow.

The dealer was face down on the ground. Tears, snot rockets and drool covered his face. The cops had the other cuff secured on him and were talking loudly. The blood rushing through my ears drowned them all out.

And down on the ground next to them, Logan and Luke were both on their knees, groaning.

"What happened?" I asked the cops.

"They tried to get him off of you and you dosed all three of them."

Luke made a retching sound and Logan choked a little, and wiped at his face.

"Guess I'm driving home," I said to no one in particular.

———

Luckily, we had some bottled water in the truck, which, combined with a roll of paper towels, helped clean most of the pepper spray and other bodily fluids off my guys. I felt terrible for dosing them when they'd just been trying to help get that lunatic off me. "I'm so sorry," I said over and over as I swiped at Luke's face.

"Jackie stop," he wheezed.

"I just feel so bad—"

He gripped my arm. "No, I mean, stop with the paper towels. You're taking off layers of skin at this point."

"Oh, sorry." I turned to Logan and began wiping him down the way I would Bessie Mae at the carwash. "Really, *really* sorry."

Logan sat quietly and let me babble out my contrition as I dabbed at his face. His eyes remained closed and he'd cough every so often but he didn't say anything.

I lowered my arm, worried that I was somehow making it worse. "Are you okay? Should we go to the hospital?"

Bloodshot blue eyes opened and fixed on me. "I'm cool," he rasped.

"Don't you want to yell at me?" Honestly, I'd feel better if he did. If they both did. Then I could shout back and stop feeling like such a heel.

"You were defending yourself." Luke pointed out. "Don't worry about it."

Shit, no reprieve there.

Once they were as detoxed as I could make them in the field, we loaded into the truck and I made a beeline for home. Luke got out and headed for the door. I turned to the backseat to look at Logan. "Do you want me to drive you home? You could probably shower sooner at your place. Barring traffic of course."

"Yeah, that'd be good."

I rolled down the window and shouted to Luke. "I'm gonna drive Logan home."

His head had been bent toward unlocking the deadbolt but lifted. He didn't turn to look at us, instead just raised a hand in acknowledgment.

"Do you want to move up front?" I asked the Dark Prince.

"Nah, I'll just hang here and be Miss Daisy."

I grinned and pulled back out into traffic. It was only a five minute drive to Logan's apartment complex so early in the afternoon. I found a space near the front of the lot and turned to face him. "Do you want me to wait?"

He scowled. "Aren't you coming up? You need to wash your hands and anywhere else you might have been sprayed."

I hadn't felt anything but it probably was better safe than sorry when it came to pepper spray. "Okay."

I climbed from the truck but frowned when Logan had made no move to get out. I opened the door and asked, "Are you sure you don't want me to take you to Urgent Care?"

"I'll be fine." He pivoted and pushed out of the vehicle.

He looked so disoriented that I had to help him. "Where are your keys?" I asked as I scooted under one heavy arm to help steady him.

Logan looked down at me, surprise elevating his eyebrows. "Left front pocket, but I can get them."

I ignored him and reached across the front of his body to dig out his keys. He shifted closer into me so I could reach all the way to the bottom and extract what I needed. To anyone looking from the outside, I might as well have been feeling him up in the middle of the afternoon in a public parking lot.

I sighed in relief when my hand closed around metal. "Okay big guy, let's get you inside."

He weighed a ton and the body armor he'd donned didn't help matters. Slowly, we made our way through the lot and up the steps to his apartment. I sort of shoved him against the door jamb so I could find the right key. He had about a zillion of them on there, but two from the front of the ring I hit pay dirt.

"What's with all the keys?"

"Women who want me to come and see them again. It's my version of notches on the bedpost."

I shot him a scathing look. "Seriously?"

He cracked a lid, revealing one bloodshot eye. "No. I just wanted to see if you'd believe it."

"Well, I didn't. If that was the case, there would be more of them." Shoving the door open, I looped his arm around my shoulders and helped him inside.

"I can walk on my own," he murmured.

"Of course you can," I soothed. "I'm just helping you for the merit badge."

He grunted something I couldn't hear and shuffled off to the bathroom. I shut and locked the apartment door and went to the kitchen sink. There was no hand soap but he had a fresh bottle of Dawn. I scrubbed my skin like I was going to operate, cleaning up to my elbows, between my fingers, around my cuticles and under my nails. Then I shut the water off and looked around.

Without the distractions of Big Joey, Luke, and Abu the

apartment was eerily quiet. I frowned, too quiet, because there was no sound of the shower running.

I went over to the bathroom door and rapped softly with my knuckles. "You dead?"

"No," came the weak reply.

"Good because I've had my fill of corpses for this lifetime." I was seriously worried about him though. Was he having some sort of allergic reaction to the pepper spray? Some people had a keener sensitivity to it. "Logan?"

"Go away," he groaned followed by the sound of vomiting.

Fat chance. I tried the knob and it turned. "You better not be naked."

He wasn't. In fact he still wore his tactical gear all the way down to his boots. And he looked more miserable than I'd ever seen him.

"Jesus, Jackie," he griped, then bent over to pray to the porcelain god again.

I reached for a washcloth and ran some water in the sink to wet it, before placing it against the back of his neck. "Be serious here, Logan, not a macho asswipe. Do you think you're having some sort of allergic reaction to the pepper spray? Because if I'm going to kill you, I want it to be intentional."

He leaned up again and hit the toilet handle to flush. "I have a bad reaction to pepper spray is all."

"Are we talking Benadryl or Epi pen?"

"Neither, I just need to ride it out."

I studied his face, then nodded. "Okay, let's get it off you."

Reaching past him, I turned on the shower to a little to the left of medium. When I reached for the Velcro on his vest his hands caught mine, his gaze locked on my face. "You don't have to—"

"If you argue with me, I swear to God, Logan Parker, I will spray you again."

His hands fell away and he leaned his head back against the wall. "Just undo one side to get the vest off so the size stays true."

I did it his way and tossed the vest to the far side of the bathroom. Next came his t-shirt then the boots, his socks until he was stripped down to his black cargo pants. Even in his less than stellar state, he was male perfection, or at least my idea of it.

Our gazes locked. The falling shower created a wall of steam that cocooned us both. *This is medical*, I told myself. *Health related, not at all sexual.* The man just threw up for crying out loud. I was not thinking bad thoughts about my brother-in-law, who I'd just assaulted with pepper spray.

So why was there an electric charge in the air, threatening to electrocute us as I reached for his zipper?

Logan was up on his feet in a second, knocking me back onto my butt. With his pants still on, he climbed into the shower and pulled the opaque white curtain across, shutting me out.

I sat there like an idiot, not sure what I should say. What I should do was leave. If Logan was well enough to get his ass up into the shower, he didn't need me here like some sort of whacko Peeping Tom looking for a cheap thrill.

I cleared my throat, pushed my hair, which was frizzing in the humidity, out of my face and called out, "I hope you didn't have anything valuable in those pants."

Way to make it less awkward, Jackie.

Evidently, the Dark Prince was off his game because he didn't say anything. With any luck he hadn't heard me or wouldn't remember this weird ass conversation at all.

The water shut off a few minutes later and Logan called out, "Will you hand me a towel?"

Glad to have something to do, I reached for the towel rack again and passed the terrycloth rectangle through to him. When he emerged he was damp and once again had the towel around his hips. He swayed on his feet and I leapt over to give him an assist, telling myself that eighty percent of all household accidents happened in the bathroom.

And why the hell I remembered that particular statistic was a mystery.

Logan looked down at me, still unsteady. "I need to lie down for a while."

"That sounds like a very solid plan." I guided him out of the bathroom and down the short hallway to the pink nightmare bedroom.

With absolutely no grace at all, Logan face planted onto the unmade bed. I shook my head, thinking that was how I crashed after a particularly arduous day. He was half lying on the quilt so I flipped it up over him so he was covered from foot to mid back. His towel was still wet but I wasn't about to strip it from him.

I backed out of the room and shut the door, then turned and lost my momentum. For the first time since Luke had left the Marines, I didn't want to go home. Didn't want to see him scanning online for apartments or pack up his stuff to leave me.

Instead, I sat down on Logan's nothing special couch, picked up the remote and turned on the television. I told myself that I was staying for the Dark Prince's sake, until he'd recovered from the pepper spray incident. Reality could wait until I was damn good and ready to deal with it.

CHAPTER 23

"Jackie, wake up."

"No," I swatted the hand on my shoulder and rolled away, only to face-plant into beige carpet. I sat up, my body feeling logier than usual, not responding to my commands. "Ouch. Where am I?"

"My apartment," Logan murmured. "I thought you'd left hours ago."

"Hours?" I squinted up at him. He was a dark shadow against the bright wattage of the dining room light. It came back to me in a rush, the pepper spray, Logan being so sick he could barely walk. Me stripping him and getting an eyeful, perving on him after he'd just upchucked. Wow, when had I turned into such a creep?

Unable to meet his gaze, I looked down and realized I still wore the bullet proof vest he'd strapped me into that morning. No wonder I felt as though I'd packed on twenty five pounds, I had, actually. My voice was thick and craggy as I croaked, "What time is it?"

"After ten. Luke called looking for you. He was worried since he hadn't heard from either of us and shit has been going sideways on a regular basis. Like I said, I thought you'd left."

"I just sat down for a minute. I guess the last few days caught up with me." I winced as a crick in my neck sang out. "Are we supposed to meet him at home?"

Logan shook his head. "He'll be here in a bit. Let me help you up."

His hand extended and I gripped it, letting him pluck me from the floor like a daisy petal. I wobbled on my feet and he reached out to steady me. "Are you all right?"

Well wasn't *that* a loaded question? Instead of answering, I asked one of my own. "Got any coffee? My system needs a serious jump start."

"I'll put a pot on." He let go of me and turned toward his small kitchen.

I let out a sigh, relieved he wasn't staring at me with those knowing eyes anymore. Things had gotten weird between us, the air crackling whenever we were sharing the same space and I wasn't sure what to do to fix it. Needing a distraction, I reached for the Velcro on one side of the body armor. It gave easily and I stretched to pull it over my head, but something seized up in my shoulder. I froze, not wanting to give the pain another toehold.

"What's wrong?" Logan asked.

"My shoulder just seized up. Could you…?"

There was a jerk and then the vest was off. Easing my arms down, I tested the shoulder gingerly while Logan studied my reactions. "It's my neck and shoulder. I must've slept at a weird angle. It's just a crick, it'll work itself out."

I rolled the shoulder a little more, then turned away to check on the coffee's progress, when strong hands gripped me. I let out a hiss of surprise, the sound like bacon sizzling on the stove. The noise deepened into a groan as Logan kneaded the sore muscles beneath his palms.

"Feel good?" he asked, his voice low, soothing.

I murmured something unintelligible in response. If he would just keep doing that for the rest of my natural life, I'd die with a smile on my face.

The knock on the door interrupted the impromptu massage. Logan's hands fell away. "That'll be Luke."

Yeah. Talk about being bitch-slapped back to reality, my husband, the man who was leaving me, was here. I chucked my thumb at the hallway. "I'm just gonna go use the restroom."

Logan strode to the door and I scurried back into the bathroom. Eek. My reflection was downright scary, with hair matted down on one side and sticking straight up on the other. There was a red blotch under my left cheek where I must have stowed my hand. My clothes were wrinkled to hell and gone and then some. I looked like a woman who slept under a bridge, not in a bullet proof vest on her brother-in-law's couch.

What had Luke thought when I hadn't come home, hadn't bothered even to call him and let him know what was doing? Did he think that Logan and I had hooked up, like I was trying to teach him a lesson? I wondered if he was hurt, or if he cared at all. Feelings couldn't be shut off like water from a faucet and I was still his wife.

Of course nothing had happened. Well, if I was being completely honest, yes there had been lusting, at least on my part, but that's as far as it had gone. I would never act on it, even if Luke and I were broken beyond repair. Too many hearts were at risk, had already been damaged, including my own. I didn't want to hurt him the way he'd hurt me. There was no, *well it serves you right, you were the one out flirtmancing the kennel bitch.* I just couldn't downshift into revenge, especially not with Logan. He deserved better.

I used the facilities and then wetted a washcloth to scrub

the sleep off my face. I found a scrunchie in the pocket of my capris and slicked my hair back into a ponytail. It wasn't a huge improvement but at least I didn't look homeless anymore. Squaring my shoulders, I inhaled a deep, fortifying breath and marched out to face the music.

LUKE STOOD BY THE DOORWAY, his hands in the pockets of his black cargo pants, his eyes on the floor. I willed him to look at me, but his eyes were focused on the cheap white linoleum.

"Coffee's ready."

I turned to face Logan, who offered me a steaming mug. My hand shook a little as I reached for it, and he reached out, steadying me.

I looked up into his eyes and swallowed past the lump in my throat. I cradled the mug to my chest and stared down into it. Milk and sugar, just the way I liked it.

Glancing up, I saw that the Dark Prince was still staring at me. The knowledge was there, and the sympathy. Considering our track record he had every right to hate me, to rub salt into my open wounds, but instead he fixed my coffee the way I liked it. "Thank you."

Luke cleared his throat. "We need to check in on our furry friend. Has there been any word on the RV?"

I took a bracing sip of coffee and then set it down and patted my pockets. Nothing. "Shoot, I think I left my cell in the truck."

Luke actually looked relieved. "Oh, I'll get it. Toss me the keys."

I did and frowned as he beat feet out of there.

"Want to tell me what's going on with you guys? Why you decided to sleep at a right angle on my crappy couch instead of going home."

"I was tired."

Logan shook his head slowly. "A month ago you would have left the truck and called a cab to get home. Now try it again, what's going on with you and Luke."

I glared up at him. "Why do you always have to do this?"

"Do what?"

"Just when I think you're being a halfway decent guy, you have to revert to your Alphahole self. It's none of your freaking business what's going on in my marriage, Logan. Butt out."

He gripped my arm and jerked me to him. "It's my business if you're using me to mess with my brother's head. You can't switch us out when you're tired of one of us like last year's wardrobe, Jackie."

My blood boiled and I jerked my arm out of his grip. "Screw you and the dark horse you rode in on. For your information, he's leaving me, all right? He's the one who wants out, *not* me. And the fact that you think I would *ever* use you shows how little you know me."

Logan stepped back, eyes wide, his expression stunned. "He's leaving you?"

"Yeah," Luke said from the doorway. His gaze went from me to his brother and back. "I am."

"Well, somebody's home," I said to the tense silence of the vehicle. "Looks like every light in the house is on."

Luke hadn't said a word since his announcement that he was leaving me. It had been my call that we come out and try to find out what was doing with the furry and I got the feeling that the Parker brothers were just along for the ride. "Can you verify that Jamel Smith is at work?"

I flipped open the file folder and used my finger to cross

Lease on the Beach

to the contact info the lease had listed for Jamel's place of employment. Punching the digits into my cell, I lifted it to my ear and waited.

"Gas and go, Jamel speaking."

"Is this Jamel Smith?" I asked.

There was a pause. "Yeah, who's asking?"

"My name is Jackie Parker and I work for your landlord. There have been some complaints about excessive foot traffic at your house at night and animal noises. You know having a pet on the property is a violation of your rental agreement."

"No pets and I work nights," Jamel said. "It's gotta be my roommate. He's into some freaky shit."

"Your roommate?" I frowned down at the paperwork. "There's no one else listed on your lease."

"His name's Harvey. Harvey Dale. He's home now, you can call if you want but no guarantee's he'll answer."

"And why is that?" Maybe because he was in full furry mode?

Jamel cleared his throat. "I gotta keep this line open for work."

He hung up and I put my phone down. "He says he has a roommate. Should I call the property owner and ask if he's aware of this?"

"Let's check out the situation first, so we have a clearer idea of what's going on in there."

In the time since we'd parked, more people had driven up. "It looks like a party," Luke commented. His tone was all business and I sensed in him the same determination that I felt to get the job done.

"So, we should crash." Logan popped his door and hit the pavement.

No one told me to stay in the car and I was curious about the furry community, so I scrambled down, clipboard in hand. Technically, if the property owner didn't know about Harvey Dale, he was essentially a squatter with no rights to be on the property regardless of whatever arrangement he came to with Jamel. But if he'd been there for some time and was receiving mail at the address, it could be a little more complicated.

We followed a group of middle aged men and women to the back door and waited for the bottleneck to clear. Even from outside the music was audible, Lady Gaga's *Poker Face*, cranked up to eardrum rattling decibels.

"I'm surprised there aren't more noise complaints." I had to yell to be heard and the guy standing in front of me turned and scowled.

Finally, we pushed through the door and into a sea of…animals.

"Holy menagerie, Batman," I breathed as I took in the costumes, each more elaborate than the one before. "It's like amnesty day in the twilight zone."

"Nah," Luke murmured. "No reptiles."

He was right. As two horses galloped by, I realized that everyone here was dressed as a mammal, including two Orca whales. There was another difference too, the creatures here were adored, some on leashes held by other animals and even a few humans. Unless those were dogs in human rig. Nothing would surprise me at that point.

"How are we going to find Harvey?" I asked the guys.

"I've got an idea," Logan said. He unzipped his tactical vest and yanked out an air horn. As the loud honking noise pierced the room, there were yelps and barks and growls, along with some very human questions.

"What the fuck is your problem, man?" One of the orcas removed his head. He looked even more bizarre with his feet and head sticking out of the decapitated costume.

Luke stepped forward. "We're here on behalf of the property owner. You all need to clear out now."

"You can't do this." A pony galloped over, his dark brows furrowed.

"Yeah, actually we can," I said. "If you don't believe me, wait for the cops to show up and explain it to you."

"No one is drinking or doing anything illegal," a big parrot said. "It's just a harmless gathering."

"Are you a lawyer?" I asked, recognizing the tone.

"As a matter of fact, I am." The bird beak came off, followed by the green and red plume. His eyes went wide as recognition hit him and the self-satisfied smirk slid right off his face. "Jackie?"

"Stan," I nodded to my old boss. "Small world. How's it going?"

It took visible effort for him to collect his wits and I lifted my phone and snapped a picture of him.

Stan puffed up, indignant as though I'd—literally—ruffled his feathers. "This is private property, you can't just—"

I flashed him the photo. "This is going to get soooo many likes on my Facebook page."

He paled and if it had been anybody else, I would have felt bad for teasing him. But the man had made a habit of grabbing my assets, forcing me to leave, and was indirectly responsible for my current job, which was ruining my marriage. I kinda liked seeing him suffer.

"Who invited you?" One of the nearby dogs reared up and removed his head. At his side, a beaver was holding his leash, a pink one covered with baby blue hearts. Sheesh, and I thought my love life was complicated.

"Are you Harvey Dale?" Logan asked.

The dog nodded. "You're the guys who were here the other day. I thought you were Jehovah's Witnesses. Why are you ruining our gathering?"

I looped one arm through one of his plush ones. "We've gotta talk."

An hour later, Harvey's guests were filing out of the house and I'd handed him a card. "Call this number and ask for Josephina. She's great, she'll help you find an affordable space to hold your gatherings."

He nodded. "I didn't want to get Jamel in trouble, but I had nowhere else to go and Marlena said it would be okay."

I'd been halfway out the door, ready to go nab something to eat when I froze in place. "Marlena?"

He nodded, which still looked weird in his dog suit. "Yeah, she's a Realtor. Marlena Cruz. She was just here, came with the parrot."

CHAPTER 24

"Where are you going?" Logan shouted as I ran for the door, knocking a bunny onto his kiester.

"Shoot, sorry, sorry," I apologized but didn't take the time to help the guy/girl/rabbit up. My focus was on the door that Stan's green feathered ass had just disappeared through. I looked up and down the darkened street but there was no sign of him. Damn it, it wasn't like he could just fly off into the night.

"What was that?" Logan had followed me out, his sidearm in his hand.

"Harvey just told me that Stan the Stain brought Marlena Cruz here."

Logan frowned and stowed his piece. "I thought you were going to let it go."

"If she's involved with Stan, there's something rotten in Miami's real estate business. This affects Damaged Goods, especially if they're taking advantage of people who don't know any better. I just want to ask her a few questions." If I could exonerate Big Joey and in the process implicate Stan Cunningham of shady business practices, so much the better.

The Dark Prince searched my face. "I've got a bad feeling about this."

I patted him on the shoulder. "You always say that."

"So, what do we do now?" Logan raised a brow.

I thought it through for a second. "I want to go check out the place where Big Joey was staying and see if we can find anything that ties him to Stan. Then when Stan opens for business tomorrow, we can confront him."

Logan nodded once. "What about Luke?"

I glanced over to where my husband stood next to Harvey, talking through a few issues with the rental. "That's up to him. Let's give him the choice."

"Do you want me to talk to him?" Logan offered.

I nodded. "Yeah, I'll wait in the truck."

I turned to walk away but he put a hand on my shoulder. "It's going to be okay, Jackie."

I smiled up at him, even though I really didn't buy into *the everything will work out just fine* set of beliefs.

In the truck I called the property owner and let him know that there shouldn't be any further incidents of excessive foot traffic at his property. He agreed to draw up a new lease with Jamel and Harvey, specifying that only non-human pets were forbidden.

After I got off the phone I saw I had a text message from Celeste. Deleting the thing without reading it, I rolled down the window and put my face out into the night breeze.

"Hey," Luke said from the shadows.

I jumped and cracked my head against the roof of the truck. "God, you scared the crap out of me."

"Sorry," he said and I could tell from his mild tone that he meant it. "Logan told me about Marlena Cruz."

"Yeah." I looked around but didn't see the Dark Prince anywhere. Refocusing on Luke I asked, "And are you here to tell me not to get involved?"

Lease on the Beach

He shook his head. "No. I know I can't tell you anything. You're going to do what you want to do no matter what I say. That's why I have to leave."

I laughed, my chest feeling as oddly hollow as the sound. "Really? You're leaving because you can't boss me around? I thought that was just a game we played, not how you wanted everything to be between us." And if it was, I would be better off without him.

"You don't understand." Luke shook his head back and forth.

I wanted to reach through the car window and shake him. "Then make me understand."

He opened his mouth as though he wanted to reply and my heart leapt. When he didn't say anything, I leaned my head back against the seat, exhausted down to the cellular level. "I'm the only one trying here, Luke. The only one fighting for us. I thought you loved me."

"I do," he whispered.

"Those are just words. Empty and meaningless with nothing to back them up." I rubbed the sore spot on my head. "What do you want from me, Luke? I'm too tired to play the guessing game so do me a favor and spell it out for me."

His voice was quiet. "I want you to be safe. To be safe and happy at home the way you were when I was away."

As I stared at him, my lips parted on a silent exhale. This was the root cause of his craziness?

"You and Logan take the truck. I'll see you later."

As he walked away, I thought about his words. They didn't make any sense, none whatsoever. How could I be safer or happier without him than with him? He was out of his ever-loving mind.

I wanted to go after him, to chase him down the street and tackle him if need be, shake him until he understood how instrumental he was to my happiness. But the safety thing tripped me up. Why would he think I'd be safer without him?

I shook back to the present when Logan opened the driver's side door. "Everything okay?"

I made a face. "At least compared to usual. Do you know where we're going?"

Logan handed me his smartphone. "Input the address into the GPS."

The place where I'd stashed Big Joey was off of Biscayne Boulevard. It was a motel /apartment building that rented week to week. Done up in classic 1950's Miami Modernist Architecture or "MiMo," the building had a blue three story high wave painted along the side facing Biscayne Boulevard. The building didn't fall in the MiMo Historic district, so the rest of it had been overdone with coral colored stucco. The building made a hard angled U shape around an empty swimming pool and the cracked concrete. Like so many bits of older Miami, the Florida sun had withered it to a bleached out shell.

Logan made a face as we pulled into the lot. "This was the best you could do for him? It's a wonder the guy didn't hang himself on the shower curtain rod."

"It's worse than I remember, especially at night." I peeked through the windshield and cracked my knuckles. "What are the chances they didn't just toss his stuff in the Dumpster as soon as the cops picked him up?"

"Only one way to find out." Logan opened the door and climbed out.

I followed him to the registration office and pushed into the vomit green space. Apparently the interior décor hadn't been updated either. An ancient looking box television was blaring out an episode of Unsolved Mysteries through tinny speakers, but there was no one in sight.

"Cigarette break?" Logan raised a brow.

Lease on the Beach

"There was no one out front."

There was a rust covered bell and I picked up a brochure on Miami's nature preserves, rolled it up and slapped it over the device. It made an off key ding.

A toilet flushed somewhere down a pokey dark hallway. A moment later a door creaked open. An emaciated woman with curly gray hair and cat-eye glasses with rhinestone encrusted wings shuffled forward. Her makeup was in hideous Technicolor—green eye shadow to match the putrid walls and pink lipstick. She had on a shapeless pink gunny sack of a dress covered in huge two dimensional daisies, which only served to enhance her thinness and a pink and poison green name tag covered with pink flowers that read Trudy. A severely overweight tiger striped cat wove between her ankles with every step.

"You want a room?" She croaked at us in a two pack a day voice and then bent over to pick up the cat.

"No," Logan said at the same time I said. "Yes."

The woman blinked and then her heavily smeared lips creased into a grin, revealing snaggled yellow teeth as she addressed the Dark Prince. "You've already paid for the pleasure of her company, you might as well see it through. By the looks of her, she's a professional girl. She'll do you right."

The cat meowed as if in agreement.

Logan made a choking sort of sound as I seethed, "I. Am. Not. A. Prostitute."

She shrugged and stroked the fat feline. "Whatever you say, Sugar."

I stabbed my arm at exhibit A for asshat. "Does he look like the kind of man who would need to pay for sex?"

She turned her bespectacled gaze on me. "He's a man, ain't he?"

I couldn't think of a rebuttal, so I let it drop along with

my arm. "Actually, we were wondering if you could let us in to the room Big Joey Santino was using."

She set the cat down on the desk and studied me. "You friends of his?"

"Yes," I said just as Logan said, "Not really."

Trudy frowned at us. "Well, which is it. You all are wasting my time. I gotta get back to my stories."

"I'm Joey's friend and he's my partner."

A knowing light entered her eyes. "So he owes you money, right?"

Out of the corner of my eye, I saw a rebuttal forming on Logan's lips. I shifted over so I stepped on his foot even as I focused on Trudy. "You caught us. We heard he'd been pinched by the Po-po's and thought we'd try to reclaim some of our losses."

Though I could feel Logan's gaze on me, I ignored him. I was the brains of this here operation, even if it only existed in my own head.

Trudy eyed me shrewdly. "And I'm expected to just let you into his room out of the kindness of my heart, am I?"

I could tell she liked me better now that she thought I was a criminal. Go figure. "I'm sure we can come to an arrangement. Is all his stuff still inside?"

She nodded. "The only one's been in there is the five-o. But they said I'd be free to clean it out whenever."

I'd left my purse locked in the utility box of the truck, so I held out my hand in Logan's direction. When nothing landed in my palm, I glared at him over my shoulder.

He rolled his eyes, but extracted his wallet and opened it. "How much?"

"A hundred?" I asked Trudy.

She stroked her Cat, who gave me a death stare. "I can't seem to recall which number he was in. It's terrible to get old, the things you forget."

"Two," I said to Logan, hoping he had that much cash on him.

He grumbled but ten twenty dollar bills hit my palm.

Trudy smiled and took the wad before handing us a key that was attached to a boat floater. "Room 308, just to the right of the snack machines."

"Thanks so much." I nodded at her and pivoted toward the front door.

"Pinched by the Po-po's?" Logan asked. "Tell me you did not just say that."

I did a palms up gesture. "I was going for criminal authenticity."

He rolled his eyes. "Maybe if they watch a lot of crime time television."

I scowled at him. "Hey, I got us the key, didn't I?"

"No, my two hundred dollars got us the key. And I hope you're planning to pay me back."

"Sure I will." Eventually. "Let's go see what we won, Johnny."

"A WHOLE LOT OF NOTHING." Logan groused as he closed the lid to Big Joey's suitcase. "Congratulations, Jackie, this was a waste of both time and money."

I ignored him as I pored over the receipts I'd found in a suit pocket. Mostly food deliveries, paid in cash. A gas station receipt and a turnpike toll receipt were all that was left. The police had confiscated his laptop and everything else he'd had other than his clothing.

"Okay let's walk through it," I said as we relocked the door and headed back down to the ground floor. "Big Joey finds out his biological mother is Evelyn Pomeroy. He promptly leaves his life up north and heads south, taking the turnpike and collecting food and gas receipts along the way." I held up the items in question.

"He had the rental all picked out via Marlena Cruz through some online scam she's working with Stan the Stain Cunningham. He moves in and plans his family reunion. Evelyn becomes aware that Joey is staying on her property and hires us to remove him from the beach house, do not pass go, do not collect two hundred dollars.

"We show up and evict Big Joey from the apartment. When he finds out that his mother was the one who chased him away from his baby sea turtles he goes to her office to confront her."

Logan scowled. "Something about that doesn't make sense. Why would he confront her at her office, not at her home?"

I shrugged. "Maybe he didn't know where she lived?"

"But you just said the man had done his research. He's here under doctor's orders, trying to reunite with his long lost mother. And he's got criminal connections. Plus where does Danny O'Rourke come in and why did they beat him and leave him in a ditch alongside route 41?"

I nodded slowly. "I asked Sargent Vasquez the same thing and he claimed Joey had himself beaten because Danny O'Rourke hasn't left New Jersey. He said that Joey's DNA matched what they found at the crime scene and that a man who could bite off his own tongue could have his crew beat him and leave him alongside the road to throw suspicion off himself. Do you think that he could have done that?"

Logan shook his head. "I treated those wounds and believe me, they weren't just for show. Some of them would have gone septic in that ditch. And I can't get past the fact that he was left there for us to find. It's too big a coincidence, that we just happened to be driving down 41 at the same time one of the tenants we evicted gets booted out of a moving vehicle."

"It's us," I whispered.

"What?" Logan frowned. "What about us?"

"All of it. Don't you see? All of it ties together and leads back to us. My old boss helps some unknown woman rent out an apartment for a client of ours, knowing Mrs. Pomeroy would call us in to deal with him. The drug user we're hired to evict drives the RV we're after into the Everglades so we would be on route 41 to find Big Joey. Who said himself he was left as a warning. A warning for *us*. My mother fakes her own abduction, supposedly to protect me. Protect me from whom?"

Logan nodded slowly. "It does make sense."

"Someone killed Evelyn Pomeroy, beat the crap out of big Joey after framing him for his mother's murder, paid Markov, probably in Krokodil or the money to buy that poison, and threatened Celeste. We've been moved around like pieces on a chess board and we can't see the end game."

"But why would Joey have bitten off his own tongue?" Logan asked. "He hasn't delivered the message."

Our eyes met and the shared thought went between us. *Unless he already did.*

"Luke," I whispered. "Luke said he wanted me to be happy, to be safe."

"Holy Mary, mother of God. Get in the truck," Logan barked, already in motion. "We need to find him. Now."

CHAPTER 25

"What the hell is he into?" Logan took a turn too fast and I slammed against the side door, jarring my shoulder and mashing my phone against my ear. "And why would he hide it from us?"

"I have no idea, I really don't." I let out an aggravated breath as Luke's voicemail picked up and his low, even voice proclaimed, "Hi, You've reached Luke Parker and Damaged Goods. Leave me a message and I'll call you back, ASAP."

"Damn it all to hell, why isn't he picking up his phone?" I ended the call and immediately hit redial. Same deal.

Logan looked as on edge as I felt, leaning forward in the driver's seat as though he could force the vehicle to go faster with his will alone. "He's been acting weird for weeks. Distant, unbalanced, short tempered with both of us. I thought it was about your abduction. Do you think it's drugs? Please say it isn't that zombie shit."

I remembered the look on his face when he saw Markov, the disgust. "I don't think so. And if he had a drug problem, the military would have picked up on it years ago."

"Unless it's recent." Logan cursed as he missed a light and we both slid forward. "What if he has PTSD or something and is trying to self-medicate? Jesus, why didn't I see it sooner?" His handsome face was anguished in the low light, a mask of self-recrimination and inner agony.

We had no proof we were even on the right track, but it made sense, so much more than anything had in weeks. "It's not your fault, Logan. He's been trying to drive me away. To drive both of us away in whatever way he could. Save me from heroes and their BS."

Even though traffic had been light, it was the single longest car ride of my life. Even as I hit redial again and again, praying for my husband to answer, I wondered why I hadn't seen it before. As the daughter of an addict, I should recognize the signs, should know when someone I loved was in over his head and had lost all control. Why didn't I put it together sooner?

After what felt like an eon, Logan turned onto our street. He didn't so much park as stop the truck in front of our house and throw the door open. Even with all his speed, I reached the front door faster, unlocked it, and threw the thing open. It bounced against the wall with a heavy thud, but Logan put out a hand to keep it from rebounding into my face.

"Luke?" I shouted. "Where are you?"

One glance verified he wasn't in the kitchen, living room, or hallway. I ran for the master bedroom while Logan beelined for the office. I checked the bathroom and then, just for shits and giggles, the closet. What I saw made my heart skip a beat. His clothes hung on his side of the walk in, looking undisturbed. He hadn't packed and bailed. I hadn't realized until that moment that was what I'd been hoping for, that Luke had made the decision and bolted. I knew from experience that was a much better alternative than him being forcibly abducted.

"Anything?" I shouted to Logan.

"Not a trace." His voice came from down the hall. I ran toward it and we crashed together in the doorway of the third bedroom. No sign of Luke.

"He said he was going to take a cab home, right?" Logan asked.

"That's what he said." Of course he'd been lying to both of us lately, so his word wasn't exactly all that credible.

I paced into the living room, my hand tapping against my thigh. "Where else would he go? To your folks, maybe?"

The Dark Prince shook his head. "No, he's trying to put distance between the people close to him, to protect them from whatever the hell he's tangled up in. He wouldn't jeopardize Mom or Dad. Maybe a hotel?"

"I can check our credit card. See if there are any new charges." I ran for my laptop with Logan hot on my heels. Though the threat was still vague, we both felt it down to our marrow and the sense of urgency spurred us forward.

It took for-freaking-ever for my laptop to boot up. Finally, I logged onto my credit card statement, then sagged back in disappointment. "Nothing unusual."

"My bike's still out front." Logan paced to the window and peeked through the blinds. "Should we head to my place, see if he took your car?"

It was something to do other than sit here with our thumbs up our butts, but it didn't feel like the right direction. Slowly, I shook my head. "I wish we had software to track his phone through GPS or something."

"Maybe you should call Sargent Vasquez," Logan suggested. "File a missing person's report."

I considered it, but then shook my head. "We don't have enough information to go on right now. He's an adult and we have no proof that he's been abducted or even coerced. For all intents and purposes, it'll look to the outside world like he left me without a backward glance."

Lease on the Beach

Logan put a hand on my shoulder and squeezed. "It's not your fault, Jackie."

I put my hand over his. "Yours either. We're going to find him."

Restless, I switched from our credit card account over to my bank statement. We'd finally gotten the check from Mrs. Pomeroy's estate for evicting Big Joey. I went to transfer two thirds into our personal savings, then blinked as I saw the numbers. All the blood drained from my face. "Logan," I whispered.

"What's wrong?" Logan ducked down and read over my shoulder.

"It's gone. All of the money I'd saved up." I scrolled down and saw periodic withdrawals of cash over the last six weeks. I clicked back into the business account. Everything seemed kosher there, which was why I hadn't noticed anything amiss. Dread filled me as I logged off and then back in to check the account I managed for Celeste. "My mother's too. Shit, that was why she was evicted. Luke drained the money from her account and the auto pay bounced. That was the excuse that weasel used to boot her out."

"He stole from your mother?" Logan's dark brows drew together and I could see him wrestle with fitting that idea into the image he had of his brother. "Why didn't she tell you?"

I reached for my phone. "I think she tried to and I wouldn't listen to her."

Celeste picked up on the first ring. "Jackie?"

I didn't bother with pleasantries. "Why didn't you tell me Luke stole from you?"

There was a sharp intake of breath and then my mother spoke in a rush. "He didn't steal from me. I lent him the money."

Okay, that was only slightly better. "Do you know what it was for?"

"No. But the two of you have been so generous with me over the years, that I couldn't say no."

"But why didn't you tell me?" My tone was shrill and I sucked in a quick breath so I didn't start shrieking. "Mom, you were evicted for crying out loud. And you never thought to mention this to me?"

"I didn't know what to say," Celeste whispered. "You think the world of that man and I was afraid you wouldn't believe me, that you'd think I was making it all up."

Christ on a crutch. And the worst part, she was probably right. I wouldn't have believed her, would have sprang to Luke's defense. "Tell me why you faked the kidnapping?"

A sniffle. "Luke asked me to lie low for a while. He said you two needed time alone and asked if I had somewhere else I could stay while he sorted everything out. He asked me to ignore your phone calls, so I shut my phone off. I had no idea you thought I'd been kidnapped until you showed up here. I'm so sorry, I didn't mean to upset you."

A great, yawning void opened in my chest, consuming my heart and lungs and various other organs down into the abyss. I thought about the messages, the voice modulator disguising the voice on the other end of the line. I could have been talking to anyone, even my husband and I wouldn't have recognized him. The two calls I'd received from the kidnapper were both when Luke wasn't around and he'd picked fights with me. Why would he put me through all that?

"Have you heard from Luke?"

"Yes, why? Jackie, what's going on?"

I ignored her question and asked one of my own. "Did he tell you anything about what was going on?"

"No. All he said was that he would make everything right between us."

I closed my eyes. Right, when his web of lies unraveled, it would fix things between me and my mother because she'd been duped by him too. "Are you still staying with John Garrison?"

"Yes. Jackie what's going on?"

"Luke's missing. He's emptied our savings account and he's not answering his phone. I think he's involved in something extremely dangerous. Just do me a favor and stay where you are. I'll call you when I can."

"Baby, be careful." Celeste whispered. "I love you."

"Love you too, Mom." I hung up and put a hand to my head.

Logan crouched down before me, his expression concerned. "You okay?"

I wanted to scream, to vomit, to hurt something the way I was hurting. But dealing with my feelings wouldn't help me get to the bottom of this mess. "He didn't steal from Celeste. She gave him the money."

His gaze met mine and I saw the knowledge there, clues pieced together from listening to my side of the conversation. "And faking the kidnapping?"

"It was all him." I shook my head, unable to dwell on that betrayal.

Logan rose, his hands clenched into tight fists. "Let's find him first. Then I'll hold him down while you beat him senseless."

I offered him a thin smile. "Not funny."

Logan offered me a hand. "It wasn't meant to be. Come on, let's go."

I let him help me up. "Where?"

"To visit your old boss."

We pulled up in front of the Neo-Classical monstrosity that my former boss had mortgaged to the hilt. The ostentatious estate boasted Corinthian columns flanking the front entryway and spotlights shined on it where two honest-to-god lions sat regally.

"Are you sure this is the right place?" Logan whistled low. "It looks more like a bank than a private residence."

"I named the lions Fred and Ethel. Apparently, they were a gift from his dearly departed mummy. His family's got more money than we'd make in five lifetimes. He just dabbles in law because he's an entitled prick with too much free time. The dressing like a bird thing is new though."

Logan popped the door but I gripped his arm, holding him in his seat. "Tell me again why you think Stan knows anything about what's going on with Luke?"

He held up his index finger and said, "One, because he knows Marlena Cruz somehow."

"That doesn't mean—" I began but he rolled right over the top of me.

"Two," he held up a second finger. "Luke disappeared right after we spotted him. And three, it's too much of a coincidence that he's at a party on a property that we were given to manage and even though he could have slunk out without us knowing about it, he made himself known. I think he was a distraction so Marlena Cruz could slip away."

It made sense in that same weird, twisted way everything else did. I was starting to believe that there was no such thing as a coincidence, at least as far as Damaged Goods was concerned.

"Get a vest on," I said to Logan. "I don't want him to shoot either of us by accident."

The Dark Prince grinned. "I'll strap on yours if you strap on mine."

"It's a good thing my Taser is in the glove box or I might use it on you," I said as I scrambled into the back seat.

"Nah, you need me to find Luke." Logan exited the car and circled around to the curb.

"What about those?" I pointed to the ski masks and gloves. "It might be better if we do this and aren't recognized."

"If it'll make you feel better." Logan pulled a mask on. We geared up. I grabbed my Taser, Logan grabbed his glock and we crossed the street into the lion's den.

"The front porch is too exposed," I murmured. "One look at us all outfitted to throw down and he'll wet his pants and call the cops. Let's go around back, see if he's left a door open."

"You know if he calls the cops on us, we're done." Logan griped. "We have no legal right to be here, and we're both armed. There'll be no helping Luke from a cell."

I stopped by the base of a huge palm and glanced at him over my shoulder. "What's our other option? Go home and wait for the police to tell us they found Luke's body in Biscayne Bay?"

I saw from the set of his jaw that he didn't like that scenario any better than I did.

"Okay," Logan nodded. "Let's move."

We crept around the side of the house, unsure of what we'd find. It was two in the morning and any normal person would be in bed. There were several lights on in the mansion but all the doors I tried were locked.

Logan gripped my arm and whispered low. His breath stirred the hairs around my ears. "Listen."

I froze and then I heard it, a distinct splashing.

"Pool," I breathed. "Behind the hedges."

He mouthed follow me and then ducked and ran.

I followed, my stride shorter but just as determined. The splashing grew louder as we approached. It sounded too choppy for someone doing laps. We peeked through the bushes, just to make sure it was Stan and not some maid taking a midnight swim.

Turned out, it was both.

"Oh for the love of Pete," I said, staring at the poor woman who was getting pounded from behind. "I could have died happy without seeing that."

From the bored expression on her face, Stan's partner didn't appear to be enjoying herself very much. Stan looked like he was on the verge of a coronary, his expression pinched, his skin flushed so darkly it was almost purple.

"No guards, at least." Logan hissed. "Must be our lucky day."

Since Stan obviously wasn't armed, Logan stowed his piece and we sauntered around the hedges as if we'd been invited for tea. I kicked a chair, sending it skidding on the patio.

Stan stopped in the middle of whatever ineffectual maneuver he was preforming and glared up at us.

"Sorry to interrupt," the Dark Prince said, not sounding sorry at all. "But we have some urgent business that couldn't wait."

"*Madre de Dios*," The woman crossed herself, her affection going from bored to frightened.

"You, get out." Logan ordered.

She did as he commanded, climbing out of the pool and shielding her nudity with a fluffy white towel.

"It's okay," I said to her. "You can just run along to bed."

She looked from Logan to me and back.

"Carmine, call the police!" Stan shrieked as he scrambled for the ladder.

"That's a bad idea, Carmine." Logan's tone was even as he drew his sidearm and aimed it at Stan, who froze midstep. "You see, your boss here has gotten himself mixed up with some very bad people and the police might haul him off to jail and he won't be able to pay you, so how about you go up to the house and hit the hay."

Carmine took off across the grass.

"Who are you?" Stan asked. "What do you want?"

"Tell us about Marlena Cruz," I said.

His beady eyes focused on me. "I know you."

I aimed my Taser at him and asked Logan. "Do you think he'd be electrocuted if I shot him with this?"

"Won't know until we try it." My partner-in-crime deadpanned.

"Don't!" Stan shrieked.

I wouldn't but he didn't know that. "Marlena Cruz. What is your relationship with her?"

"We do business together."

"What kind of business?"

"All legitimate—" he began.

"Bull," I stepped forward, aiming the Taser so it aligned with the bits under the water. "What sort of business?"

"Real Estate scams!" Stan shrieked. "I'd find an empty property and she'd go in and say she represented the owner. Then we'd split the money. It was all her idea though!"

Out of the corner of my eye, Logan tapped his wrist. I got the message loud and clear. The clock was counting down on us, I knew it. If the cops caught us here we'd have a lot of 'splaining to do and there'd be no one to help Luke. Time for one more question and then we had to skeedattle.

"What's her real name? Where can I find her?" I asked the Stain.

"I don't know her last name."

"Maybe you should shoot his man parts off." I said to Logan. "I'm sure poor Carmine would thank you for it."

Stan's voice was reedy as he squeaked, "Justine! Her first name is Justine and she fronts at an animal shelter over off of Coral Way."

Justine? The skank I thought Luke had been flirting with was also Marlena Cruz? Oh, Luke, what have you gotten into?

"Fronts what?" Logan asked, his voice tight with emotion.

"Bets mostly. Dog and horse racing, major sporting events. Anything Danny O'Rourke wants."

Danny O'Rourke. Jesus, Mary, and a bag of holy chips. I wanted to follow up, ask for more information, but Logan was yanking me backwards.

"We got what we came here for. Let's go."

CHAPTER 26

"So Marlena Cruz is Justine, the hottie from the shelter where Luke's been spending all his free time," Logan said as we drove back the way we'd come.

With the substitution of rank-skank bitch for hottie, my thoughts were following the same path. "And she works for Danny O'Rourke, the guy who worked over Big Joey. Justine is in bed with Stan the Stain, who likes to target Damaged Goods properties. Hell hath no fury like a weenie scorned. Justine pretends to rent Evelyn Pomeroy's beach house to Joey and pockets the money Joey thinks he's paying to his long lost mother. Making bank on someone else's family tragedy."

Logan scowled. "Why would O'Rourke have Joey beat though? And how does Luke fit into this?"

"He must have seen something at the shelter." I said. "Something he wasn't supposed to see. Maybe he told Justine he'd go to the cops and then when we showed up, she threatened my life to keep him in line."

"We've got nothing else to go on at this point." Logan's tone was flat, but there was an edge of disbelief I chose to ignore.

The truth was, I had doubts too. We had nothing to go on but a loose string of chaotic events, Luke's erratic behavior and a coerced confession from a bottom feeding lawyer.

"Do you think she'll hurt him?" I asked as Logan turned onto Coral Way.

"It's not Justine I'm worried about."

I frowned. "Vasquez assured me O'Rourke wasn't in Miami."

"Look, it's not that I doubt Vasquez, but it's not out of the realm of possibility that O'Rourke has his police detail in his pocket. All it would take is one dirty cop to go on a coffee run and let O'Rourke slip out. Next patrol shows up, dirty cop says there's been no sign of the guy and the next thing you know, O'Rourke is on a plane to Miami with the local LEO's none the wiser."

I cracked my knuckles. "So you think it was O'Rourke that has been pulling Justine's strings all along?"

Logan shot me a sideways glance, then pulled over into a fast food parking lot. "I think there's a lot we don't know. It's one thing to scare the information out of a dweeb like Stan Cunningham, but O'Rourke is a different animal. He's armed and has guys, you know it would take a vanload of muscle to snag Luke off the streets. We need more manpower."

"We can't call the police. For one thing, Stan might have reported us. And like you said, all it takes is one dirty cop." I thought about it for a beat. Where could we find muscle for hire that would haul ass out of bed in the middle of the night and help rescue my husband. As soon as the thought occurred to me, I blanched even as Logan uttered, "John Garrison."

I didn't like it, but what choice did we have?

I held my phone in one hand, but couldn't remember how to work it. "I need coffee."

Logan took the phone from me. "What you need is sleep.

Lease on the Beach

We're both too raw to do this right now. We'll head back to your place, get a few hours shut eye and go in right before dawn."

I shook my head, ready to argue, but Logan held up a hand. "They've already had him for five hours. Two more won't make a difference to him, but it could mean life or death for us."

I stared at him, noting the dark circles of strain. He didn't like waiting any more than I did, but he was right. We needed to take a combat nap, marshal our strength, and come up with a plan. "Okay."

Logan changed gears and headed back towards our house. "Call John Garrison and ask him to meet us across the street from the animal shelter at 5:30."

I did and to my astonishment, Garrison agreed to the scheme, for a hefty fee of course. "There goes the money from Evelyn Pomeroy's estate."

"I have a little saved up," Logan said as he turned into our driveway. "I can help you guys out."

I'd never take his money but was too tired to argue. "Thanks."

We went into the house and Logan was sure to bolt the front door. I stood in the living room and stared into our bedroom. I didn't want to go in there without Luke, didn't want to imagine what it would be like if I never shared a bed with him again.

"Come with me." Logan gripped my arm and towed me down the hall to the third bedroom. The futon was still made up from when Celeste had been staying here.

"What are you doing?" I asked as Logan undid my bullet proof vest and then his own.

He pushed me down onto the bed and then dragged the boot off my left foot. "You're going to sleep with me."

"The hell I am." I kicked out with my right foot but he caught that easily and removed that boot as well.

"Sleep, Jackie. That's all. If we're alone, we'll be turning everything over and over for the next hour and fifteen minutes. At least this way we won't be alone."

Logan shucked his own vest and boots and climbed on the bed. I made to get up, but he slung one arm around me and pulled me in tight until my head rested on his shoulder.

"Let me go." With the fatigue thickening my voice it sounded too much like a plea, so I shoved at him.

"Go to sleep." He pinned both of my hands with his free one and then shut his eyes.

Like I could? The man was out of his mind. He had me pulled in tight against his body and I could hear the reassuring beat of his heart. So I'd just wait for him to fall asleep and then I'd sneak out and crash on the couch.

Okay, solid plan. My tense muscles eased as I let myself relax against him. The sooner he thought I'd fallen asleep, the sooner he'd drift off and the sooner I could get away from him. I sighed as though I'd given up the fight and closed my eyes, trying to ignore how warm and comfortable he was, how well we fit together. His chest rose and fell evenly and before I knew it, my breaths had synced with his. Inhale, one, two, then exhale, one, two. My eyes drifted closed.

An infernal beeping sounded in my ear. I bolted upright, jarred out of sleep. Disoriented, I glanced around the room, looking for something familiar.

"You okay?" Logan's voice was rough from sleep. The noise came from his cell, which he'd left on the nightstand. He reached forward and shut it off.

"Yeah." I rose stiffly from the bed and this time he let me go. Picking up my boots and vest, I asked, "Do I have time for a shower?"

"If you can take one in five minutes."

Lease on the Beach

"Okay." I moved for the door but then paused. He'd been right, I wouldn't have slept any other way and I did feel clearer for the nap. Without looking back I choked out, "Thank you."

"You didn't do anything wrong, Jackie."

A smile actually snuck out and I had to glance back at him. The sight of him there, rough and rumpled from sleep actually made my chest ache. It was the same feeling I'd experienced when I thought about never sleeping beside Luke again. What if this was the last time? Logan could die, would die if his death would save his brother. The two had a fierce bond of loyalty, which was what made them such an effective team. And I had no doubt in my mind that Logan Parker would sacrifice himself for me as well.

"What?" he asked. "Why are you looking at me like that?"

I shook my head and kept my response on par with our usual banter. "Considering you're usually first in line to criticize me, I guess I can take that to the bank."

I left before he could respond.

WE HIT a drive-thru for coffee and still hit the parking lot five minutes ahead of schedule.

Logan had gotten out and done a quick recognizance on the buildings. The first words out of his mouth when he climbed back in the truck were, "You won't believe this."

He showed me a photo he'd taken with his phone. "You've got to be kidding me."

"Is it the one we've been looking for?" Logan reached into the back and shuffled through the files of our open cases. He flipped open the one labeled Markov, glanced at the photo he'd taken of the RV and then back. "License plate is a match. This could be easier than I thought."

"Or more complicated." I pointed out. "Remember the Garrisons were after the RV, too. "

"They can have it, if we get Luke back. There are no guards as far as I can see but there's a camera mounted on the Southwestern corner of the building. I pulled up my hood and strolled by it and no one came out to look, so either no one is watching or they didn't see me as a threat."

A Range Rover pulled up alongside us and the window rolled down.

"Garrison," Luke nodded at John and his two meathead sons.

"Parker. What's doing?"

"We think we found Markov's RV. The tenant handed the keys over to his dealer. That's at least one more body we have to contend with to get to Luke."

John Garrison nodded thoughtfully. "What we need here is a diversion."

Logan nodded in agreement. "Jackie, wait five minutes for us to get set up and dial 911 on a burner phone. When they pick-up, report the Krokodil at this address. That bitch needs to be behind bars and the police presence will have the wise guys scattering like roaches. The Garrisons will grab Luke and pull him out of there."

I frowned at him. "What are you going to do?"

He flashed me a white smile. "I'm going to let the dogs out."

Garrison barked out a laugh. "That is one hell of a distraction."

I thought about it, then shook my head, swallowing down the lump of fear that had risen from my gut. "No. You need to be with the Garrisons in case there are more people there. I'll take care of the dogs. I can use the burner phone from inside as easily as from here."

Logan glowered at me. "You're terrified of dogs. And I want you here, safe."

"I'm going. Either with them or with you. The people are more dangerous than the dogs and you're a better shot than I am."

Logan cursed and John said, "We're losing cover of darkness here, Parker. If she wants to go in, the kennel is the safest place for her."

Logan swore long and loud in a combination of words I'd never heard before. He closed his eyes, then they flashed open and he shot me a hard look. "If you get bit, I'll be really pissed."

"Same deal if you get shot." Impulsively, I leaned forward and kissed his cheek. "Bring him back safe."

Logan appeared completely nonplussed and he actually raised a hand to the spot where my lips had made contact. Then he shook himself. "Let's move."

Four big men skulked off into the night. I grabbed a burner phone from the bin in back and then strode across the street to the entrance of the kennel.

There were two ways in. Through the main office, the way we'd gone in last time and over the chain link fence about six feet high. At this time of day the office would be locked and I was armed with only a Taser, a disposable phone and my determination so shooting the lock off wasn't in the cards. I pulled the hood up, hiding my face from the camera mounted on the roof of the building and strolled by. About halfway down the length of the kennel, I checked to make sure I was out of the camera's range and set to scaling the fence.

Climbing with double D's and a bullet proof vest was no easy task. Logan could have scrambled up and over fences twice this size in about two seconds flat. The thought that he and the Garrisons were counting on me pushed me up and over the top and I landed on top of the cage below in an uncoordinated heap.

The rattling startled the dog who'd been sleeping inside into a frenzy of barking. Dogs in nearby cages picked up the war cry. I scrambled off the cage and ducked behind a shed, just as someone opened a window and shouted. "Shut it, you filthy mutts!"

The voice was male and had a distinct Jersey accent. My heart stopped as I caught a glimpse of his profile. No way. It couldn't be…could it?

The man in the window looked exactly like Big Joey Santino.

CHAPTER 27

I ducked down low so the man wouldn't see me. My heart thundered, trying to make a break from my body and this bizarre twilight zone it landed in. How had Big Joey gotten out of police custody, never mind how he'd regrown his tongue?

He couldn't have.

There was only one viable explanation. Twins. The man who'd just threatened to skin every resident of the kennel and then slammed the window wasn't Big Joey Santino, but his identical twin brother.

Shaking myself firmly, I decided that for now, it didn't matter. I had two tasks to accomplish and more than the five minutes Logan had allotted me had passed. If the dogs kept barking, someone would soon come out to find out what was up. To the east, the sky turned the colors of blood and gold. I had to move fast.

I didn't try any of the nice doggie speech that I usually fell back on when I approached canines. Instead, I hid my fear and pictured Abu, just another of God's creatures wanting a little love.

Luckily the cages weren't padlocked. The dog inside was

a Boxer. He was all white with chocolate spots and had a big square head and sad looking brown eyes.

"You're not going to bite me." I told him as I undid the latch on the cage and opened his door.

Though I'd expected him to bolt for freedom, he didn't budge. I wasn't about to reach inside and haul him out so I moved on to the next cage, leaving the door open.

The next dog was of indeterminate species, possibly part Sasquatch, judging from its massive size and the amount of dark hair. The creature whined pitifully as I unlatched the cage. This one came right over and bumped its massive shaggy head against my leg. I yelped and then clapped a hand over my mouth so no more noise would escape. The dog kept pace with me, sticking to my side like a shadow as I moved on down the row.

The dog in the first cage poked his square head out. He sniffed and then let out a high pitched bark before scooting out of the cage.

In the cage to my right a dog growled and I shivered at the low threatening sound. It was the German Shepard, Adonis, who'd scared the crap out of me the last time I'd been here. His hackles stood stiffly all the way to his tail, his canine teeth bared in obvious threat.

Sasquatch dog growled back and I stepped away from it hurriedly, afraid it had changed its mind about being my pal. But the massive mutt's focus was on Adonis, not me. All the dogs quieted, as though they were watching prime time TV. After a brief staring contest, Adonis lowered his head and whined.

Sasquatch dog looked up at me and wagged its tail, as though letting me know it was okay to open the cage.

"Um, thanks?" I said to my shadow creature and reached for the latch.

Though I expected Adonis to lunge he simply stepped outside and turned the way the Boxer had gone.

The rest of it went smoothly, and I had twelve dogs of all breeds milling about the compound by the time the sun came up. Sasquatch dog stayed with me, almost as though she was offering me protection. I actually got up the nerve to pat it on its shaggy head.

Logan was probably wondering if I'd been eaten by the dogs, so I shot him a quick text. *Done, not bit. Calling 4 help.*

He hit me back with an *Okay*. Seriously, who spelled out the word okay, especially in a text message?

I extracted the burner phone from my back pocket and dialed 911.

"What's the nature of your emergency?"

"There's a woman dealing drugs out of an RV. She's parked at the animal shelter off of Coral Way."

"Ma'am, are you in immediate danger? Because this line is for emergencies—"

I hung up and stuffed the phone back in my pocket. Technically it was an emergency but with any luck, we'd be long gone before the police discovered that tidbit.

It was a little scary, how easy I took a nosedive from upstanding patron of the community to operating in the shadows. Then again it wasn't like I had much choice, not if I ever wanted to find my husband.

It was quiet in the yard, too quiet. I scowled as I scanned the rows of cages. Where were all the dogs? Even Sasquatch had vanished. Logan had told me to hop the fence and go straight back to the truck, but I couldn't just leave them milling about the yard. What if they'd found a way out to the street and got hit by a car? I'd let them out and I felt responsible for the canine contingent.

Decided, I wound my way through the yard, listening for

any signs of the pack and on the lookout for shuffling curtains.

The rows of cages funneled into an open yard. There'd be no cover for me if I went through the grassy area and it was in full view of the house behind. I stopped by the corner of a shed, the one I'd seen Luke come from the last time I'd been at the shelter.

I tried to whistle for the dogs, but my lips were too dry. I licked them and had just sucked in my breath for a second attempt when a soft, whimpering sound came from inside the shed. Had one of the dogs managed to get in there?

The door was on the far side from where I stood and as I crept around the small structure, I saw it was unlatched and partly ajar.

Voices came from inside the shed, one male and one female. Though I was too far away to clearly hear what they were saying, it was clear they were in the middle of an argument.

"Too soon... find where he hid it." The woman said.

I was sure that was Marlena/Justine/ whoever the woman was who was involved with all this.

"Boss said...," the man's voice was much lower pitched and I had a hard time making out his words. Then more clearly, "...do with Parker?"

I stopped breathing. Luke. They were talking about Luke. I closed my eyes and concentrated everything I had on hearing what they said next.

"Leave him in the RV. He's served his purpose."

Purpose? I wondered. What purpose was that? As curious as I was, I had to let Logan know what I'd found out.

Taking my cell from my back pocket I saw that I'd missed another text from him.

Where are you?

I typed back, *L in RV. Guards?*

A moment later, *Get back to the truck. I'll get him.*

A loud bark from behind me made me jump. Sasquatch had snuck up on me unaware.

I patted at the air in the universal take it easy gesture, trying to calm the massive mongrel so she wouldn't give us away. From inside the shed I heard Justine say, "That sounds close. Are you sure you locked all the cages?"

"Yeah. I don't want those things getting out."

The dog barked again. Shit, I had to boogie or risk discovery.

I'd taken three steps away from the shed when the back door to the office was flung open and the Big Joey Doppelganger leveled a barrel of a very deadly looking semiautomatic at me and Sasquatch dog.

"What the hell is going on here?" He barked. "Whose is this bitch?"

"Well, well," Justine said from behind me. "Nice to see you again."

I had one card to play, the one Luke had dealt me. I could only hope I had enough of the drama queen gene to pull it off.

"Where's Luke, you husband stealing hussy?"

Justine put her hands on her slim hips. "I thought he left you for good? And aren't you afraid of dogs?"

Doing my best to ignore the gun pointed at my head, I rounded on her with all the fury of a woman scorned. "No, and I'm not afraid of some two bit harlot who set her sights on my man, either. I'm here to fight you for him."

Justine grinned. "Isn't that sweet? True love conquers all, yeah. Too bad I'm not more of a romantic."

"Where is he?" I pressed, even though I knew. My only play was to stall for time and hope like hell I bought enough time for Logan and the Garrisons to get Luke free of the RV.

The guys needed a distraction and I aimed to give 'em one.

It was going to require I dance on a fine line between crazy and stupid so they didn't just shoot me in the head.

"Who the hell is she?" The guy who looked like Big Joey asked. The weapon he held in his beefy hands must be heavy because he lowered it slightly.

"This is Jackie Parker, Luke's wife." Justine smirked. "Or, former wife."

If I hadn't already heard her say that Luke was in the RV, I would have reacted badly to that. They meant to kill him and Justine acted like it was a done deal. Not exactly good news for me that she'd admit that out loud. The chances of my chalking this up to the crazy jealous wife who would be sent on her merry way when the throw down was over were looking smaller and smaller.

The guy with her looked like the missing link. Arms like a gorilla with tufts of black curly hair spouting from various spots and curling out over the top of his wife beater. He wore several thick gold chains around what passed for his neck and had one hell of a unibrow. It pulled into a hairy V as he scowled at me. "Maybe she has—"

"Shut up, both of you." The Big Joey Clone said. He wore a palm printed robe and matching boxer shorts, which looked way too casual with the gun. I wondered idly if fashion challenged ran in the family.

I froze as I met his ice cold stare with that word echoing in my head. *Family.*

"Who are you?" I asked the lookalike.

"Show some effing respect!" No neck backhanded me. My lip split on impact and I staggered back several steps. He raised his hand to hit me again and Sasquatch dog lunged for him. Her triangular head opened and massive jaws clamped around the threatening arm. He yelped in pain and she bull-

Lease on the Beach

dozed into him, taking him down to the ground. Justine danced back, waving her arms in classic *what the hell do I do* gestures.

"That's enough!" The other man brought the business end of the gun up over our heads and fired several rounds. Sasquatch dog let go and bolted at the noise, her dark form disappearing back around the shed. Everyone froze, as the collective focus shifted back to him.

"I'm Danny O'Rourke and you," he said, stabbing a beefy finger at me, "know too much. Bring her to the RV. She wants her husband so badly, we ought to reunite them."

―――

Though I'd petitioned the universe that Logan and the Garrisons would have sprung Luke, I knew they hadn't when I saw the two massive guards flanking the door.

They both carried weapons similar to O'Rourke, harbingers of death. Logan's handgun didn't stand a chance against that kind of heat.

I wondered if the Dark Prince was watching me being hauled up the RV stairs. The smell wafting out of the vehicle was awful, half hot garbage, half acrid chemicals. All thoughts of the rest of my team fled as I caught sight of my husband.

"Oh, Luke," I whispered. He was lying on his side on a filthy mattress all the way in the back. Even from a distance I could tell he'd been badly beaten. One eye had swollen shut, and bruises covered his exposed cheek. The clothes he'd been wearing were torn and blood oozed out of several rips and stained the filthy mattress beneath his head.

He let out a sound when he saw me that was half groan, half sob. "No. Jackie, no."

And I knew. All his weirdness, the scheming, the lies, had

been to prevent this exact situation. My big, strong dumbass of a husband had been desperate to protect me. He was heartbroken, because he couldn't keep me safe.

I rushed to his side and knelt down. "Luke, it's all right. Everything will be fine."

"You see, that's what I'm talking about." Danny O'Rourke said to Justine and Cro-Magnon Man.

I glared at him over my shoulder. "Why would you do this to him?"

"It's how we treat rats where I'm from."

Rats? I wasn't about to stop and analyze his words. "You mean, like your twin brother?"

O'Rourke got in my face. "My brother was warned, but no, he had to go tearing off to find Mommy Dearest. He thought that selfish gash could tell him something, maybe explain why she gave us up for adoption. She didn't just abandon us, she separated us from each other to be raised by separate families. What kind of a sick bitch does that to her own flesh and blood?"

That explained the different surnames.

"It took us years to find each other, seeing as how the Santinos and O'Rourkes don't exactly get along. She musta planned it that way, planned to keep us apart. Do you have any idea what that's like, feeling like there's a part of yourself missing all the time but not knowing how or why? And then to get him back. I was so damn proud of him, coming up in his family the same way I did. But then he had that heart attack and everything changed."

His expression turned ugly as he reminisced. "He started hiding things from me. Me, his own brother. Making noise about reconnecting with our dear mother. So I had to show him."

Danny O'Rourke had a full head of steam going and clearly, he needed to vent. It was all well and good for me that he monologued until the police arrived. "Show him what?" I croaked.

"That she was a cold, heartless woman. Justine was here, running my Miami interests and she had no problem finding a crooked lawyer to set it all up. Real estate scamming is a profitable side business, but there's a hell of a lot more paperwork than with blow."

"So you set your own brother up to be evicted by his birth mother? That's so cruel."

O'Rourke got in my face, spittle flying. "She's the cruel one. I didn't make her hire you, didn't force her to evict her own flesh and blood. That's on her."

"You killed her." I could easily see it. The rage was threatening to overflow from every cell in his body. "You beat her to death."

"Yeah, and I only wish I'd done it sooner."

"So you're gonna let your brother go to jail for your crime?" I asked. "How's that showing family loyalty?"

"Joey only has six months to live. He bit his tongue off as a clear message to me that he'd rather die in jail than rat. Unlike your miserable fink of a spouse, running off to the feds." He turned his wrath on Luke. "Did you think we wouldn't catch on? You're not a junkie or a gambler, you're a straight arrow. Of course we knew who the rat was."

"Oh, Luke," I whispered, my heart breaking. He'd been trying to bring down a drug ring. By himself. "Why didn't you tell me?"

"Don't worry, doll. You'll have the rest of your lives together. All five minutes of it." With that he exited the RV.

"What does that mean?" I whispered to Luke. "Where's he going?"

Luke pointed to the kitchen table where various chemicals omitted noxious fumes. "The feds are closing in, thanks to my intel. They're going to blow the place, with us in it. Set the distraction to get away while they're picking up our body parts. Meth labs blow all the time and with a gas tank right under us..." he tried to make a shrugging motion then grimaced in pain.

"Where's the Krokodil pusher?" I asked. "Arlene Lipinski."

"Behind the wheel. I found her OD'ed along the side of the road. She's gone."

"Can you walk?" I asked.

"I'm so sorry, Jackie." He exhaled the words as though wrenching them out of the pit of his soul.

"We'll talk about it later. Right now we need to get ready to move. On your feet."

One of his shoulders hung lower than the other and he hissed in pain when I got near it. Deciding to leave it alone, I propped myself up like a human crutch beneath his other shoulder.

I'd just gotten him to a precarious standing position when the door opened and Logan stuck his head in. "Jackie, what the—?"

"Later," I interrupted. "They rigged this place to blow. Help me get Luke out of here."

To his credit, the Dark Prince handed me his sidearm and took Luke's battered body against his own. "We'll have to follow you until we reconnect with the Garrison team. Don't take any unnecessary chances but move as fast as you can."

"If you're done giving me contrary orders," I murmured as I moved down the steps. "I'd like to get the hell out of here."

I moved down the steps and poked my head out. "All clear."

Logan was almost carrying his brother as he maneuvered down the steps.

Sirens pierced the night and I sighed. "Twenty minutes, really? Is it any wonder tourism is down?"

"Shit, go!" Logan yelled.

Something pinged off the side of the RV and it took a moment for me to realize it had been a bullet. I glanced around, trying to pinpoint the shooter's location. More gunfire sounded from the other direction, and I saw John Garrison, rise up from behind a crate to gesture us in his direction. "We'll cover you!"

"Jackie, run!" Logan shouted, his voice tinged with panic. He dragged Luke past me.

I ran, with my hands flung up over my head. I was almost to the wall of crates when I heard a growl and a scream as back up arrived from another corner. "Sasquatch! John, don't shoot the dogs!"

Logan cursed at me profusely, shoving me forward. "Run, damn you!"

"Look out!" John yelled.

I turned and saw Justine, with a handgun aimed straight at my head.

"No!" Luke's voice ripped through me as she fired. Everything slowed, every breath took an eon, every heartbeat a millennium. And then a big male body dove in front of me, taking the impact of the bullet and knocking us both to the ground.

"No!" It was my turn to scream. The Garrisons converged on Justine and police cars roared into the lot. I was barely aware of any of it. "God damn you, no!"

"Better this way," my hero looked up at me, warm brown eyes filled with pain. And love.

"Luke," I sobbed, then Logan was shoving me out of the way, doing everything he could to staunch the flow of blood and save his brother's life.

The same way Luke had just saved mine.

CHAPTER 28

"Idiot," I seethed as I plopped down in the chair beside Luke's bed. "You are such an idiot."

"I'm sorry I scared you, Ace," Luke croaked. "Could you get me some water?"

I rose and circled the bed to the side where the pitcher of ice water rested. I poured it into a cup and opened a straw then jammed the thing between his cracked lips. "You're sorry you scared me? How about not taking a freaking bullet for me, okay? Could you maybe do that next time instead?"

With the straw still in his mouth he held my gaze out of his good eye and then slowly shook his head no.

"Stubborn man," I murmured with affection. My gaze softened as I looked at his battered face. Two inches to the left and the bullet would have pierced his heart. I could have lost him. For a few agonizing moments I thought I had lost him. "This does not by any means wipe the slate clean. I want answers and as soon as they let you out of this hospital bed, I intend to get them."

He released the straw and settled back against his pillows, eyelid drifting shut. "I know."

Setting the cup aside, I reached down and smoothed his hair. "I'll let you sleep."

"Don't go," he gripped my hand, holding it tight, almost ripping out his IV in the process. "Don't leave me."

It was on the tip of my tongue to point out that he'd been the one about to leave me and in the most permanent sense of the word. Though I'd stripped off my bullet proof vest, I still wore the same grubby clothes that I'd had on for the last thirty six hours. I itched to go home, to change my clothes and take a long, hot shower.

"I won't," I said instead. It was nice to be wanted again and I wasn't about to start taking his yearning for me for granted. I could do all the thinking I had to do right here if it would make him feel better.

He released my hand and I circled back to the chair and pulled it closer to the bed. The hand on this side was free of tubes and wires so I put mine over his, to let him soak up the connection.

A connection we could have lost. I leaned my head back and shut my eyes, willing myself not to cry.

"Ace?"

"Yeah?" I looked at him. He'd shifted on the bed, turning until he had a clear view of me.

"I love you."

I shut my eyes again, a small smile curving my lips. "That's no excuse."

He laughed but the sound turned into a cough. "I know," He wheezed.

"Easy," I said, sitting up. "Do you need more water?"

Luke shook his head reached for me through the bars of the bed. "Your face."

I leaned forward until he could touch me. "Yeah, I know, I'm a mess."

"I wanted to keep you out of it." He whispered. "Wanted to keep you safe."

"I know that."

Luke drifted off. Yeah, I knew that he had my best interest at heart. Still, he'd lied to me, made me feel like crap, intentionally put distance between us. I was too tired to decide right now if the ends justified the means. Instead I was just glad he was going to live.

"Jackie?" Logan stood in the doorway to the room, his expression grim. "Sargent Vasquez is in the waiting room. He wants to talk to us, if you're up for it."

I nodded and rose stiffly out of the chair. "Yeah. Might as well get this all wrapped up."

Logan stared down at me, his penetrating blue gaze assessing. "You sure you're up for this?"

I blew out a sigh. "I'm fine."

"Liar," he replied, but didn't press further.

We walked down the hall to the waiting area. Enrique Vasquez was there along with two people in dark suits, one man, one woman, both sleek and polished looking. One glance at them and I knew they had to be feds.

"Mrs. Parker, this is Special Agent McInnis and Special Agent Gray from the FBI." Vasquez said.

I cast him a sharp look, wondering if it was for my benefit or the feds that I was Mrs. Parker all of a sudden.

"Mrs. Parker." Special Agent McInnis nodded to me. "We hope your husband is all right."

"He was beaten," I said flatly, "While working with you. My brother-in-law and I had to rescue him while you were nowhere in sight. He took a bullet meant for me and it just missed his heart. So no, he is not all right."

Logan's warm palm landed against my neck, either as a warning or a way to keep me from attacking the feds.

"We understand your frustration," Special Agent Gray

said. Her voice was cool and smooth, almost soothing. I wanted to grab her by the hair and smash her face against the wall.

"What about the money?" I asked. "Luke took money from my mother, from our own personal accounts. She was evicted for not paying her rent."

"We advised him to hide all of your assets, in case O'Rourke did an income check. Call our office and we'll get you the account information." Gray handed me a card with not so much as an "our bad."

"Why?" I whispered, staring at the block letters on the card. "Why him?"

"He came to us." McInnis said. "A few weeks ago, he said he had a lead on Danny O'Rourke's Miami based drug trade being run out of a local animal shelter. He was gathering evidence for us, helping us build our case against O'Rourke. But then he went off the radar. We thought he'd been scared off and we didn't want to blow his cover by approaching him if it hadn't already been blown."

Logan's eyes narrowed. "So you abandoned him? Left him to deal with the fall out by himself?"

"The decision came from over our heads," Special Agent Gray stated blandly. "O'Rourke has slipped the hook too many times and too many lives were at stake."

I stared at her incredulously and not only because she didn't look like the type of girl to bust out a fishing metaphor. "So he was what, your sacrificial goat? The good of the many outweighs the good of the one and all that happy horseshit?"

They stared at me blankly and then turned to Vasquez. "Maybe we should wait until Mr. Parker is up for visitors."

"Probably a good idea," Vasquez said mildly.

"You enjoyed that," I accused him after the Special Agents had gone off to be special someplace else.

"Maybe a little," he grinned. "They've been stonewalling me this entire time about Santino and O'Rourke, acting like a homicide investigation is just small potatoes or whatever else white people eat."

"Cheese." I told him. "White people like cheese."

"And bacon." Logan added helpfully.

"Everybody likes bacon." I told him.

"Noted," Vasquez said. "So, it looks like our homicide is still matricide and we have the DNA evidence along with a confession to back it up."

"Wait, I thought you said the DNA matched Big Joey? How can it be a match for Danny O'Rourke too?"

"Because they're identical twins," Logan mumbled.

Vasquez nodded. "Right and because Santino is on heart medication we couldn't get a fingerprint off him, which is the only way to identify one identical twin from the other."

"So what happens now?" I asked.

"Well, the feds can do whatever they want, but I'm booking O'Rourke with murder one. With your testimony we can send him to jail for life. Justine Marples is being charged with attempted murder, real estate fraud and animal cruelty so you won't have to worry about her anytime soon."

"And what about Cro-Magnon man, or the two guys that were guarding the RV." I frowned, thinking it through. "For that matter, what about the RV. It belongs to one of our clients."

"The feds have them all in connection to the drug case. I heard through the grapevine that the DEA was in on it too, so they'll be looking at serious jail time. And I'll call you when we release the RV from evidence."

I was swaying on my feet and Logan put his hands on my shoulders to steady me. "Can I bring her home?"

Vasquez nodded. "We'll be in touch."

"Luke," I said turning to go back to his room.

Lease on the Beach

The Dark Prince held me in a firm grip. "Is asleep. Besides, Mom and dad are on their way, so they'll be here by the time he wakes up and you won't get a word in edgewise. Time to take care of yourself now, Jackie. Come on, I'll buy you some cheese."

"With bacon?"

He kissed the top of my head. "Whatever you want."

Hours later, I opened the door to my bedroom to find Logan fast asleep on the couch. Tip-toeing past him, I made my way to the coffee pot and set up a full pot. When it was ready, I poured myself a steaming mug and took it out front.

The strong brew helped clear away the cobwebs and I sat, staring out at Miami and wondering what came next.

"Hey," Logan said from behind me.

"Hey yourself." I made an undignified noise when he plucked the mug out of my hand and took a large gulp. "Get your own."

He raised a brow. "Mug or pot?"

"Both." I took another sip and sighed. "Was this a win for us?"

Logan frowned. "Why do you ask?"

"It doesn't feel that way." I shrugged. "I want to be happy that Luke is going to be all right, that we closed most of our cases and that the bad guys all got locked up. But Big Joey lost his shot to know his mother and he has only a few months left. Arlene Lipinski and Gary Markov are dead from that horrible drug. I think I might have irreparably damaged my already screwed up relationship with Celeste and Luke…." I shook my head. "I know he did it for me, for us both but I don't know if I can get past the fact that he lied to us, stole from Celeste, from me. A few days ago I wondered if

I ever knew him at all and now I'm sure that I don't. No matter the reasons, the man I married wasn't capable of all the shit he pulled."

Logan nodded thoughtfully. "What are you going to do?"

"I don't know. What do you think I should do?"

He laughed. It was a hollow sound. "I don't know what to say. I mean, on the one hand he's my brother and you're his wife so it could be argued that for the sake of his happiness I'd encourage you to stay with him."

"Yeah. I guess you're not exactly unbiased, huh?" I turned to smile at him and was completely taken off guard when his lips met mine.

It was a searing kiss, the kind that could brand you down to your soul. His hands cupped my face, holding me still as his mouth molded mine. He tasted of coffee and sin and he stole my breath and made me dizzy before finally releasing me.

"Logan," I whispered, shocked.

"And on the other hand," he said, blue eyes searching my face, "I'm in love with you. I want the best for you, I always have. That might not be me, but it sure as hell isn't my brother. Not anymore. He almost got you killed this morning and him taking a bullet meant for you doesn't change the fact that if he'd told us what the hell was going on, you wouldn't have been in the line of fire. His hero complex is going to destroy him and you along with him if you let it."

He rose and pulled a ring of keys out of his pocket and tossed it down on the porch steps. "Keys to my place."

I scooted back from the thing as though he'd thrown a scorpion at my feet. "Your apartment?"

He shook his head and chucked his thumb at the bungalow next door. "No, my new place."

"You bought the house next door?" I asked, confused.

He nodded. "I'll be gone for a little while, but if you need to get away, it's yours to use."

My heart thudded in my rib cage and I watched him move down the sidewalk toward his motorcycle. I rose to my feet, my breath huffing out in ragged breaths.

He strapped on his helmet and backed out of the driveway.

"Logan!" I shouted, just as the motor thundered to life.

There was no way he could have heard me but he looked over his shoulder. Sunglasses covered his eyes but I could feel him drinking me in, the same way I was doing to him. He turned his head away abruptly and my lips parted. I didn't know what I had to say but I knew I had to say something.

Then it was too late and I could do nothing but watch him ride off, a shadow fading into the rising sun, leaving me alone with decisions I didn't want to make.

~The End~

IT'S NOT MY WORDS THAT COUNT. IT'S YOURS!

Please consider leaving an honest review for this book. Reviews help readers like you select the kind of books they like and help authors like me sell books to the right readers. I found one of my favorite series from a two star review.

Thank you for reading!

Jennifer L. Hart

WANT MORE DAMAGED GOODNESS?

Cure or Die Book 3 in the Damaged Goods series

Certified Process Server Jackie Parker could do a case study in bizarre human behavior. Like the time the Damaged Goods property management team found a man fermenting his own fecal matter to get high. Or the angry downstairs tenant who threatened to spit on her. And that was just one building in the Miami art's district.

Returning to the scene of the crime a year later at the request of the landlord, Jackie believes she's ready for anything. Since the Dark Prince left the team, she and Luke have gone through an amicable divorce and maybe just this one time she can manage to not land face first in something foul. But what they find in the vacated apartment is far worse than on their earlier visit and Jackie's situation is about to get a whole lot messier.

Cue Logan.

Want more #Mysterieswithhart?

> *Cleaning has never been so much fun! Hang on for the zany thrill ride of the*
>
> *Misadventures of the Laundry Hag mystery series!*

ABOUT THE AUTHOR

USA Today bestselling author Jennifer L. Hart writes about characters that cuss, get naked and often make poor but hilarious life choices. A native New Yorker, Jenn now lives in the mountains of North Carolina where she's learned how to say y'all with the best of them.

Sign up for Jen's Author Newsletter Hart's Hitlist and receive a free ebook!

Made in the USA
Monee, IL
23 April 2021